The Last Customer

A Novel by

Daniel P. Coughlin

A HellBound Books LLC Publication

Copyright © 2025 by HellBound Books Publishing LLC
All Rights Reserved
Cover and art design by Tee Arts for
HellBound Books Publishing LLC

www.hellboundbooks.com

Dedication

This book could not have been possible without the inspiration of my brother Ryan Coughlin, my wife Kelli-Rae and my son Kasey "Mad Max" Coughlin.

I also dedicate this book to my parents John and Kris Coughlin, thanks for fighting through it. You know what I mean.

And to Jeremy "Pendleton Actual" Steinell, Brian O'Reilly, Cody Frett, Eric Moore, and Natalie Kuhl, thanks for the training!

And to Eli, Cortney, Elijah, Cherokee, and Destiny, DeeDee, Ray, Jerry and Jerrin... thanks for making work an awesome spot to be!

Part 1: The Introduction

Chapter 1

1

Father Leslie Gardner, standing six foot two inches tall with stout posture and shaggy brown hair—and a bit of a dark complexion—ran his brown eyes across the twelve-by-twelve-inch paper calendar pinned to the far wall of his small dorm room. The calendar's bottom corners were faded and curling. His pointy right index finger traced the thick glossy paper until it fell upon the square box which revealed the date as August 18, 1980. He double tapped the box with the pad of his finger.

He was staying in a Catholic rectory. His living quarters were standard at best. The room was a basic eight-by-eight cube with no windows and baby blue walls. The rectory sat to the side of a beautifully constructed Catholic church. In this small town, the steeple was visible for miles. It gave the panoramic view a picturesque quality. The interior of the holy structure held a vaulted ceiling.

The body of the church was accented with brand new pews, freshly tarnished. Every inch of the building was polished to perfection. The freshly waxed floors shined bright. The stained wooden pews and marbled floors gave off a lemon scented glimmer. And the statue of Christ held not a speck of dust.

Father Gardner had only been residing in this small Iowa town for eight days. The town rested forty miles west of Sioux City. His assignment was to assess, evaluate, and conclude whether or not a young woman had been seized by a demon—a foul presence.

Within ten minutes of meeting Donna Shaney, an average sized woman of thirty years, he'd concluded that she'd been the victim of demonic possession. All the symptoms were prevalent. Her eyes held a ring of white fire.

Upon entering Donna's room, on the first day, Gardner immediately wanted to cup his nose. The stench was awful. The odor hung in the air like fog. But he wouldn't allow the demon to sense any weaknesses. He refused to cover his nose. Even a small gesture such as masking-a-scent would reveal a weakness to the demon. And the demon would prey on it. Breathing deep, Gardner allowed the foul air into his nostrils. He became accustomed to the smell. And then he was over it.

Gardner had conducted many exorcisms. He knew the demon was looking for any avenue to exploit him. And if the demon found a weakness, it would certainly do just that. And the exploitation could interfere with the rite of exorcism. And that was unacceptable.

Father Gardner went into every assignment clear headed. At least he tried to. Over the years, he'd developed a thick shell. He'd enabled himself to disregard foul smells and insults. He'd been desensitized to the ways of the demon.

Donna's room was freezing. The wallpaper had begun to peel because the pores had dried up, which was the result of the unnaturally cold temperature. Gardner shivered. He made eye contact with the demon and walked to the right side of the room. He took a seat in a wooden rocking chair near the queen-sized bed. He leaned forward toward the girl. The chair creaked. As he moved closer, he glanced at the bed. The sheets were covered in yellowing sweat stains and foul waste.

And then he spoke to the evil presence inhabiting the girl—*the demon.* And as always, the demon lied. At first, it had claimed to be a serial killer from the nineteen fifties. Gardner knew this to be false. Serial killers were unable to possess the human body. Possession was the fallen angel's game.

The demon recited many subjects the young junkie woman could not have known. For instance, it spoke both Latin and German languages. And it insulted Gardner with both. It laughed when asked questions about Judas and other biblical characters. The demon spouted out specific instances in which it had possessed others. And then it laughed as it threatened to destroy Donna.

Gardner found this threat valid.

After taking vital signs—a strenuous chore—it was revealed Donna was badly dehydrated. Every organ in her body revved on failure. Her skin had turned a sickly yellow. Her liver was failing.

Gardner visited with Donna every day for a week. He needed to perform psychological testing. In the past, Gardner had disproven many possessions. Mental illness was often misconstrued as possession. But after going through his checklist, Gardner approved the exorcism.

On the eighth day, Gardner awoke early. He forced down a decent sized breakfast of toast and eggs. He needed his energy. Then, he prayed intensely for over an hour. He begged for strength. In his heart, he felt the awareness of the power of good. The Holy Spirit was breathing within him.

After leaving the rectory kitchen, he jogged down the cement stairs from the second floor. The nuns had gathered in the small rectangular shaped lobby near the coffee table. They stood from their seats as he entered the room.

They were frightened and intimidated by his presence. None of them said a word. They stood erect with their lips sealed. Gardner could feel their judgment. It was written amongst their cold gazes and faithless expressions; not faithlessness in God, but faithlessness in Father Gardner.

Gardner didn't wear the traditional uniform of a Catholic priest. Or any other priest for that matter. He was dressed in simple black slacks and a cheap button-down white shirt with a black tie.

Nodding toward the middle-aged women dressed in their traditional gowns and hoods, he stepped into the light of the new day.

The brisk morning air refreshed his clean face. His lungs filled with crisp oxygen. His heart rate quickened. He continued down the walkway.

Gardner was a handsome man of thirty. There were no prominent wrinkles in his skin. His face appeared vibrant, soft skin accentuated the candy-brown eyes that were set neatly on his face. His jaw was blocky, which gave off a masculine appearance, along with his hair, which had growth, but wasn't too long. He continued toward the sidewalk.

His thoughts and attention deviated when the pigs from the slaughterhouse across the street screamed as he walked past. Gardner picked up his stride, moving quickly past the large cement warehouse that contained the swine about to be processed. The squeals of fright and terror spilling from behind the thick concrete walls were nowhere near as unnerving as the sounds he would hear upon entering the house on Cleveland Street.

2

The morning walk through town was pleasant and much needed. It gave Gardner a chance to review his thoughts and settle his nerves. Before he knew it, the sidewalk ended.

A Dead End sign stood to the right, in the center of the street's end. A cluster of Elm Trees led way to the forest behind the long rectangular wooden plank with a large reflective orange octagon bolted to the middle.

Gardner glanced up at the sky and gave thanks before turning to the two-story brick home on his left. He always gave thanks for the gift of life. Every day was a battle. But Gardner cherished his life. He understood his purpose. Purpose was a luxury most people didn't have. And his was to fight evil—to destroy it before it spread like disease.

Gardner had traveled across many countries conducting the business of holy cleansing. At first, it was hard to accept—*His calling.*

Gardner grew up in a good home. He was raised by a fine family of God-fearing parents. Both Ethel and Peter Gardner were strict and loving. His childhood was ordinary, happy even. Then he discovered his gift.

The spiritual world, which existed beneath the earthly plain of existence, showed itself to Gardner at the age of ten. At first, he wasn't able to grasp what was happening. His life had suddenly become different from the other children. For a boy of Gardner's age, that was hard to accept; impossible to talk about. Even at the age of ten, he acknowledged he was special. It was frustrating. He wanted to be like the other children. Playing kick ball at recess and baseball after school, he tried his best to hide the things he knew.

The first awareness of his unique gift had been revealed to him on a warm September morning while he walked to school.

Lolling down the cracked sidewalk of Elm Street with his schoolbooks tucked under his left arm, he was struck by a blinding vision. At first, his sight went hazy. He dropped his books and stumbled back a few steps. Everything went bright as if a light bulb had exploded. His gaze washed white. He was blinded. Scared, he waved his arms in front of his face. He wiped his eyes, hoping the feeling would stop. He quit moving. Darkness set in. Everything became silent. There was no movement. No wind. The passing cars seemed to stop. The air became still. The sky parted and peeled back as if the world was merely a two-dimensional painting. Before him, he saw more dimensions. A realm of existence was exposed beneath the world's surface. The silence turned into a whirlwind of pain and screaming. Gardner was scared. The parallel world where demons and angels battled had opened to him. Good and evil clashed. Everything was fire orange or black. The world in front of Gardner had become a supernatural warzone. There was torment and agony. Even the angels fought with brutal tenacity.

Gardner tried to run. His legs wouldn't move. He stood frozen while many snarling creatures surrounded him. They circled in on him with glossy eyes and watering mouths. Their fangs jutted from their scaly mouths. Some looked like wolves. Others appeared as dark shadows with razor sharp teeth.

Gardner feared he'd lost his mind. A scaly creature snarled while galloping toward him. He closed his eyes and prayed to be somewhere else.

Again, there was silence. And when he opened his eyes again, he was back on Elm Street. His schoolbooks were strewn across the sidewalk. His math book lay in the grass near the curb. He picked up his belongings.

Glancing around, he saw no one and no one had seen him. There were no worried neighbors. No dogs barked and no bullies laughed. He blew a long sigh of relief and wiped away his tears. He took a deep breath and continued to school.

The images he'd been shown that day scared him. He wanted to tell someone. *But who would believe him?* He figured it would be best to keep the vision a secret.

The entire experience had only lasted seconds. It was gone. And it wasn't until years later he would be given another. And on that day, he was given his first guiding vision. From then on, he was given visions of the future— images of places and people that he would need to help. The visions called to him, and the answers were revealed. They eventually led him to the ministry. And from there he'd been able to meet others like him. It was comforting to know there were others with the *gift*. Together, they were able to organize their supernatural gifts and assignments were distributed. His life as a holy warrior began.

Now, turning away from the sidewalk, Gardner glanced up at the street sign.

Cleveland Street.

He spun his head and peered down the street. His gaze opened to a neat row of small homes he'd passed, oblivious, on his way to the Shaney's home. There was nothing off-kilter about the aesthetics of the house. It was a standard brick home with a screened-in porch. The brick was a fading cream color in need of a pressure wash. The lawn was bright green, a bit overdue to be mowed. But other than the slight lack of upkeep, the house didn't stand out. Furthermore, it didn't reflect the evil burrowed inside.

When Gardner's heels clicked together at a forty-five-degree angle before the first cement stair leading up to the porch where an older woman, Silvia Shaney, Donna's grandmother, was standing with the screen door propped open, he felt a familiar rush of energy course through his system. It was the Holy Spirit. It was preparing him to fight.

Silvia tried to a smile. The exhaustion and angst beneath her expression wouldn't allow comfort. It was obvious she hadn't slept in days. Her eyes were dark circles. The creases in her skin were unnaturally deep, the moisture had been depleted. Still, as haggard and tired as she appeared, the deep love she held for Donna was unmistakable. It radiated from her sunken glare.

"Thank you for being with us, Father Gardner. Please come in," she said in a pleasant, but shaky voice. She held a hospitable nature. She stepped aside, her light blue dress fluttered above her ankles as a breeze whisked past. Her silver hair danced across her forehead where it had fallen from her braid. She was a good woman. Her abundance of life exceeded her age.

Upon entering the quaint home, Gardner immediately heard shuffling and thunderous stomps from the upstairs bedroom. It was the sound of bouncing bedposts.

Quickly, he shuttled up the hardwood steps and landed on the second floor, ready to face his opponent. Through research, prayer, and the visions God had shown him, he knew the entity living within the girl was the demon *Sammael.* Gardner had never been challenged by this particular demon. And, as always, he hoped today would be their last meeting.

Making the sign of the cross, Gardner peeked out the hallway window. The view opened into the neighbor's yard. There was an aging wooden fence separating the Shaney's property from the nearest neighbor. The day was bright. There were many rays of sunlight bending and refracting through the Elder trees outside. It was pleasant and comforting, if only for a moment.

Gardner continued down the hall.

He entered the room.

The evil entity called him a pig.

3

The bedposts ceased slamming against the hardwood floor when Gardner entered the room. The demon spun its head toward Gardner, quick and concise. Their eyes met. Her lips were livery and gray. A large tear had settled in the center of her bottom lip. Crusted dry blood branched downward from the abrasion. The split in her lip broke further when the demon smiled.

The odor permeating the room was horrendous. Gardner couldn't get used to it.

He didn't.

Maintaining his composure, he moved to the edge of the bed. The sheets were soaked and stained yellow with waste.

Donna sat upright against a soggy pillow with her back arched. Every muscle in her body flexed and strained. Her ashen skin had become so dry the top layer broke. There were lesions crossing her sunken cheeks. The restraints on her wrists held crusty brown streaks where her skin was rubbed off. Her blonde hair was wiry and matted—caked with sweat, blood, and vomit.

She opened her mouth and smiled maliciously while licking her broken, bleeding mouth. "Go away. You haven't the strength to fight me."

Gardner received a vision. Fairly often, he received visions during the course of exorcism. They didn't come to him during every exorcism. And every exorcism hadn't been successful. On more than one occasion, Gardner expelled the demon but lost the host. A few victims had died during the rites of exorcism. The body could only take so much fight before it quit. It disappointed Gardner when the physical body became so worn-out that its soul couldn't maintain its ground. Luckily, with Donna, her body wasn't to the point of terminal exhaustion, *yet*.

Falling back a step, Gardner's vision became clear. The blinding light cleared. He saw *her*. It was Donna. And she was beautiful. They stood in the light. She held her arms out, inviting him to cleanse her body of the demon. There was fight within her. Her soul was capable of beating the entity. And Gardner was the catalyst needed to lead the evil spirit out.

Confident of what his duties entailed, he smiled at the face of the demon Sammael.

The vision cleared. Gardner adjusted his tie. He stepped forward, extended his arm across the bed and rested his palm upon Donna's forehead. He pulled out a small silver vile and dribbled holy water down her forehead. The demon hissed. Gardner's face lowered to the demon. Sammael spit in his face. Yellow mucus and brown blood dripped from Gardner's face. He wiped it away, unfazed.

Staring into the demon's eyes, he whispered, "I cast you out. The power of good…that which is greater than *you*, casts you out." The octave of Gardner's voice heightened. "The Holy Spirit casts you out!"

The demon growled. It shook furiously on the mattress, shredding the tangled blankets. The bedposts rose and fell successively on the wood flooring. The demon continued hissing. It swore. It didn't want to leave this young woman. It wanted to rip her insides to pieces and kill her earthly body. Nothing would satisfy the demon more. It wished to take her soul to the depths of eternal pain.

Gardner was contended as he took part in the demon's defeat. As the evil began to separate from Donna's body, it looked to Gardner and gnashed its teeth. It spoke in a deep harmonic tone that made Donna's grandmother writhe and back away. It spoke: "I will come back for you. I will tear the skin from your corpse and burn you in the eternal flame. It will hurt more that way."

The demon closed its eyes. In an instant, color returned to Donna's face. It was as if she'd awoken from a deep sleep. And then her body sprung upward from the bed.

Gardner closed his eyes. He prayed. There were no certainties in life—he knew that more than anyone.

With grace, Gardner stepped aside while Donna lurched above the bed. The demon howled as it shed from her body.

Donna landed softly and bounced on the mattress. Her voice rattled and huffed.

As if waking from a horrible nightmare, with clear eyes, Donna peered around the bedroom. She was confused. This was a normal reaction. Her eyes fell upon Gardner. "What happened?"

Donna shook her head. Her face contorted. Her pain struck. Gardner went to the bedside. He ran his hand down the side of her exhausted face. She groaned. She grabbed at her aching back and fell to the bed. The physical aches had set in. The demon had stretched and torn Donna's organs. Her body had been twisted and depleted for weeks. Donna had very few recollections of what happened during the short period in which she was possessed. In time, she would be enlightened of the encounter with her evil entity. *Sammael.*

Silvia went to Donna's bedside. She didn't care about the filth-soaked bed sheets or the awful scent her granddaughter gave off. She only saw her beautiful Donna.

The awful parasite that preyed on her had been cast away. Her granddaughter was clean. She could continue life with a clean slate.

Gardner stood. He backed out of the bedroom and into the hallway.

He didn't say goodbye.

The longing between these two women—to bond and love one another—was too strong. Gardner refused to interfere.

And so he left.

4

Moving down the stairs from the second floor, Gardner glanced to the neatly framed family photos that hung staggered across the walls. The captured images were sweet. There weren't many pictures of Donna and her parents, but there were many of her and Silvia. It was easy to see that Silvia loved her granddaughter like a mother.

Gardner left the Shaney's house.

The soft hum of the summer afternoon felt right. From here, Gardner would drive until he found a nice café to stop at. He enjoyed small diners. He could relax with a nice cup of coffee. Small town greasy spoons were a treat.

The screen door creaked as Gardner pulled the latch and swung it open. Stepping down the cement staircase, he looked back to the second story of the brick house. He heard sniffles. He smiled. His joy came from their happiness.

Gardner continued down the stairs toward the base of the sidewalk. A shadow spilled over him. He glanced at the sky. A dark cloud crept over the house.

In that moment, Gardner felt the damning power of Sammael. His presence hovered above. And he was angry. Demons became furious after being expelled.

Sammael had been defeated but not destroyed.

Sammael would find Gardner again.

Their battle was far from finished.

Gardner could feel it.

Part 2: The Vessels

Chapter 2

1

The sky was clear on that sunny summer day in August, 2010. Not a cloud hung in the sky. The canvas above was a perfect blue. A humid gust of wind blew through Dodge Junction, a small town of eight thousand in the southern region of rural Wisconsin. The humidity hung thick in the air, making the day hazy. The temperature was ninety and rising. With the added humidity it was scorching, almost unbearable.

Downtown Dodge Junction was deserted. The line of old stores, diners, repair shops, banks, and gas stations were dried up and desolate. Even the industrial area north of town seemed to be lifeless. The generator factory—where the town's livelihood stemmed from—was shut down for the weekend. The remaining townsfolk had retreated to their air-conditioned homes, or at least fanned living rooms. Sprinklers danced across many of the freshly mowed yards creating a scenic glaze across the suburban neighborhoods. Fresh green lawns popped nicely against mild colored houses. Even the paint laminating the white picket fences seemed to sweat on this particular day. The wetness made everything appear glossy.

It was peaceful.

It was Saturday.

In a town forty miles north of Dodge Junction, the heat held something perverted, dreadful, retched, and nearly unspeakable—

2

Rod Barton and Patty King baked in the summer heat of a posh Midwestern living room. The couch where they sat was comfortable. The covers were made of satin. They were stained with sweat. Patty and Rod had access to air conditioning but didn't bother. They'd been camped out in this nicely polished Victorian home for three days. The heat was fine. The two *deviants* were invested in heinous acts they sought pleasure in committing. They were experiencing too much pleasure to worry about a thing like *heat*.

Patty watched Rod's eager eyes peer down, intensely, at the glass pipe. The small bulb on the end was smudged with a thin layer of blackened burn marks. The black ash spread as he ran a cheap lighter underneath the round ball at the end of the straw-like tube. He slowly turned the tube between his index finger and thumb. The crystal methamphetamine was melting and creating a ribbon of smoke that tumbled like a miniature tornado within the small glass circle with a tiny hole in the top.

Patty watched attentively as Rod's full red lips puckered around the base of the straw. He began to suck. A heavy cloud of the uppity smoke left the bulb and entered Rod's mouth.

Leaning back in his chair, Rod turned to Patty. His piercing blue eyes met hers. His pupils dilated and blackened. His cheeks sunk in. Pulling the pipe away from his lips, he leaned toward her. He extended the pipe to her.

Patty's heart leapt when his eyes met hers. She felt her affection for him funnel. Her hands began to shake and perspire. She loved him. He understood the hate in her heart and accepted it—loved it. She'd never—in her short life—felt as complete as she did with Rod. They'd been together for four years. She would never, willingly, leave his presence. She couldn't. The bond they'd created was unbreakable. The things he'd shown her made the flesh on her arms tingle and the hair on the back of her neck jump. Sex was just part of it. The journey, as Rod called it, was the excitement. It was an intense relationship. Her father would have called it a perversion. *But who cared?* She and Rod took care of *daddy* years ago. Patty had gotten the last words in on him.

The last time Patty King had seen her father, she was staring directly into his sunken brown eyes. She was swaying back and forth from her right leg to her left. She was excited, unable to sit. Rod held a freshly sharpened straight razor beneath his chin.

Rod was smiling.

"I never loved you, Dad. And I'm enjoying this. If you want to make me happy, Dad, then you should scream," Patty told her father. And while she said this, she remembered the beatings she'd endured at his hand. When Patty was a child, her father had locked her in a dog kennel. He'd kept her there for days at a time. He starved her. She would faint from dehydration. He'd put her there whether she'd been bad or not. He enjoyed watching her suffer. He even told her she'd thank him one day. He was doing this for *her own good.* She'd frozen out there, in the kennel, behind the barn. The fenced-cage was freezing at night.

And time was slow. Each minute seemed like an eternity. Her hatred was given plenty of time to develop.

And now, while she watched Rod suck on the glass pipe, she enjoyed the memory of her father's demise. Murder was invigorating. The meth accentuated Patty and Rod's experiences. It was a tool. It heightened their sensations.

Patty had wanted to kill her father for many years. She'd thought about it day and night. She even played out scenarios, in her head, of killing him. Finally, Rod talked Patty into moving forward, killing him. He'd sat her down, explained that she didn't have to feel guilty for enjoying the nasty things she so loved doing. He told her to achieve happiness she would have to accept the sick thoughts swirling in her head. She needed to enjoy her sickness. With acceptance came happiness. It helped, as he said it would. Her wall of inhibitions crumbled when it came to Rod. Rod made Patty happy. And she would do anything for him. Just thinking about the beautiful crimson blood as it drained from her father's neck allowed her to feel sensations of love and hate intertwined. Her thoughts were good, orgasmic even. *She loved her hate.*

A blooming cloud of amphetamine smoke erupted from Rod's mouth. His throat bulged. A huffing sound escaped his lips. Although his T-shirt was white, Patty could see a hint of yellow. It was sagged from the weight of his sweat. They'd been sitting in the ungodly heat for the past three days. Sure, they showered, but as soon as the sweat washed off, it was leaking from their pores again.

Patty took the pipe, then the lighter. She put it to her lips. She sucked. She retracted the pipe, smiled, and set the glass tube down on the coffee table. She let the rush of amphetamine pump through her blood system. Immediately, her veins jumped with life. She shook her head. Her own cloud of smoke barreled out from between her parted lips.

She leaned forward and ran her fingers through her bleached blonde hair. It was damp. Rod liked her hair to be blonde. He liked her skin to be tanned. He'd told her every day that she was beautiful. And when they made love, it was strong and intense. The drugs accentuated the sensation—the ferocity of the sex—but not the passion of it. She could near climax—most of the time—when she locked onto his blue eyes. They were calm, the color of the ocean. They reminded her of the warm water of Baja Mexico. That's where they intended to live after they fled from the states. Before they could do that, they would need to leave this house. A manhunt would be assigned to them soon. They both knew it. They felt it coming. They'd left a trail of bodies across three or four states. Each victim looked the same. They were all tied up in the basement and missing limbs. Surely, there was a detective who had picked up on the similarities. And they knew they wouldn't be able to stay in the country for long. It was only a matter of time before they would be caught.

The house where they resided belonged to a young woman. She was maybe thirty years old. The woman was attractive. She was a lawyer.

The young, attractive, professional woman had been sipping on chardonnay from a large wine glass at a cozy little tavern in Middleton, a town just outside of Madison, Wisconsin. The bar was nearly empty. Only a few patrons inhabited the bar on that fateful night. Like always, Patty had taken her seat near the end of the bar. It was her job to *watch*, nonchalantly, while Rod made the young lady's acquaintance. He would charm the young woman, entrance her with his eyes. His eyes won him the girl every time. Patty knew this. It was how he'd won *her*. Rod probably would have killed Patty too if he hadn't sensed the *sickness* within her.

His eyes were magnificent.

The woman continued relaxing at her small candlelit table in the dining section. Rod walked to her table. He inquired if she'd like company. He'd already asked the bartender what she was drinking. When he approached her, he held another glass of the chardonnay she sipped on. When Rod and the girl, Judy, left together, three hours later, the bartender was oblivious to the fact that Patty had any relation to Rod.

Rod would soon tie Judy to a metal post in the basement of her nice Victorian home.

And now, sitting in Judy's living room, passing the pipe back and forth, Rod and Patty decided it was time to do away with her. This *thing,* Judy, had been fun to play with. But it was time to move on.

They'd removed both of Judy's arms with a hacksaw that they'd found in the garage. To stop the bleeding, they'd cauterized the stumps against the red-hot bottom of a frying pan. They found the black pan in the kitchen cupboard below the microwave. They'd held it over an open flame for an hour before cauterizing Judy's stumps with it.

Judy wore a gag. It was merely a rag stuffed in her mouth. It muffled her screams while they laughed at the agony she displayed.

Judy didn't have neighbors. Her house was isolated. For the three days Patty and Rod had taken residence in Judy's home, no one had come to check on her. The mailman delivered but didn't venture past the mailbox at the end of the driveway. Not once did he think to come to the door and ask why she hadn't picked up her mail. And Judy had no friends. There was no one to hear her masked sorrows. No one would help her. She was vulnerable and alone.

After the second day, Judy explained that she'd taken a week of vacation from work. She'd recently finished an important trial she'd been working on for two years. It was over. And she was taking a week off to recuperate and celebrate.

Not quite the celebration she'd hoped for.

Rod removed his shirt. It peeled off. The sweat ridden cloth stuck to his back. Patty watched him disrobe. She admired his chiseled body. He wasn't overly muscular. But his muscles bulged from beneath his skin. He had no fat. He was tan. Not dark. His tan was the kind of beach boy orange that accentuated his boy-next-door looks. To the living dead of society, he was a male fantasy. No one saw him or understood him the way Patty did.

Rod and Patty could enjoy their sickness undetected. They could take pleasure in their *sinister deeds* without the predetermined flood of guilt that waved-in with societal standards.

When Rod pulled the basement door open, a cool musty breeze shot up the stairs and kissed Patty's face. It was refreshing. Faintly, she heard Judy attempting to scream. The scream was diluted by her gag.

Patty followed Rod down the creaky wooden stairs. The basement was dark. It was dank. The space was large. There were round, red, posts cemented along the sides and at the center. A washer and dryer were neatly aligned behind the staircase, in the right corner. All the amenities of a fine Midwestern basement were present. Beneath Judy's *stink* was the pleasing scent of dryer sheets and laundry detergent.

Judy's legs rested flat on the cement floor, beneath her pool of urine and excrement. The smell was bad. Patty and Rod's excitement allowed them to disregard the odor. The stench was a minor inconvenience. Torturing this woman for the past three days was enlightening. The power that came with controlling Judy's demise was spiritual.

Patty watched while Rod knelt beside Judy, his abdomen flexing. Patty was enamored.

Rod gazed into Judy's eyes and smiled.

"I want to thank you, Judy," he said politely. "Sorry." He turned to Patty and nodded. "*We*…want to thank you. You've given us the greatest gift. *You.*"

Judy cringed. Her face was caked with dried sweat, blood, and tears. Her skin was haggard and pruned. Her stumps flailed, comically, as she struggled. The heavy rope wrapped around her slim naked waist prevented her from escaping. Her body convulsed. She lowered her head and sobbed.

Patty's lips stretched wide. Her pearly, bleach-white, teeth jutted forward. The ultimate excitement was at hand. Fulfillment was coming. The torture, sex, and foreplay *of murder* had risen. It boiled to a head.

Rod extracted a straight razor from his back pocket. The blade was spotless as he retracted it from the handle. It was recently sharpened. He placed it beneath Judy's chin. It sunk into the soft flesh of her neck.

"Guh…guh…guh…" billowed from her mouth.

Her throat heaved upward. It riveted when the razor sunk into her neck. Her skin parted in neat slices. Smiling, Rod slid the blade lengthwise. Blood spilled like a theater curtain and painted her naked breasts and stomach red.

Patty's excitement grew while the woman convulsed. Judy's life drained along with the color from her face. Patty knew what came next. The end of the ritual was Patty's favorite part. She and Rod would smoke more amphetamine and then make love for hours. The power of what they'd done would peak and sex was the only way to settle their restlessness.

Patty felt a moment of fear when Rod twisted his neck toward her. His scowl was intimidating. He strutted in her direction, his face intense. He grabbed her by the waist and lifted her. She straddled him. She felt the stiffness below his hips. He carried her upstairs to Judy's bedroom.

They engaged in carnal pleasures for hours.

3

A pleasant breeze swept through the house. The sun began to set. In the bedroom, Rod and Patty watched out the window while the blood orange sun fell below the hilly terrain to the west. It cast a wonderful glow over the countryside, over the endless acres of forest.

Naked, Rod and Patty held each other. They lay in bed until sleep found them. The amphetamine had kept them awake for three days. Even so, their bodies demanded rest. Their eyes drooped. They were out. After a long sleep, they could continue their morbid journey with fresh energy.

They awoke twenty-four hours later to another sunset. Sobriety was unkind. They felt drained, exhausted, and depleted. They were experiencing the tolls of the amphetamine. Getting up from the bed, Rod made his way to the kitchen. He could smell Judy's stink. She was rotting in the basement.

Reality sunk in. They couldn't stay in this house much longer. The stink would travel fast. This was a fact Rod knew well. He was certain Patty would agree. The hunt, capture, and kill had been amazing. But the evolution of their experience was complete. Rod had a familiar feeling. He'd experienced this feeling many times. Staying in this house was risky. They were on borrowed time. Every moment they stayed was another moment they could get caught.

Rod wouldn't go to prison. He'd eat a bullet or cut his own throat before he'd go to jail. He and Patty needed to recuperate. They needed to fuel up, and leave.

Night was beginning. They could enjoy each other for one more evening. Then they would have to travel on. Their plans were to drive south to Chicago, west to Arizona, then down to Mexico. They'd saved a good amount of money along their destructive path, close to two hundred thousand dollars. Robbing liquor stores, gas stations, and even a few small banks had given them a plentiful bounty.

Rod gulped water from the kitchen sink faucet. It tasted good. It was smooth. It hydrated him. Midwestern water tasted clean. *Maybe it was the lack of chlorine*. He didn't know for sure. Water moaned through the old pipes. Patty was showering. The creaking pipes from the upstairs shower drifted into the kitchen. Rod smiled. He went to the living room, hit the glass pipe, and went upstairs.

The bathroom door was open. The lights were off. There were three candles set across the sink and on the back of the toilet. Candlelight danced across the blue walls and reflected elegantly across the clear glass shower door. Rod removed his clothes.

Naked, he stepped into the warm water. It was soft. The last hit off the pipe had renewed his energy.

Patty's hair was slick, wet, and neatly pulled back. It came to a point in the center of her back. Just above her nicely shaped backside. Her skin was flawless. It radiated in the candlelight. Her body shimmered. Her beauty aroused him. She was a stunning woman. He was a beautiful boy. Their looks would run out with time. But, for now, they enjoyed each other's vanity. They were both appealing and took pleasure in carnal activities, hungered for each other's flesh.

"We'll leave tomorrow night. I'll take care of the smell in the basement. The best I can, anyway. We'll smoke some bowls and fuck tonight," Rod explained while he placed his fingers under her chin. He lifted her face.

Patty nodded. She grabbed a washcloth and began to scrub Rod's back. She focused on the fast streams of water that ran between his loins. His backside was well formed and hairless.

She liked to touch him.

"I'll do whatever you tell me." She nodded while kneading her fingers into the flesh of his tense back.

She *would* do anything for him. She'd slit her own throat with his razor if he asked her to.

And he knew it.

"I know, babe. That's why I love you."

She smiled affectionately. She grabbed the green bar of soap from the ledge beneath the showerhead and lathered him up. They held each other beneath the warm beads of water, bodies rubbing together.

They made love again.

4

The early morning hours evaporated. So did the continuing ribbons of smoke from the glass pipe. Wound and sped up, Rod saw imaginary shadows dance across the living room walls. Shadows were nothing new. Rod had seen things that *weren't there* many times while in the depths of a meth binge. It was part of the psychosis. This time there were noises. Silent screams drifted into his ears. When he saw the frightened look upon Patty's face, his blood rushed. He froze with fear.

Rod stood fast. He ran through the kitchen, pulled the basement door open and hurried down the stairs. Stopping at the bottom step, he turned back to the top. Patty gnawed on her fingernails. Obviously, she was frightened.

"I heard it, too. Is she still alive?" Patty called down.

Rod didn't answer. He was afraid to talk. His mouth was dry. He crept toward Judy's body. Her love-handles hung over the blood-soaked rope-binding. The thick hemp length dug into her stomach. Her chest folded forward. At first glance, she looked collapsed. Her stomach was bloated, forcing her back to arch. Her bony spine stretched a line along the middle of her back. Her bloated and blackening stomach poured over the rope.

Still scared, Rod forced a nervous smile. He wobbled to the back of the basement. His knees were weak. It was dark, visibility was nonexistent. His footing was staggered. He nearly tripped over Judy's left leg.

Judy was motionless. Rod was relieved.

Maybe he imagined the screams?

Maybe they were delayed death throes?

Neither would have surprised him. The methamphetamine tricked his sense of sound.

The upstairs light switch clicked on. Rod spun, quickly.

"You want the light on?" Patty called down in a shaky voice.

Rod was annoyed. He stared at Patty. She descended down the stairs. The creaking wood was unnerving. Each time she took a step, Rod's heart pounded.

Rod stood near Judy's corpse.

Patty hit the last step. She stood, gawking at Rod from the bottom of the staircase. Her hand was wrapped tightly around the railing. From this distance, Rod could see the whites of her knuckles. Her eyes widened. She was terrified.

Confused, Rod spun toward Judy. She rose from the floor. Her dead legs lifted parallel to the cement. She was levitating. The rope began to stir, unwrap, and then fall to the ground.

Rod's mouth dried up. He could taste dry saliva clinging to the roof of his mouth. It created a paste. He pried his tongue from his cheek and swallowed.

Judy's head jerked forward. The color of her eyes rolled over white, fiery. Her lips peeled back. She smiled. The corners of her mouth tore upward. Her teeth pushed forward. A harmonic cackle escaped her lips. Rod ran for the stairs.

Something heavy grabbed his neck, picked him up, and threw him with great velocity. It wasn't Judy. She was across the room. Whatever it was, it felt like he'd been hit by a truck. His body slammed against the cold cement wall at the far end of the basement. His jaw was broken. His organs burned. His joints felt like they were on fire. The pain was unbearable. He coughed up blood. It splashed against the cold cement. He didn't know if he could endure the pain. Looking to his right, with his peripheral vision, he saw Patty being erected from where she stood. She was smashed flat against the wall. It was as if gravity had sucked her against the cement bulkhead. Given the stretched look upon Patty's face, Rod knew she was experiencing the same excruciating burn he felt.

Judy glided toward them as though she was being operated by a pulley system. Rod's heart thumped out of control.

Judy slid in front of Rod. She laughed the sweet laughter of a demonic child. Her voice sounded synthesized.

He tried to scream. His lips wouldn't part. They were locked together.

Judy stood between Rod and Patty with her arms spread open. Snake-like vines slithered from the stumps where her arms used to be. The snakes glistened. They were covered in dark ooze. The slimy end protruding from her right arm wiggled between Rod's lips. It forced his mouth open. Tiny razor-sharp hooks poked out from the center of the scaly snake. He felt the slimy vine forcing itself down his throat. It felt like a serpent was slithering into his stomach. It tore the moist flesh of his esophagus. It ripped the lining of his stomach. Blood gushed from the fissures. His heart knocked hard, not fast.

Relief suddenly swept his mind. This thing was going to kill him. And being dead was better than living with this degree of pain and agony. He thought he was going into cardiac arrest. The slithering thing wrapped around his heart. It squeezed. The burning intensified. The hooks ripped through his ventricles. They ripped through his aorta. Rod's sanity fled. He watched a blazing hole open in the wall. Another world opened to him.

He was afraid. He fell forward into the lack of color.

He was in Hell.

5

Patty watched on while Rod's corpse slumped forward onto the floor. The swaying, pulsating vine—that looked very similar to a raw muscle—retracted and then shot back like an elastic band into the remaining length of Judy's arm.

Patty wanted to die. Closing her eyes, the burning seized her.

Patty fell to the ground like crumpled trash next to Rod—what was left of him.

Chapter 3

1

Rod felt his limbs tingle and tighten. The muscles in his legs, arms, back and chest flexed. The tendons in his neck stretched. His fists clenched. His chest cramped. Every fiber of hair stood tall. His skin pulled taut, like it was about to shed. His organs burned. His heart hammered heavily. Even his ribs felt like they would break and burst through his skin. He wanted to scream. He couldn't. His eyes opened wide. He couldn't shut his eyelids. Panic set in.

Rod stared across the length of the basement. He fell forward onto his face. The cold cement hurt when his forehead pounded into it. Blood trickled from his mouth, staining his lips. He tried to move but couldn't. He was flat against the ground, lying on his stomach. He tried to wiggle his fingers. Nothing. Then his toes began to move, but something else was moving them. The communication between his brain and limbs no longer functioned. He was paralyzed yet moving. Something else was driving the vessel, his body.

Whatever movement took place, now had to be some kind of nervous twitch. He thought. He felt the sensation of movement, but control didn't exist. The burning sensation spread through his veins. Fire pumped into his heart. Then he was being lifted. His body cranked ninety degrees and his feet planted on the cement. He walked toward Patty. He was still only a passenger, in *his* body.

He picked up Patty's head. His face lowered toward hers. He peered into her eyes. He felt his own eyes move but wasn't controlling the movement. His optic nerves seemed to invert. Then he felt *something* within him, an indescribable presence. Whatever it was, it laughed at him. And the laughter humiliated him. Rod's mouth opened. He began to speak. He felt the sensation of his tongue lolling and his vocal cords stretched. But still, he wasn't in command of his functions. He wanted to scream. And then his mouth vocalized. His voice was deep, rich in tone. It sounded synthesized.

"Rise, Jezebeth," the voice commanded.

Patty stood and peered into Rod's eyes. Rod was staring at Patty through the empty windows of his eyes. Patty held a glowing ring of white fire around her pupils. The circle outlined the blue coloring.

"We've been given time," Patty said.

But it wasn't Patty.

2

Sammael stood in the dark pit of eternity. He brooded over the lake of torment and flames, enjoying the endless screams of the vile spirits surrounding him. They splashed in and out of the fire, begging for his hand. He only laughed.

Without warning, he began to levitate from the rock he stood upon. He was being beckoned by the Unholy. Pleasure sizzled within him. He was being sent up. He enjoyed being sent to the plain of human existence. People were tantalizing when tormented.

They were fun.

Sammael had walked with humans of the earth many times. He took pleasure in possessing them and killing them. It had been three years since he'd been granted existence on earth. The last time had been spent pleasurably. He and the demon, Lilith, were sent to an isolated Farmhouse where they tormented a young married couple who had killed their infant child. They'd killed their young son simply for the insurance money. It was fun to toy with the couple. The newlyweds had done awful things. And in return for their sins, Sammael and Lilith had drowned them, cut them, and brutalized them. Afterward, they sent them into the searing pit of darkness.

Sammael felt a familiar sensation while he sunk into the flesh of his newest human. The feeling was pleasant. His focus was lost. He saw the Priest. *Father Leslie Gardner.* Sammael was being sent to earth to take revenge on the priest, Gardner. Excitement coursed through him. This would be a great redemption. It had been decades since the priest expelled him from the body he'd stolen. And being sent *back* had hurt. Sammael's rage burned for a long time. It stewed inside of him. The last mission, torturing the married couple, had been a good release, but it hadn't eased his anger toward Gardner or the junkie whore whose body he'd borrowed.

Peering down at the strong arms of the body he now possessed, he admired its flesh. The body was strong, youthful, and attractive. This boy was muscular and physically able. Sammael looked over his new vessel. He flexed his new muscles and saw the world through human eyes. Then he took in his surroundings.

He was in a basement. There was a dead woman lying on the ground at his feet.

How nice.

She was missing her arms. Blood seeped from her orifices. Her skin was blackened. She smelled foul. And there was another woman. She began to rise.

It was the demon Jezebeth. Sammael knew this demon well. She took the body of the other woman, the younger one with blonde hair. This woman wasn't missing her arms. Both Sammael and Jezebeth wore attractive new bodies. Their vanity was very pleasing. Jezebeth had blue eyes and blonde hair. Physically, she radiated beauty, fit and attractive. But as Sammael looked inside the eye of the woman's mind, he saw how retched her soul was. The boy and girl who Sammael and Jezebeth *took* had been torturing the woman with no arms. The two of them had taken pleasure in tormenting her. They'd inflicted hell upon her.

Sammael would enjoy this young man. He was a worthy vessel. Reading through the boy's thoughts, he found a name. This boy was Rod. And the girl was Patty. But Rod and Patty were gone. It was only Sammael and Jezebeth, now.

Jezebeth had destroyed whatever life was left of Patty. She was only Jezebeth now. They could remain in these bodies until they were destroyed. Destroying human bodies was fun. Possession was a regal experience. The only trouble with possession was that the body rotted. It could only be inhabited for a short time. Once it was deteriorated, it couldn't hold the evil spirit any longer. The body would quit, and the demon would move on. They needed to get busy.

"We must go. We don't have much time," Sammael told Jezebeth.

They climbed up the stairs and exited out the back door. They stepped into the dark of night, moving through the wet grass, and strolling down the driveway. Their new bodies were exceptional.

When they reached the mouth of the driveway, they halted.

Sammael flicked his fingers. The beautiful Victorian house ignited into explosive orange flames. The flames painted the morning sky with magnificent ribbons of orange.

They continued past the base of the driveway. A white Ford Explorer was parked at the foot of the driveway. Within minutes, Sammael and Jezebeth were speeding down a deserted country.

They headed toward Gardner

Chapter 4

1

Every few minutes, the roar of a passing car whisked down Highway 26 near the edge of Dodge Junction. Buggy's Liquor store sat off to the right side of the highway. The white brick building rested at the base of a rolling hillside. The hilly terrain held acres of cornfield. A narrow gravel road led to a farmhouse on top of the hill.

Winny and Garth Gasper stood behind the counter of their liquor store munching on Corn Nuts. They were silent. Garth read an automotive magazine with a 1969 Ford Mustang on the cover while Winny watched the sun fade below the small town of Dodge Junction. The day had been a nail-biter. A real bore of a Saturday afternoon. Both Winny and Garth were tired. They'd done nothing all day. And boredom was tiresome.

Winny strolled around to the front of the counter. He stopped near the entrance doors and gazed out at the vast acreage of farmland, which rested beyond the parking lot. His sullen green eyes quickly adjusted to the setting sun.

The fields and forest held many luscious colors. The greens and rustic tones captivated his sights. The evening glow of sunset highlighted the treetops and fields with a golden tint. The pink tint and shadowing of the evening was magnificent. Staring through the aluminum framed window, reality became a painting. The sun's fading orange glow splashed across Winny's long, bony face. His figure was bony, too. He'd bulked up over the past few years, placed a few layers of meat beneath his skin, the result of acquiring athletic routines like running and mild weightlifting. He had a modest bench press and dumbbells in his garage. But he was still wiry.

Winny loved the small town of Dodge Junction. He was proud of its German and Irish heritage. He appreciated that his immediate family and most of his friends lived within five minutes of anywhere and everything in the community. Meeting up for a beer with an old high school buddy was never a problem and always satisfying. Winny didn't want for anything. His family and friends were all he needed, and they were close.

Winny sensed his brother's desire to leave. Garth had been very vocal about *getting out* since before they'd graduated from Dodge Junction Senior High School five years ago. On many occasions, Garth had confided in Winny that he was sick of small-town life. He wanted to see the world. Experience new things; meet new people. Personally, Winny didn't agree with Garth's philosophy. To Winny, family and friends were everything. Small-town life was enough. It was easy. The way life was meant to be.

Buggy's Liquor was passed down to the Gasper boys two years earlier after their father retired. Their father had spent many years running it. Buggy's Liquor was the town's most successful booze outlet.

Buggy Gasper, Winny and Garth's father, retired at the age of sixty-eight and he was proud to have set up a successful business for his sons. The store continued to make a good amount of money. It would be enough for his boys to raise their families and live a comfortable life, if they ever settled down.

The people of Dodge Junction took a liking to the Gasper boys. They were charming and witty. They displayed an ideal family dynamic. For this reason, the other liquor stores in town weren't as profitable. They only wanted to make a buck. The Gasper's were part of the community. In small towns like Dodge Junction, people were more than willing to go out of their way to buy beer and spirits from people they trusted. The Gasper boys held a warm relationship with the town. Winny appreciated this. He didn't know why Garth was so ashamed of living *the good life.*

Winny shook his head.

Usually, Saturday nights were busy, but not tonight. Most of the townsfolk stocked their booze on Friday. The county fair was being held in Watertown, which meant the weekend would be slow. The town was dead. When the county fair came around, the lively crowds, from town, usually made their way up to the Rock River Camp Grounds, near Watertown. Everyone was stocked up on booze for the three-day celebration. The majority of Dodge Junction's townies were camped out in tents and RV's by Rock Lake. They were drinking, camping, and boating. Still, Winny and Garth expected Saturday to be a bit busier than it was.

Maybe tomorrow would pick up?

Winny set his half-eaten bag of corn nuts on the counter. Crumbs sprinkled out across the counter. He made his way toward the bathroom at the back of the store. Along the way, he grabbed his wooden mop. It rested in a yellow bucket. The bucket wheels were loose and they whined every couple of feet and the back right wheel spun back and forth, lazily. It wasn't closing time yet, but Winny figured he might as well mop the floor, get it out of the way.

"It's my turn to clean the crapper, right?" Winny hollered.

Garth blew his shaggy brown hair away from his tan face. Peering to the back of the store, he stood up and directed his dark brown eyes at Winny. "Yeah, bro. It's your turn to clean the crapper. I'll sweep up when we close."

Nodding, Winny pushed his mop bucket toward the restrooms.

Stopping in the middle of the brightly lit hallway, which separated the men's room from the lady's, Winny propped the large blue door open with his plastic bucket. He quickly dipped the stringy cloth end of the mop into the hot soapy water. Tiny white bubbles popped at the surface. He stirred the handle until a thin layer of foam spread across the surface of the swaying water. It smelled piney and pleasant. Moving from the far end of the hall to the mouth of it, Winny swabbed the mop from side to side, never missing a spot.

2

The store's automated doorbell chimed loud when Father Leslie Gardner entered the store. Shaking his head, he blew out an exhausted breath. He waved his arms up and down like a bird. He sighed when the cold air conditioning surrounded him. Standing beneath the vent, he closed his eyes and inhaled deep. His light gray T-shirt was sweat stained underneath his armpits and lower stomach. He wiped his forehead with his forearm then turned to Gath and smiled.

"Man, is it hot out there. It's nearly dark out and I'm sweating like a hog," Gardner said cheerfully. He continued to wipe sweat from his brow. "I got *this* sweaty walking from the house."

"You only live up the hill," Garth returned, subtly sarcastic. He barely looked up from his magazine to acknowledge Gardner.

"I know," Gardner said matter-of-fact like. He had a corny excitement in his tone. A grin curled across his aging face. "Where's your brother?"

"Back here!" Winny shouted excitedly from the back hallway.

Father Gardner turned to the back of the store. He raised his right hand and waved. "Good evening to you, Winny. Why is your brother so cranky?"

"Evening, Father! He's always cranky. You know that."

Shaking his head, Father Gardner winked at Garth, who looked annoyed, and went to the cooler. He headed past the cold beer and stopped near the milk. He pulled out two gallons of two percent from the bottom rack, strolled back to the counter and set the milk jugs next to the cash register. He dug through his pockets. A moment later, he held out a crisp twenty dollar bill while Garth rang him up.

"It's sure been a scorcher, wouldn't you say?" Father Gardner prodded. He ran his hand through his damp silver hair.

"I wouldn't know. I've been in the nice, cold, air conditioning all day." He set his magazine down and looked out the window. "I might go for a run after work." He turned to Gardner with an inquisitive expression. "Say, can I ask you a question?"

"Sure thing."

"You're a priest? I mean we call you *Father* and all. So, where's your church? I thought you worked in a flower shop?" Garth asked as he took Gardner's twenty dollar bill. He put the twenty in the register and then counted out Gardner's change.

Gardner nodded. He briefly skimmed over his change. He put the money in his pocket then looked up at Garth, "Excellent question. I retired about eighteen years ago. I still work with the church, but on more of consultant level. I spent a lot of my days traveling…setting up aid in third world countries and less fortunate parts of America…That kind of thing," Gardner responded, vaguely.

He didn't think it was necessary to tell Garth he'd spent most of his time fighting heinous acts of evil; exercising demonic spirits and battling those who lived their lives along a disturbed path. That, in fact, was why he'd retired in the first place. The exhaustion that came from fighting unholy enemies had gotten to be too much. He couldn't handle it anymore, didn't want to.

Neither could his mind. He wanted to experience a bit of happiness. He desperately wanted to relax before he left this world. Now, he lived with his beautiful wife Donna, the love of his life. They were happy. They still worked. They owned a garden nursery in town. They didn't make much money, but the work was relaxing. It was easy.

Given the things Gardner had seen, he didn't think it was too much to want a little peace before he passed. Not that he would pass anytime soon. He was well and in good shape for a sixty-year-old man. He didn't drink—maybe a glass of wine with dinner—and he was an avid runner.

Given the stress of his career, he was lucky he hadn't had a heart attack, yet. The average man would have dropped dead if he'd seen an eighty-year-old Hispanic woman crawl across the ceiling of her one bedroom apartment on the Mexican side of Tijuana. The many faces of evil were burned into Gardner's memory. His thoughts were scarred from the evils he'd fought.

"You want a plastic bag for your milk?" Garth asked.

"No thanks. Say hi to Buggy for me. Tell him to stop drinking so much beer. Every time I see him… he's drinking beer."

Garth aimed his index finger at Father Gardner like a gun and then pulled the trigger and said, "He's pretty happy, Father. And beer isn't the worst thing in the world." He raised his finger to the sky. "Say hey to *your* father… for me."

Gardner smiled, gently. He left the liquor store with his milk jugs. A hot gust of humid air bellowed into the store as he left.

3

The sun disappeared. The moon had risen. It was dark. Inside the store, Garth ran his palm along the rough edge of the wiry metal rack that ran the length of aisle one. The rack neatly displayed all the sugar-based snacks like candy bars and gummy candy.

He made his way toward the restrooms. Along the way, the yellow wrapper of a Butterfinger called out to him. He hadn't eaten a candy bar in a long time. It wouldn't kill him to have *just one*. He thought about it. He passed.

Garth hated to clean. And he didn't want to help Winny, either. But he was bored and craved some company. After rounding the corner of aisle two, he grabbed a bag of potato chips from the corner shelf, ripped the bag open and began to munch. He moved into the men's room doorway and leaned against the open doorframe. He kicked at the wooden door stop wedged beneath the chipped door and tiled floor.

"How can a guy as smart as Gardner believe in something as silly as God? You'd think he'd be smart enough to acknowledge the facts."

Winny stopped mopping. Garth knew he'd struck a cord. He sometimes forgot, or chose to forget, Winny was a *believer*.

Slow and precise, Winny set his mop against the off-white tile wall. He frowned.

Garth rolled his eyes. He knew he shouldn't have said anything. Now, he would receive a lecture about how Jesus died for our sins and blah, blah, blah. There was no concrete evidence God existed, let alone had a child.

"Why are people who believe in God stupid?" Winny asked. He steadied the mop and crossed his arms. "I believe in God. I'm not a genius, but I don't think I'm stupid."

Here it was. He should have kept his fool mouth shut.

"You want to stay in this town and keep working at this stupid liquor store, that's stupid, too," Garth hissed back. He didn't know why he put it that way, either. The words just came out.

"So you *are* saying I'm stupid?"

"You're *acting* stupid. I don't think you *are* stupid. It's stupid that you've accepted this store as your destiny," Garth enlightened his brother. He didn't know why he'd said all this. For one reason or another, he was antagonizing his brother.

"And why did you change the topic from religion to geographic location?"

A long silence followed. Winny stared at the floor. He prodded his toe at the edge of his mop. Then, his eyes swept upward and he said, "This store's been in our family our entire lives. I have fond memories *in* and *of* this place. In a way it's a *living thing*. This store provided our family with a home, money, and a life. That's not stupid, it's a success. And if you see a success as stupid, then you might want to ask yourself if *you* aren't the one *acting* stupid."

Garth gritted his teeth. He hated it when Winny came at him like this, making him feel unappreciative. It was degrading. It made him feel selfish. It was belittling.

"I guess I want more than this. Think about it. We run a liquor store in a stupid little town no one's ever heard of. Don't you want more out of life?" Garth returned.

"Like what?"

And that was the problem. Garth Gasper didn't know what he wanted. He only knew *it* was more than *this.* He was better than *this place* and he wanted to prove it to the world. Even more than the world, he wanted his family to know it. Their father, Buggy, originally named William, had technically given the store to both of them equally, but everyone knew Winny was in charge. And it wasn't because Winny was smarter. He wasn't. He was the oldest and it just seemed right to let Winny run the place. He was more assertive.

"I want to move out to California, live by the ocean," Garth finally said, with no conviction. And living in California wasn't necessarily a plan, it was a place. The only difference was California's weather was great.

Both Garth and Winny had friends who had moved out to California in search of the American Dream. Tom Hopkins moved to Los Angeles shortly after graduation. He had intentions of becoming a famous actor but had only become cynical. He moved back home two years later. He'd developed a nasty drug problem to boot. And he'd blown his savings. His only success was a small role on a television show about homosexual men in rural Texas.

"What do you want to do in California, Garth? I'm not trying to be mean; I just don't know what you want to do with your life. If you don't want to stay here, that's fine. Just because I'm content here doesn't mean you have to be. But it would be nice to know you have a goal and that you're trying to achieve it."

Winny always had a way of asking questions which in turn made him appear angelic. He talked like he'd already done it all, seen everything there was to see. Winny could be self-righteous. He liked taking the high road and did so whenever he had the chance.

Still, Winny had what he wanted out of life; he was happy living on a pedestal in this one horse town. He was able to look down at his misguided little brother and hover above the simple-minded population. It made him feel superior, Garth thought.

"You're really getting mad at me, aren't you?" Winny asked as he squared off with his disgruntled sibling. He placed his hand on Garth's right shoulder. "I'm serious. I just want you to be happy. I wish working here, with me, was enough. But if you need to go… and see the world… then that's what you need to do. I get it. I admire that. You're a dreamer."

Garth genuinely felt bad. Sometimes his thoughts got the best of him. His idle mind allowed his paranoia to spin out of control.

"And as for the God thing, I just like to think there's more to life than just eating, sleeping, procreating, and going poop," Winny concluded. "Otherwise, what's the point? None of this would mean anything."

At *poop* they both busted into laughter.

Chapter 5

1

The full moon hung high in the night sky. It was yellow. And around it, the stars danced brightly across the cloudless black canvas. Below the magnificence of the universe, a beat-up old truck drove down the empty highway. The headlights illuminated the fading yellow dash marks in need of fresh paint. Each dash shot beneath the rusted red truck as it sped forward.

Inside the vehicle, Timmy Sutter, a thirty-two year roughneck biker-type with ice coursing through his veins, drove at a steady pace of fifty-five miles an hour. He cruised easy down Highway 26. The driver's side window was rolled halfway down. The subtle breeze blew Timmy's dark brown hair back and around, and whipped his thick beard.

The fresh air was comforting. It made him feel easy. And he was careful to drive the speed limit. He didn't want to get pulled over. Especially, since Timmy and Terrance

Morton, an African American biker thug with no hair on his face or head, and Cherri Joyce, his beautifully disturbed blue eyed, redheaded girlfriend, had just knocked off a gas station on the Wisconsin side of the Mississippi river.

Timmy's two accomplices were sleeping on the seats next to him. And they wore their seatbelts. The seats were small and everyone was scrunched in tight. They were over a hundred miles away from the gas station they'd recently robbed.

The station they'd hit was located at the edge of a small river town. It was an easy *target*. The clerk was scared. She didn't worry about protocol. And she hadn't risked her life for what was in the register. She gave every cent to Timmy. She would have given them anything they wanted, so long as they left fast.

As usual, Terrance stood as a lookout inside the station, near the door. This way, he could identify and deal with anyone who entered. He could control the situation while Timmy conducted the armed robbery.

Cherri sat on the curb, outside the front door, drinking a coke or licking an ice cream cone. Her job was to look innocent. She would warn Terrance if anyone threatened to enter. And Terrance would inform Timmy. Cherri looked young for her age. She was twenty-three, but easily passed for seventeen. Like Terrance, her job was to act as a lookout while Timmy did the gun work.

And the last job had been easy. When the gas station attendant saw Timmy's gun, she calmly opened the cash register and retrieved all the money. She stacked the green bills neatly in her shaky hands. She even put the change inside of a plastic bag and zipped it shut. She'd handed the cash to Timmy as if he were a paying customer.

Timmy appreciated her cooperation. In all truthfulness, he didn't like hurting people. He didn't like struggles. He'd knocked off quite a few gas stations and cooperation was always welcome. Struggles usually occurred when the pump jockey got itchy and felt the need to be a hero. Those were the jobs that ended up messy. In situations like that, someone always got hurt. Luckily—so far—no one had gotten dead.

Timmy hadn't killed anyone. But he'd gotten violent on more than one occasion. A few of his *uncooperative victims* had spent a good amount of time in the hospital. He could be rough.

If it had to be done, he would clock the clerk with the butt of his pistol. A good crack to the nose left the hero dazed. During the course of his criminal career, Timmy had broken a few noses and knocked a few people unconscious. Thankfully, that's all the violence that had been necessary.

Now, driving down Highway 26, about thirty miles west of Dodge Junction, Timmy realized they needed more cash. More money would be necessary to continue their travels. The last gas station had been a success, but it only amounted to four hundred dollars. Not a lot. Four hundred was chicken scratch. It would only carry them for a day or two. They were headed to Detroit, which was a couple hundred miles east.

Timmy's brother ran a Chop Shop in downtown Motor City. He'd been attempting to get Timmy to work for him for a couple of years. But a few stints in county jail and a few years of probation had hindered the opportunity.

Terrance was along for the ride. Terrance and Timmy met in county jail. They were cellmates. And after they were released, they'd worked a couple of jobs together. They weren't a team, but they collaborated well.

Terrance was outgoing. There would be plenty of opportunity for him in Detroit. He could unload product; drugs, guns, stolen goods. Many of the abandoned neighborhoods around inner-city Detroit were serving as cook houses for the manufacturing of drugs. Terrance was the kind of guy who could sniff-out a good operation and excel at it. His high wasn't the drugs. It was the action. It was the thrill of making a deal, holding up a station, getting away with it.

Cherri, on the other hand, was Timmy's woman. Despite how badly Timmy treated Cherri, he loved her. She was loyal. She whined about his career choice, but that was her job, to nag.

He'd only gotten rough with her a few times. Usually, after she'd suggested he find a new line of work. She believed in this fairy tale where she could change him, that she could manipulate him into settling down and working a real job. And they could live happily-ever-after, on love.

What a joke.

He wondered how long she'd stick around. His lifestyle would eventually turn her away or get her killed. In this line of business, relationships had a shelf life. Sure, he'd thought about quitting the criminal life and settling down. He wanted to give Cherri everything she desired. But she didn't understand that this lifestyle was *it* for him.

He didn't know how to do anything else and, truthfully, he didn't *want* to do anything else. His brother's chop shop *was* the compromise. She would have to respect that because that's the way it was. Plus, his brother's chop shop was a steady job. It wasn't legal, but it was structured and organized.

2

Cherri woke up when the low rumble of the truck's engine grew louder and the cab began to shift. The tires juggled over the jagged shoulder of the highway. Small rocks kicked up under the floor panels.

The pebbles sounded like marbles on wood. The current terrain was bumpy. Obviously, these roads were in need of maintenance. There were potholes scattered everywhere. In the dark, you couldn't see where the road ended. The paint markings were faded, almost non-existent.

Cherri focused on Timmy. He pulled a brown paper bag from beneath his seat. He dug into the bag, pulled the tab off a can of Pabst Blue Ribbon beer and sipped from it.

Terrance was asleep next to Cherri, on the right. She sat in the middle. Cramped was an understatement. She wished Timmy would have boosted an SUV or even a car. That would have been more comfortable. But Timmy liked trucks. And now, they were stuffed shoulder to shoulder inside of this heap-on-wheels. A dumpy Chevrolet with rusted *everything*.

"Where are we headed?" she asked, knowing he didn't like being bothered while he was driving.

"Saw a sign for a liquor store. It's about thirty miles ahead. I think we should hit it."

She looked to the digital radio face. It was ten o'clock. Most liquor stores closed up at this time of night. In places like California, you could buy alcohol until two o'clock in the morning. The laws varied from place to place. But around these parts—the Midwest—you usually had to purchase your booze slightly before or after ten o'clock, unless you were in a bar. Bar time was two-thirty.

"If you think we can do it."

"What the hell's that supposed to mean?" Timmy snarled. He stared at the road, never turning his head toward her. He continued sipping from his beer.

"I just meant it's late. Liquor stores usually close early around here."

His jaw was sliding back and forth. His teeth faintly chattered as he ground them together. He chugged the rest of his beer and tossed the can out the window. "I guess we'll see."

This was her cue to *shut it.*

There was nothing else to say. She adjusted, slumping back against the cloth seat covers. The seat cushions were held together by shredded padding. The truck was old. They'd stolen it from a farmer who probably didn't know it was gone yet. It smelled musty like a stale fart. The white covers were stained sweat-yellow. Cherri closed her eyes. She wanted to sleep. Unfortunately, her dreams, too often, took her back to childhood. A place she'd rather forget.

Cherri's mother, Dawn, was a nice woman. She was pretty. And she loved Cherri. But she loved her abusive husband more. And booze came in second.

On more than one occasion, Dawn was taken to the hospital for alcohol poisoning. Dawn drank in extreme when she needed to ignore what her husband was doing. She needed to ignore him because he often ventured into Cherri's bedroom.

Her husband was doing things to Cherri he should have been doing with Dawn. On those nights, Dawn would suck down a fifth of Jim Beam, sometimes more. She would sit at the crappy wooden table in the middle of the kitchen. There was a huge crack running down the center of it. She'd slump down over her elbows, lean into the bottle, and wait for the sting of alcohol to dull her sorrows.

When Cherri's stepfather, Garry, was done with her, he'd go to the kitchen, grab a beer from the fridge, and sit with Dawn. They would remain silent. Gary would stare at her. The stare, Cherri thought, was to confirm Dawn knew what would happen if she ever told anyone about what was going on in her daughter's bedroom.

The rest of the world wouldn't understand Garry's needs. That's how he explained it to Dawn. And Dawn never bought into the argument. But she was powerless against him, and her rage was silent. She hadn't the nerve to do anything about it. She couldn't.

Cherri shared only one bonding moment with her mother. It was the night Dawn killed the vile son of a bitch.

Garry came home from work. It was winter and he was drunk. He stumbled to the bedroom, shrugging his shoes off as he tripped down the hallway. After he undressed, he made his way into Cherri's bedroom. Dawn was waiting for him in there with a Remington double barrel shotgun.

The gun was neatly polished. Garry flew out of his boots. The lead slug that Dawn unloaded into his chest sent blood splattering across the walls. Garry hit the wall and slid to the floor near the door. He left a trail of crimson gore. The skin around his sucking chest wound sizzled from the heat of the round.

Cherri hadn't been scared. In all honesty, she was glad, relieved. Gary would never *have her* again. Cherri felt her mother's humility. She watched her mother take a seat on the edge of the bed. The sad look in her eyes suddenly gleamed and her mouth perched into a smile. She'd forgiven herself. She quickly turned away from Cherri and lifted the barrel of the shotgun to her lips. Her eyes, again, turned toward Cherri. She attempted to say "I'm sorry" and then wrapped her thumb over the trigger. Her face caved in. She punched the contents of her head across Cherri's bedroom. Some of her brain matter stuck to the ceiling.

Cherri stared at her dead mother, lost. After a few seconds, she spit on Garry and kicked his lifeless corpse, furiously.

When she finally settled down, Cherri inspected the grotesque scene. Broken skull fragments peppered the floor, wall, windows, and drapes. Leaning down, she gazed into the wide hole ripped through Gary's chest. For a moment, she thought she could see his heart. It looked black.

Once her fascination was curbed, she became frightened.

What came next?

She would have to call the police and explain what had happened.

A short investigation ensued and not much occurred. The police took Cherri at her word. At one point, they'd asked her if she pulled the trigger, but they didn't pursue her further once she said "no." Cherri wasn't capable of murder. She was a scared little girl, and the crime scene had told the story.

Within a year, Cherri was shuttled into foster care. And that was where she met Timmy. He was nice. He had a violent temper, but nobody's perfect. Cherri and Timmy became friends. During social time, they would play board games. They would talk until lights out or until the foster care givers sent them to their state sanctioned dorm rooms. Sometimes they would get split up and sent to random foster homes, with random families.

Timmy would run away. Sometimes, the family he stayed with would prove to be unreliable. And Timmy always found Cherri, no matter where he was sent. He'd get kicked out or run away, and he'd find her. After a few years, he was finally sent to a juvenile facility. And they didn't see each other for a long time.

A few years later, Cherri landed a job as a waitress. It wasn't much. She worked at a small bar and grille, a road stop in Clyman—a map-dot town in southern Wisconsin. Timmy happened to pop in for a burger and fries. It was pure coincidence. They both read it as fate.

The burger was fine, the fries were good, but the girl was great. After paying the tab, Timmy took Cherri away. She hadn't even changed out of her uniform.

And over the course of the first few months, he'd given her everything he could, which wasn't much. He earned his living off robbing people. Once in a while, he landed an odd job. And he didn't want her to work.

He could be sweet like that. And when they made love, it was gentle; mostly. When money was tight or non-existent and stress levels were high, he would drink heavy and slap her around. Once in a great while, he would punch her. He always apologized. Sometimes he'd cry. And Cherri knew he loved her. He didn't mean to hit her. He felt awful about hitting her.

How could he possibly be such a bad guy?

He lacked self-control. He couldn't help it. And he punished himself for abusing her. He would cut himself with razors or sharp knives. Usually he would slice into his shoulders and arms, but sometimes he'd cut his legs. The pain settled him.

Now, cramped in the truck between Terrance and Timmy, Cherri's eyes drooped. Her head bobbled to the side. She rested near Timmy's shoulder. And soon she dreamed of a normal life, a boring life with a small house and a cat. Maybe, in this dream, she could have a secretarial job in an office and Timmy could work at a mechanic shop. They could reside in a small town where they could live easy. She dreamed.

3

Terrance was startled awake. The late-night wind had gone from soothing to chilly. He looked out the passenger side window. Not a car in sight. They were turning into a gas station. No, it was a liquor store.

Timmy tapped the brakes. The truck slowed down. They turned right, no left, yeah, right. Terrance rubbed his eyes with his fists. Light gleamed in through the windshield. A green neon sign blared from above. Peering out the back window, then the front, Terrance saw cornfields, road, and the store. The neon sign read "Buggy's Liquor." Beyond the store, past an acre of cornfield, there was a small farmhouse resting on top of the hill. The windows were dark.

Sitting up, Terrance turned to Cherri. She, too, was awake. She stared at the store.

Timmy meant to rob the place. Terrance knew it and he was excited. They were running low on cash, and the store was more than ideal, it was perfect—far away from everything and anything. It was too rural for a fast reaction force from the local police. They could take their time. Terrance and Timmy had knocked off enough liquor stores to know the only real security in a place like this was the infamous gun that always and stereotypically rested beneath the cash register.

"You want to stop and scope it out, or just rush it?" Terrance asked. He slowly crooned his head toward Timmy. Terrance rubbed his hands together, successively.

"I say we rush it. Cherri was right. They're about to close. We'll be the last customers, grab what we need, tie up the clerk, and take off. The morning clerk will let them go. We'll be well past the state line by then. And no one gets hurt."

"Sounds like a plan," Terrance said. He leaned forward and retrieved his nine millimeter pistol. It was stuffed below his belt loop. He slid the chamber open and made sure it was loaded. He set it on his lap and flipped the safety off.

"I don't want to do this," Cherri chimed in.

Terrance wondered why Timmy was so in love with Cherri. It was obvious and apparent she wouldn't continue with this lifestyle. And this lifestyle was Timmy's destiny. It was all he knew. If Timmy really loved Cherri as much as he said he did, then he should leave her. In the big scheme of things, leaving her was the most unselfish act Timmy could perform. He could leave her on the side of a road in some offbeat Podunk town. Maybe she would find a job. She could make a little life for herself. As for Terrance, he was living his dream, his destiny.

Terrance grew up privileged. He'd always been given everything he could have wanted: money, cars, girls. But he didn't want any of it. The thrill of crime got him off. It fit him. He loved it. And he was good at it. The underworld fascinated him. It lured his desires. It captured him. Nothing was more exciting than the rush of a robbery. The energy that pumped through his veins when a police chase was involved felt better than any orgasm. Crime was his drug of choice. It made life worth living.

The truck slid into the last parking spot near the back of the liquor store. Terrance jumped out of the passenger seat. He stomped toward the front door, gun in hand. Timmy walked to the right of him, shotgun at the ready.

A smile stretched across Terrance's lips.

Timmy and Terrance pulled the glass doors open and slid into the store.

Part 3: The Robbery

Chapter 6

1

The store was quiet. It was calm, too calm. Winny finished mopping the bathroom floor, pushed the bucket toward the far wall, and emptied the dirty water. The bucket rested on the white plastic drain cover, which prevented water from splashing onto the floor.

Up front, the electronic buzzer chirped. Someone entered. Garth's voice rang out as he announced the new customer.

"You're the last customer of the night. Congratulations. Try and make it quick, will yah? I have a six pack of cold beer waiting at home," Garth called out.

Winny hated it when Garth rushed the customers. Winny's theory was that if you rushed the customer, they didn't take their time inspecting the goods. If they didn't take their time, then they didn't buy stuff. And then no one made any money. Added to which, the lack of charm, could, in theory, prevent new customers from returning.

Winny set his mop next to the neatly stacked cases of Diet Coke. He pushed the bathroom door open and made his way into the store area.

He stopped dead in his tracks. He stared forward. A large man with a thick beard was pressing the barrel of a shotgun against Garth's chest.

Suddenly, someone screamed at Winny, "Get on the ground motherfucker!"

Standing near the front of the store, a muscular black guy held a nine millimeter pistol.

"We don't want any problems," Winny pleaded. He looked to Garth. "Garth, give him the money."

Although there was a gun pressed against his chest, Garth looked annoyed. He was aggravated with Winny for suggesting they give in to the gunman's request. But there wasn't another choice. If they disagreed with these people, they might end up dead. Never, in the history of the store's existence had Winny or Garth been robbed—never at gunpoint. Their father had been robbed. A few of the employees had, too, but never anything this serious.

Those robberies were more like extreme shoplifting. The standard operating procedure was to give the assailant all of the money. Buggy Gasper preached that life was more important than a couple of bucks. And right now, Winny was afraid the gunman would shoot his brother. The cold realization that Garth might get shot and meet his demise sank in like sharp hooks.

Garth couldn't die. That would be more than Winny could bear. The thought of his brother dying hurt. It felt like metal flakes were blowing through his stomach. Quickly, he tried to dismiss idea.

Winny felt faint.

The black man holding the pistol skipped toward him.

Instinctively, Winny raised his arms above his head and waved his hands in surrender.

"Ain't nobody need to get hurt here! You understand? Now, fork over your cell phones," the black man hollered.

Garth rolled his eyes as he pulled his black flip-top cell phone from his jeans pocket and tossed it in the air. The bearded man caught it, removed the battery, dropped the phone, and stomped it into smaller pieces.

The black man took Winny's cell phone and slammed it on the floor. It broke, neatly.

"Yes, we understand. I assure you neither of us will be a problem. So please, don't hurt us. There's a couple hundred in the register and another thousand in the safe," Winny said.

He sounded much cooler than he felt. The wet surface of his palms was icy. The beads of sweat threatening to tumble down his face expanded and grew heavy. He wasn't shaking, but he quaked on the inside. His vision was becoming hazy. The front of his head began to pound.

"I'm not giving him what's in the safe," Garth called out in a cold tone. "Take the money from the register and get out."

The large, bearded man jammed his shotgun into Garth's chest again. Garth jumped back.

"This ain't my first rodeo, dickweed. And this boom-stick is ready to go…boom!" the bearded man cried out. A maniacal grin swept his face. His teeth sparkled beneath his beard. He raised his shotgun.

The black man weaved behind the counter. Something from the parking lot caught his eye. The large man with the shotgun stared out the window.

The doorbell chimed. A girl walked in. She had silky red hair. Her neatly lined jaw descended into a beautifully slim angle. Her complexion was slightly tan, different for a redhead. He didn't see any freckles on her face. She looked to the large, bearded man and commanded, "Someone's coming. They came out of the cornfield. A guy and girl…I think they're together."

Winny hadn't the slightest idea why anybody would be in the cornfield at this time of night. Then he saw their silhouettes. They bobbed forward, walking hand in hand through the parking lot. They were halfway to the door.

The large man leaned in toward Garth. He whispered loud enough for everyone to hear, "If you let-on to what's going down in here…I'll start blasting away at everything, anything, and anyone." He pointed to Winny. "Your friend gets it first. Then I'll shoot you in the kneecaps and hands. It'll hurt like a son-of-a-bitch, and it'll cripple you for life. Got it?"

Garth turned to Winny with a cockeyed, arrogant, glance. He nodded.

"I'll keep my trap shut," Garth said.

"Good." He placed his shotgun behind his back. He turned and moved down the hygiene aisle. He stopped in the back corner. He fingered a few toothbrushes and picked up a bottle of mouthwash. He tried to look inconspicuous.

Winny found it curious that the robber took interest in the hygiene products. After the bearded man picked up the toothbrush and mouthwash, he made his way over to the deodorant. Strangely, Winny wondered if his selection of deodorant was sufficient.

What kind of anti-perspirant did the typical armed robber wear?

Maybe he could call his supplier and have them drop off a few more brands. As of now, they only carried travel-size Speedstick.

Maybe the customers would like Old Spice or Brut?

The doorbell chimed as the couple entered the store. Guilt swept Winny. The nice-looking young couple had just walked into serious danger. And all Winny could think about was making a few bucks by broadening the selection of underarm deodorant.

The young man with shaggy brown hair walked toward the glass cooler. He stopped near the Gatorade and opened the slim see-through door. He fingered the fruit punch bottle and then dipped his hand down to the grape flavor. He pulled it from the plastic rack. He tossed the bottle in the air, spun it, and caught it.

"There ain't nothing like a grape Gatorade to refill those depleted electrolytes—you have to drink a bottle of water afterward though, or it'll just dehydrate you from all the sugars." The attractive young man said, smiling, as he slowly made his way over to the next glass cooler that encased the bottled water.

Winny watched the good looking, blonde woman make her way toward the wine racks. She picked up a bottle of chardonnay. When she bent down, Winny couldn't help but watch the way her backside creased in her jeans. She wasn't too thin. She had a nice bump in her rump.

Stop.

Winny glanced at the large man holding the shotgun behind his back. He took position near the restrooms. He was fidgeting. The sweat on his forehead gleamed under the bright fluorescent lights.

The black man stood near the back, left, corner of the liquor store. He stood parallel to the larger man. The black man wasn't sweating at all. In fact, he held back a smile. He looked as though he was enjoying the intensity of this situation. The redhead looked nauseated. *She must be some kind of a lookout.*

Winny turned to Garth. He heard a stack of papers shuffle behind the cash register. *Garth was going for his gun.* He kept it hidden beneath the register. It was in the knick-knack drawer behind the plastic scissors.

Tiny bulbs of sweat beaded up beneath the skin of Winny's forehead. His cheeks were burning. He tried to shake his head. He couldn't. He was frozen.

Garth glanced at Winny.

He turned to the large man with the shotgun. The large man hadn't noticed Garth's hands moving beneath the register. Garth dropped the magazine he'd been reading earlier. As if on cue, the shotgun emerged from behind the bearded man's back. It swooped forward, crisp and tight.

The young man, who recently entered, slowly moved toward the large man. For a quick moment, Winny thought he might be the police.

He shook the notion.

They couldn't be cops. They're too young.

The young man looked up, quickly. He turned away from the large man. He smiled at the black man. He cocked his head toward the good looking redhead and then stopped at the blonde girl he'd entered with.

"Man, it sure seems…tense in here." He smiled big. "Did I walk into the middle of something naughty?"

Winny's bowels felt like they were filled with ice.

2

Sammael's laughter echoed through the liquor store. He'd walked into the middle of an armed robbery. His intention had simply been to cause noise, create racket. All he wanted was for the liquor store clerk to scream.

Merely institute enough noise that Father Leslie Gardner would run down from his little house on the hill. But this was fine. He enjoyed the violence. Walking into a robbery was amusing. The look upon everyone's face was priceless. The folly of human expression was comical. It was silly. And he enjoyed it. The more uncomfortable these people became, the more pleasure Sammael received. For centuries, Sammael had psychologically tormented the human race. It was so easy.

Sammael looked to the muscular fellow standing in the corner near the restrooms and asked, "Can I ask why you're crouched over there in the corner of the store like that? You look mighty suspicious. If you can't afford something, my lady friend and I would be more than happy to buy it for you. We'll require that you pay us back with your life, but hey, is a deal ever as good as it sounds?"

Sammael turned toward the wine rack. Jezebeth held up two bottles of wine: one white, one red.

"Do you really think we should offer money to strangers?" Jezebeth asked back. She was smiling, almost laughing.

Again, Sammael looked to the muscular man in the corner. A smile stretched across his mouth. He locked eyes with him. Sammael watched dark blood pump through the large man's chest. He could see beneath his skin. Beneath the large man's racing heart, Sammael saw the man's thoughts.

This guy was a criminal. Sammael could see into his past. He'd done bad things. He wasn't as bad as Rod or Patty, oh no. Rod and Patty liked to kill people. Rod and Patty were as evil as evil could get. Sammael looked even deeper. He saw the beginning. He saw a name.

Timmy Sutter.

Timmy Sutter was twenty-five years old and bad. Bad, but wished to be good, and what was this? He loved the red-haired girl standing near the entrance.

Sammael looked to the redhead standing at the doors. He read her thoughts. *Yes, Timmy and...what is her name...Cherri. He loves her, but she doesn't love him back. But she's loyal. With love in one's heart, one cannot be completely evil.*

Sammael began laughing again. He laughed at Timmy. Behind Timmy's tough exterior, he was a romantic; the kind of guy who might give up his life of crime to settle with the woman he loved.

How cute.

"Timmy, why don't you rob the place already?"

And as Sammael expected, Timmy became confused.

Sammael had been playing these little games for centuries. He'd gotten very good at them. Usually, when he called a complete stranger by name, they held a tendency to become peculiar, confused.

"How do you know my name?" Timmy barked.

"I know everything about you, Timmy. I know about your mother's suicide, your father's incredibly limited intelligence…and yours…while we're tackling that subject…"

"Shut up!" Timmy yelled. "Just shut the fuck up! Who are you?" Timmy continued. He jumped forward, shotgun raised.

Marching straight toward Sammael, Timmy held his shotgun at eye level. He stopped three feet in front of Sammael. Sammael chuckled.

"Why are you getting so upset? We're just getting to know each other. Do you want to know who I am?" Sammael asked calmly. "It would only be polite."

A stack of bottled beer crashed on the floor from the back of the store. Terrance screamed, "What's going on, boss?" His gun was exposed and raised. He didn't notice— as Sammael had—that the cashier, Garth, had retrieved a gun.

"Garth, don't!" Winny shouted.

Garth's eyes shot toward Winny.

Sammael smiled when he saw how annoyed Garth was. It had to be annoyance, as though he'd been told "don't" a million times by this person. Sammael dug into Winny's thoughts.

What was this man's name?

"Winny!" Sammael finally called. "You should let your brother shoot the black guy—he's actually enjoying this. You'd be doing many other liquor store attendants a huge favor." He turned to Garth. "Just pump a round straight into his face. We both know you can aim. You practice every day, behind the store, before work. And…given the situation, you wouldn't have any problems getting away with it. No one cares about him."

Something sliced through the air. It sounded like the air had been cut in half. Terrance had fired a shot at Garth.

The tiny stack of breath mints wrapped in blue paper and aluminum foil exploded into a powdery mist. The powder sprayed across the counter. It blinded Garth.

Winny jumped forward. He fell to his stomach, crawled to the cash register, and then slid behind it.

"Are you having a good time?" Sammael called out to Jezebeth. She stood near Terrance. Terrance grabbed Jezebeth. And she laughed.

"Oh please, Mr. Scary-black-robber-guy…please don't hurt me." She pouted her lips. "I'll do anything. I'll suck your big black dick and let you come on my face."

"What the…? Who the hell are you fucking people?" Terrance screamed. He dug his pistol into Jezebeth's side, above her love-handle.

Sammael's laughter ended. He turned a quick inquisitive eye toward Terrance. "What did you say, sir? We are merely trying to diffuse this highly intense robbery, and you have to ask 'who are we?' You're placing us in a box. I don't think I like it. Look, I know you want to hurry up and get this job over with…you and your pals can run off to Detroit and do…whatever it is you do. I'm just stating that if you kill everyone in this store, take all the money and then flee in Timmy's truck, you will totally get away with everything."

Terrance hung on every word expelled from Sammael's mouth. He was considering this. Terrance gripped his pistol, tight. His eye-line traveled with Timmy.

Sammael turned to the left.

Timmy held the barrel of his shotgun to Sammael's face.

"You and your girlfriend need to shut your damn mouths…and quick." Timmy stated.

"If you shoot me…then Rod—the man who so *ungracefully* let me borrow his body—is going to be awfully upset. He's a good looking fella. He doesn't deserve to be disfigured. I have many people to tempt with this face. If you caved it in, you might ruin my charm." Sammael spoke in a cheerful manner.

Frowning, Timmy stepped back and asked, "What in the hell are you talking about? You're not making any sense."

"I'm making so much sense…I'm making dollars. I just have a little more insight into, well, everything."

3

Gunshots echoed through the store. Garth and Winny lay in the prone position behind the counter. Their ears rang. They were deaf from the gunshots. They stared at each other, hoping to communicate on a speechless, brotherly level. They knew what the other was thinking. Garth was scared and annoyed. *Winny had no balls.* He'd end up getting them both killed.

He shouldn't have interfered. Garth could have shot Terrance. Now they— and the robbers—were being held hostage by the strangest people he'd ever come across. The too good looking blonde and her bizarre boyfriend troubled his already exhausted thoughts.

These people were psychic or something. Somehow, they knew everything about everyone in the store. Garth didn't know how this was possible. Regardless, it was happening.

Winny motioned his head toward the back door. The door led into the back room, which led to the employee parking lot. If they could get through the second door, through the open parking lot and into the cornfield, they could get to Father Gardner's house. From there they could call the police.

Garth whispered softly, "I'll fire a shot at the glass door. When it shatters, they'll turn their attention to it…run like hell out the back door."

For the first time ever—Garth thought—Winny was agreeing with him. He bobbled his head *yes*. Garth crouched on his knees. Another bullet sliced through the air. And the blonde woman screamed.

Garth hopped onto his feet. He raised his gun as he peeked over the counter and aimed at Terrance.

To his surprise, Terrance had shot the beautiful blonde woman. She was staggering backward. Her hands were moving fast near her stomach. Blood seeped through her fingers. She was trying to hold her guts in. She fell to the floor. She collapsed near the base of the wine rack, her mouth gaped open in an O-shape. Blood pumped out from between her lips in thick eruptions. Oddly, she looked like she was laughing.

Garth tried to remain calm. His heart thumped wildly in his chest. It felt like it would burst through his rib cage. He placed the index finger of his right hand on the trigger.

"Get the fuck out of here!" Garth screamed.

The redhead screamed. Her hand landed on the door handle. She flung the door open and ran outside.

Another shot rang out. Timmy shot at Sammael.

"Shit!" Sammael barked.

Garth watched as Sammael fell to the ground. Timmy's bullet shredded a crater through Sammael's chest. The wound spewed blood. It painted the floor and merchandise racks with beads of crimson.

Timmy sprinted behind the counter. He raised his shotgun like a soldier entering a terrorist infested combat zone. His aim dropped to Winny.

"Drop it or your brother has no more than two seconds left on this earth!" Timmy shouted at Garth.

Garth was furious and scared. He should have taken his shot. He had the chance, but he let it go. He was too slow. He jeopardized his brother's life.

Trying to hold it together, but shaking badly, Garth set his gun on the counter. He stepped back.

"Get the money!" Timmy screamed.

Garth went to the cash register. There was no point in doing anything heroic at this point. Timmy and Terrance had already killed two people. Garth's opportunity was over. He'd blown it.

Garth hit the "sale" button. The register drawer flung open. The bell rang. The black plastic drawer slid to a halt. Garth scraped the cash out with both hands and handed it to Timmy. Timmy stuffed the green bills into his pockets.

"Thank you. Now lay down with your brother. And we'll be on our way."

Garth lowered himself to the ground.

Timmy dropped his shotgun to the side, leaned forward, and grabbed Garth's gun off the counter.

"We good?" Terrance called out.

"We're good. Grab some snacks and let's get the hell outta here," Timmy shouted. He ran around to the back of the counter.

4

Timmy jogged down aisle two. His feet squeaked across the clean tile, leaving black streaks from the soles of his shoes. He stopped at the spot where he'd shot the crazy guy. He slowed down and looked side to side. He stopped moving.

There should be a body lying in the aisle in front of him, the crazy guy's body.

For the first time in a long time, Timmy felt real fear. A puddle of blood settled on the white tile floor. The smeared crimson liquid seeped into the slim creases between the square tiles. Peering down the aisle, there was more blood. It was peppered across the top row of motor oil, on the right. Still, there was no *dead-psychic-lunatic*, or whatever the hell he was.

Timmy turned to Terrance and yelled, "Where'd he go?"

Glancing around, shakily, Terrance knelt beneath the row of shelves. A moment later, he bobbed up, shoulders elevated in an *I-have-no-idea* shrug.

"I didn't see a damn thing. He must have crawled away."

"He crawled pretty damn fast for a dead guy," Timmy explained softly. He might have been talking to himself. He was frantically searching aisle two with wild eyes.

A few seconds later, his neck elevated. His eyes swam toward the restrooms.

"Watch those kids," Timmy called.

Terrance ran behind the counter. He aimed his pistol downward.

Heart racing in his chest, Timmy thought of Cherri. He glanced out the window. To the side of the building, he saw her standing next to a light-post. She was smoking a cigarette. Ribbons of smoke billowed up into the frothy night.

Focus.

Timmy lifted his shotgun. He put his eye to the rear site. Whatever he saw, he would shoot it. Thoughts of Sammael raced through Timmy's mind. What was that guy? *Why did he choose to show up at this liquor store at the exact same time they robbed the place?* And how had he known so much about them? He knew everything. For a paranoid moment, he thought they might be the family members of someone he'd harmed.

It was true, he'd created enemies. He had a checkered past. Maybe one of his victims had followed him. Maybe, somehow, they'd picked this place to take their revenge. *That would take a lot of planning.* Plus, he'd never killed anyone. He'd hurt people, caused financial problems for some, but was that enough to take it this far?

He guessed there were a few stores that had closed shop because of the financial loss they'd taken due to his robberies. Not everyone carried insurance. Maybe one of the store owners had somehow tracked him. Maybe they wanted revenge. The authorities never handled robberies very well. He shook his head. His paranoia was on idle. For now, he needed to be rid of the current problem, whatever it may be.

Foot over foot, Timmy made his way toward the restrooms. When he got to the corner, he stopped. He looked back at Terrance.

Terrance had control over Garth and Winny. Timmy took a deep breath. He closed his eyes and stuck his head around the corner. He retracted quickly.

Nothing.

Relieved, he swung into the hallway. The women's bathroom was on the left, men's on the right.

Which one would he go to first?

He chose the women's. It might be a bad idea, it might not. Either way, he pushed the door open with the barrel of his shotgun and slowly stepped inside.

The fluorescents were bright. The electrical buzz coming from the numerous overhead light bulbs was unnerving. There were three stalls on the right side across from the large vanity mirror. Odd to notice, there wasn't much graffiti on the tiled walls. The mirrors were in good shape, too. It didn't seem right for a liquor store bathroom to be this clean. Most liquor stores held drunken literature scrawled across the walls.

Lowering himself to his knees, he scanned the floor of all three stalls. No feet. There was no trail of blood, either. Come to think of it, there wasn't a blood trail leading to the men's room.

Maybe the guy had stopped the bleeding.

Still, where else could he have gone?

Timmy stood in front of the first blue stall door. He didn't hesitate. Nervous, but too anxious to wait, he kicked the door open. He aimed his shotgun at chest level.

No one.

The next stall: same thing, empty.

No one was in the third stall.

Relieved, Timmy left the women's restroom. He crossed the hallway and entered the men's room.

As the women's door closed, he heard Terrance yell, "Hurry up! We need to fly!"

"I'm on it. Give me a minute," Timmy shouted back. He didn't know why he cared anymore. *So a guy disappeared with a gaping hole in his chest.* Maybe it was a good thing. He didn't want to kill anybody. If the guy was dead, he would be Timmy's first homicide. But he'd disappeared into thin air. Obviously he was still alive. And Terrance was right. They needed to *fly*.

Timmy stared at the men's room door for a moment. He backed up a couple steps. For a number of reasons, he was becoming frightened and paranoid. A scenario played out in his head: *He'd turn around. The psychic guy would be standing behind him. He'd have that queer grin on his face. He'd be bleeding from a grapefruit sized wound in his chest.*

Timmy closed his eyes. He put his right foot behind the left and leaned backward. He spun around. His feet landed steady.

Every light in the store suddenly went out.

5

"Fuck this!" Terrance yelled as he leaped over Winny's legs, rounded the corner, and shuffled to the door. "I'm out, Timmy! Enough is enough!"

Just before leaving the dark store, he placed his hand on the front door handle. But he stopped moving. The store had become eerily silent. It felt creepy. He felt like he was alone, yet if he were to turn around, everyone would be standing right behind him, staring at him, ready to kill him. He closed his eyes. His shoulders shifted, then his neck.

He opened his eyes.

There was nothing. No breathing. No shoes shuffling. It was dead silent.

Something must have happened to Timmy.

He knew it. That crazy guy was alive and he'd killed Timmy.

Terrance opened the front door. As he stepped outside, he met Cherri's gaze and said, "We need to leave. Timmy or no Timmy, shit's about to go down in a bad way. I've only had a feeling this bad once in my life, and it was fuckin' bad. So let's go." He grabbed Cherri's arm and pulled her off the curb.

Cherri moved forward, shrugged, and stopped. Terrance was suddenly tugged backward. Cherri tried to shuck her arm free. With three quick jerks, she finally yanked her arm from Terrance's grip. She tore away from him and disappeared into the darkness of the store.

Shaking his hands as he left, Terrance continued across the parking lot toward the truck. "Better off on my own, anyway."

Chapter 7

1

Father Leslie Gardner sat in the darkness of his living room staring out of his picture glass window. The view was panoramic, and it soothed. From where he sat, he could see miles of rolling hills, Highway 26 (until it disappeared into the largest of the hills),the radiant light of the small downtown area, and he could see Buggy's Liquor.

The moonlight illuminated Gardner's distinguished face. It gave the room a bluish hue. Often, when he couldn't sleep, he'd sit in his reclining chair and watch the world through his window. It calmed him. It relaxed his aging mind. But tonight was different.

Something was happening at Buggy's Liquor, the small *mom and pop joint* that sat four hundred yards from his property line.   Leaning forward, he ran his calloused fingers through his silver hair. He thought he heard screaming. Gunshots had rung out.

He was quite sure of it. And the lights at the store were out. *Was there a power outage?* If that were the case, then his lights would be out, too. They weren't. Turning in his creaky gray recliner, he assured himself his kitchen lights were on. The dim light bounced a glare off the lime green walls in the hallway—the wall that separated the kitchen from the living room.

Gardner turned to the window. Again, he heard screaming. *Maybe it was the air conditioner?* Sometimes, the vents let out a slow hum. The vent at the base of the hallway hissed and the flow of air whistled. But he didn't want to call the police unless he was sure something bad was happening.

Straining to see, Gardner witnessed a black man holding a pistol come barreling out of the liquor store. The man had a bald head that glimmered in the moonlight. He ran toward an old pick-up truck that was parked near the back of the lot.

"What's going on down there?" Gardner whispered to himself. His forehead scrunched into a frown. He felt morbid concern. Misguided as they were, he appreciated the Gasper boys. His concern turned into something stronger. He felt eyes watching him. He'd felt this upsetting intuition many times during the course of his career as a holy man. It was evil's eyes upon him. He felt the same intuition when he met his wife, Donna. His wife wasn't evil, no. But she'd been possessed by an evil similar to what he felt now. He wanted to wake her, but she was asleep in their bedroom upstairs.

Donna was thirty-two years old when Gardner was called in to exercise the unholy presence that had invaded her body. She was his twenty-seventh exorcism. That was thirty years ago. Now, the memory seemed close. He remembered the day well. That had been his last exorcism.

For years, Gardner traveled across the country fighting evil. Some cases were fraudulent. The twenty-seven he counted were authentic. The ceremony and rites of exorcism which were written in the holy books were not as useful as he'd been educated to believe. The power to expel the *unholy* was in the strength of one's faith, faith in goodness. Gardner had much of that. Sure, he had impure thoughts. He was a self-proclaimed sinner, but he fought for good. He acknowledged its strength. He denounced the weakness of evil. When someone saw as many miracles and demons in their life as Father Leslie Gardner had— they had no other choice, but to believe in the higher power of good and evil. With Gardner's faith came strength. He could pull the unholy parasite from its prey. A demon could only inflict as much damage as God allowed. And if God allowed Father Gardner to seek out and help the possessed, then usually *He* had said *enough* to the Unholy One.

Donna Shaney spent her youth as a drug addict. She laughed in the face of God until one day she looked in her mirror and didn't recognize her appearance. The reflection was only a resembled image. There was something evil living inside her. She could feel it gnawing at her soul. Her eyes were black. Her reflection laughed back at her. She was being taken over and couldn't stop it. Finally, she was unable to battle the evil which possessed her.

The decision to get alternative help occurred on the day she nearly devoured her brother's infant child. Silvia Shaney, Donna's grandmother, discovered Donna wandering the streets. She'd brought her home. The Shaney's hadn't seen Donna in a long time. She'd been reported missing years earlier, but her family knew she was around. She'd been spotted by relatives and acquaintances lurking in the darkness with her criminal friends.

Donna's brother fainted when he witnessed his sister's eyes bulge forward from their sockets. Her face stretched forward, pulling her skin. Later on, when asked about that horrible day, he said he thought her skull was going to rip through her face. Donna's sister-in-law grabbed the infant. She ran out of the house with the baby. The evil that possessed Donna wasn't able to harm the child.

Silvia called the first Catholic Church in the Yellow Pages.

Silvia called many churches. Finally, through the network of priests, Silvia found Gardner.

He flew in the next day from Miami. He'd been working with survivors of a very sinister cult. They had lunch, but neither of them ate their food. Then he met with Donna.

Upon their first encounter, he became aware that the demon Sammael had possessed her.

Many of Gardner's counterparts disapproved of Gardner's unstructured methods. And in turn, he disagreed with some of their organized beliefs. But they let him conduct business. None of the other priests could deny that Gardner carried out the Lord's supernatural work.

He was special. Many of the priests and cardinals determined that Gardner was no longer Catholic. He'd gone through the process and been educated as such, but his line of work had taken him to a higher state of holiness. He only believed in God and his son. There was no difference between religions.

There was God and Jesus and everything else was human interruption. God dwelled in the hearts of all his children. The strength of evil was only as strong as the Father permitted.

Why would he permit this kind of evil?
To test.
Like a professor tests his students in the classroom, God tested his children in life. By testing high, his children could fulfill greatness. There were no certainties in life,

never. But Gardner believed striving for goodness was the way to eternal happiness. Tests came every day. They ranged from white lies to murder.

And Gardner was placed in the presence of Donna Shaney for more than one reason. One of them being she'd ignored the goodness inside of her. She had been seduced by darkness. She had let her gift of life shrivel up and burn. The gift of life was fragile. And now, her life was draining with each passing second.

Gardner didn't know if he could save her. But he would try. He prayed he would be successful.

After a person was exorcised, they usually came around to believing again. Often, they strived for goodness. The latter—insanity—didn't set well. If the victim accepted their possession as insanity, in the end, insanity would take them. And the Evil One would be pleased.

Donna was near death when Sammael was extracted. When the unholy got close to killing its host, its anger was overwhelming. And it was frightening when it failed. But evil had no strength over the greatness of God.

Sammael had to go.

So Gardner studied Sammael. And upon first meeting the unholy demon, Sammael tried to convince Gardner he was anyone but Sammael. He said he was the devil. He promised he was Saint Christopher. He even claimed to be Donna's aborted child.

The true identity of the demon was revealed to Gardner in one of his visions. His strength created a tunnel of communication. God spoke to Gardner. Only a few possessed this gift. The purity of God's voice revealed Sammael inhabited Donna.

The exorcism didn't last very long. After Sammael left, Donna was severely dehydrated. She was unable to hold liquid or food. Her tendons, bones, and organs were fighting ultimate failure. The twisted physical agony and torment was too much for her physical body. Gardner had made it just in time.

Donna fought to keep her life.

One night, about a year after the exorcism, Donna tracked down Father Gardner. She wanted to thank him. She found him by way of the priest who had originally assessed her situation, Father Denton. Having been in the area, Gardner agreed to see her.

He was taken by her beauty. They met at a small diner in Iowa. It had a view of the Mississippi River which was across the river from Wisconsin.

Gardner barely recognized Donna. The last time he'd seen her, she'd been weary and beaten. When one is borrowed by the unholy, their physical features change. Donna didn't look like the woman he'd seen in pictures before the exorcism, either. She was stunning. Gardner's heart rate began to speed. His ability to stay calm was strong. He was used to witnessing great evils and could usually remain so, but Donna managed to stir him.

The diner was bright as Gardner sat in the back at his table near the exit and stared out the window. He glanced to the front of the diner when the glass doors opened. The cold air vacuumed out.

He then locked eyes with her. Her skin was vibrant, not pasty and dry. There was a touch of sun to her. Her skin was lightly tanned. Her shoulders were freckled. Her hazel eyes danced with life. Gardner was nervous. His heart fluttered.

He couldn't turn away from her. It seemed she was sent from Heaven. In that moment, Gardner knew Donna would be his wife. She would take him away from the underworld and the demons he fought. She would become his destiny. She would show him how beautiful life could be.

She wore a light yellow dress with straps over her tanned shoulders. Her shoes matched in color. She wasn't made-up with blush, mascara or any other dressings. Still, it was apparent that she'd taken her time in the mirror. There was a natural art to her appearance.

She smiled as she entered the diner. His cheeks burned. He stood, showed her to her seat.

"Thank you for seeing me," Donna said.

It was odd to hear her speak kind words. Before and during the exorcism, she'd only said foul things to him. But that wasn't her. That was the demon.

Stunned, but slowly settling his attraction, he said, "I think maybe I should be thanking you. You look better than well. You look wonderful, lovely." And for the first time, in a long time, he was embarrassed that what he'd said sounded corny, and maybe inappropriate.

"Thank you." She reached out and wrapped her slender fingers around his hand. She squeezed gently.

The warmth of her hands felt good. He felt life beneath the skin of her palms. Her fingers held a touch of callous. It was comforting.

Donna peered down at their intertwined hands, at the center of the table. When her gaze lifted, he saw tears spilling down her cheeks.

"I'm thirty-three years old now…but I have only lived for one of those years, this past one. I've been clean, sober, and good. I work in a garden nursery. The sun feels good on my back when I plant flowers. And I know God is shining his light upon me. I never knew life could be so wonderful." There was a wild amazement swimming behind her moist hazel eyes.

Gardner allowed tears to spill down his cheeks. He couldn't help it. Watching Donna—full of life—explaining true happiness was a rich feeling. He didn't know if he was crying because he was happy for her or if he was sad because he wanted to live life as she did.

"It sounds like this last year has made up for the past."

They sat silent, for nearly ten minutes enjoying each other's company. They were comfortable, as if they'd known each other their entire lives.

After lunch, Donna sat up straight, and peered out the window. She said, "When I was taken…I was weak. I wanted to kill myself. I was miserable every day I was alive. I took drugs. Not to feel good, or because my body depended on them, but because I wanted to torture myself, slowly.

I wanted to punish myself. And when I was taken, I went to a place where I couldn't escape the pain. I was in a place where I felt extreme sorrow. It tormented me." She peered up at Gardner. "And then you helped me…"

Out of habit, he cut her off by saying, "It was God…working through me." He was being rude. "I'm sorry, please continue."

"I was able to come out of that place, where pain was everything. It burned where I was. And then I came back to life. I felt its beauty. In an instant, I knew how precious life was and I'd taken it for granted. The first thing I saw was frightened faces, but everything was better. I walk in the light, now. Life is exciting. It's a gift."

Over the next few weeks, Donna Shaney and Leslie Gardner met for breakfasts, lunches, and dinners. They went for walks. They talked about life and faith. And finally, he asked her out on a date. It was the most nerve-racking question he'd ever asked.

He'd gone to battle with demons, the most unimaginable evils; they were nothing compared to the fear of asking this beautiful woman out on a date. Everything had to be perfect. He didn't want to push her away or be unprofessional. He had to be careful. He was a professional man of faith. If this went wrong, he would embarrass the church, himself, and his faith. Added to the fact that if they continued courting each other, he would have to leave the church.

Donna didn't skip a beat. She was delighted. And their first kiss occurred on the back patio of a nice Italian restaurant in Genoa, Wisconsin. They sat near a cozy fire pit gazing out at the Mississippi River. It was sunset. The warm evening wind gently caressed their bodies. Her lips were careful, magical, and filled with love.

Donna and Leslie were married on May 30, 1985. His constituents were unhappy with his decision to leave his practice. They held a job for him, but the job was more of a courtesy than real work. They called him a consultant.

There was no one to replace him. No one else could do what he did. There was evil to fight, and the church had lost their most valuable weapon. They were aware he couldn't fight forever. The evil he battled would have eventually broken his will. It would have exploited his weaknesses and attacked him and destroyed him. In the bottom of their hearts, they were glad he'd been given Donna.

Now, they lived in their nice country home in the rolling hills of Wisconsin. Gardner's pension from the church wasn't much, but he and Donna were people of faith. They were enriched and rewarded by their fellowship. They opened a garden nursery. It did okay, enough to live off, and they were happy.

But now, looking out the picture glass window of his lovely home on the hill, Gardner felt an evil presence residing below.

Turning toward the staircase, Gardner stood from his chair. He strode upstairs, shuffled down the hallway, pushed the bedroom door open, and lightly shook his wife's shoulder. She was startled, rolling over to face him.

Donna focused when she saw Gardner's seriousness.

"What? What is it? You look scared."

He didn't know if she was fully awake yet. She obviously knew things were going bad. The severity of his expression told all.

"I need you to pack only what you need, get in your car, and drive away from here. Now," Gardner explained. He was calm yet silently frantic.

"Where will I go? When can I come back?" she asked calmly. He knew she trusted him. She wouldn't argue.

"I wish I had time to explain, but I don't. Go as far away as you can. Then, call me in a day. If you can't get a hold of me, call the police."

"I'll do as you say," she agreed while caressing the side of his cheek. "Are you sure I can't help you with…whatever this is?"

"You cannot and I would not ask it of you. The less you know, the better off you'll be."

She got out of bed, put on a pair of jeans and a white T-shirt.

"I'm not scared. I have faith." She kissed the side of his head, below his temple.

"You have nothing to fear…if you go. But I feel there is a fight ahead. Something evil is among us, and I won't put you in harm's way."

Gardner hoped he wasn't contradicting himself. If there was nothing to fear, then she shouldn't have to leave.

She got ready, quick, anyhow. She trusted him on a deep level. It didn't matter if he contradicted himself or not. He knew what he was doing. He knew she understood this.

Walking her to the door, he couldn't help but stop at the window and glance to the store. Evil resonated in the air. It was like an invisible tornado, dangerous and undetected. There was something very familiar about this evil. This was an evil he'd fought before. He'd known this day would find him.

He knew the evil waited for him.

Gardner stood in the garage. The door opened. Donna drove her Jeep onto the driveway. He heard another scream from the liquor store.

Gardner watched Donna drive down the hill. Cornfields surrounded her Jeep on both sides. Unaware he was doing so, he held his breath.

She stopped at stop-sign. It reflected in the moonlight.

Gardner prayed Donna would make it past the liquor store.

She did.

Her headlights disappeared down Highway 26.

Chapter 8

1

Winny and Garth crawled forward along the cold tile floor. They moved slowly. Every inch they pulled seemed louder than the next, their bellies lightly squeaking against the coldness of the tile. They maneuvered toward the back door, just beyond the rusty rack of cleaning supplies. They both stopped moving, startled and scared.

Stomping through the front door, the redhead ran inside.

What was her name?—Cherri.

She was calling out into the darkness of the store. Her voice trembled. Obviously, she was nervous.

Winny grabbed Garth's ankle. He crawled a few feet ahead. He whispered, "The phone in the back office…we'll call the police."

Garth turned to Winny, annoyed. He'd already thought of calling the police. It was the only thing on his mind since the thieves had smashed their cell phones.

"No shit, Sherlock. Can we get the hell out of this warzone first? Do you mind?"

Winny looked dumbfounded. He removed his hand from around Garth's ankle. They continued crawling toward the door. Garth popped to his knee. He staggered, settled, and then wrapped his fingers around the doorknob. He turned in the direction of the store area.

Cherri screamed.

"Timmy, where are you?" she begged.

Garth appreciated that Cherri was calling attention to herself. She was drawing the psychos away from him and Winny. Since he didn't care for the redhead, this was great. He hoped she would continue hollering.

Garth found it difficult to shake his thoughts of the sadistic young couple. There was something disturbingly wrong with both of them. In fact, their behavior was so disturbing he didn't want to know what was wrong. Obviously, they were dangerous. The farther Garth and Winny could get away from them, the better.

Twisting the doorknob, ever so slowly, Garth inched the office door open. When the space between the door and the jamb was wide enough, he slid through the small opening. He didn't make any noise.

The pressure from the door was uncomfortable. It was squeezing his ribs. Garth's hand was replaced by Winny's and then Winny was sliding through the door. Once on the other side, they let the heavy door slide shut. It whined, ever-so-slowly, until the lock clicked. It was secure. Garth flung the switch to the right. There wasn't much relief that came from locking the door, but a secured door was better than an unsecured one.

Given what had happened, nothing was very assuring when considering the madness on the other side of the door. Garth could only imagine the harm those bastards could inflict.

2

Cherri's knees weakened with each step she took. She wanted to sit but knew she couldn't. She was sick. Her head pounded and she was thirsty. She stopped in front of the cashier counter. She rubbed her damp hands together. She was frazzled, scared, and shaking. She wanted Timmy to hurry up. She wanted to leave.

Where was he?

She'd never seen anyone die before tonight. And it was even more frightening because she was in potential danger. The murderous psycho could easily kill her, too. She wanted to vomit, her stomach flipping. She would do anything to be far away from here.

Maybe, if given the opportunity, she'd turn herself in to the police. She hoped they would come. Right now, she'd feel safe in custody. Better yet, jail was an even better place to be. She imagined *this was what waking up meant?* She was certainly awake.

She was dizzy, but alert. If she could go back in time, she'd have jumped out of the stolen truck. She would leave Timmy and never look back. She'd never even cuss again if it meant she could get out of this nightmare alive. But that wasn't the case. She knew it. There was trouble ahead. The young *psychotic* couple who had come in from the cornfield was somewhere in this store.

They were maniacal, deranged. And they were shot, badly. They were out of sight. They'd disappeared, but still, she feared them.

Where could they have gone? They'd both been wounded. They should be dead. Cherri didn't understand how they were alive. She didn't want to understand.

Heavy as cement, her legs stiffened. She could barely walk. Somehow, she did. She stepped toward the restrooms. That's where she'd last seen Timmy.

Why would he still be in there?

Maybe he was hiding.

The cops would surely be there soon. Too much time had passed. Too much of a disturbance had been made—gunfire and screaming. Someone, somewhere, must have heard something, even if this was the smallest town in America. Someone had to have called the police.

She hoped.

If Timmy didn't come out soon, Terrance would leave. He was loyal, but not loyal enough to stay and see what happened next. Not in a situation like this. Sooner or later the police would be here, and if not, they had other problems lurking in the darkness of this store. In the end, he'd play it safe. He would leave.

Cherri's head was spinning. Her nausea was becoming uncontrollable. She wanted to leave, fast. She couldn't take much more of this. Her anxiety had peaked. She had to stop and rest, catch her breath. She wondered why she even cared about Timmy, at this point.

Leaning on the snack rack—which held various brands of potato chips—she tried to breathe. Her lungs were restricted. Her breathing was raspy and short, which made her panic more. Death crossed her mind. The thought terrified her. Dying before she had a chance to turn her life around, that was her worst fear.

She wasn't a good person. Her upbringing had been traumatizing, but that was no excuse. She made poor decisions even though she knew right from wrong. Most of the time, she knew the reaction to her poor actions was going to be bad. Still, she did what she wanted to do and didn't care who got hurt. Maybe she did it for attention or maybe she just couldn't help herself.

And now, scared out of her mind, she pushed herself up from the snack-rack. She shuffled toward the bathroom.

Something dripped on her.

It was cold and wet and hit her forearm like rain drops. It was heavy, thick. It landed halfway between her elbow and her hand. She rubbed her finger in it. It looked black against her skin. She smeared it. She brought her finger up to her nose and smelled it. There was a slight metallic odor to it. Maybe it was oil. No.

Her eyes went wide.

It was blood.

She slammed her eyelids shut and tilted her head up. Blood continued to drip on her. It fell on her other arm, her chest, the side of her face. It fell faster now. It was a stream. Once her head had completely tilted upward, she opened her eyes. Hazy at first, her vision allowed her to visualize the *thing* hanging from the ceiling. It appeared to be about the size of a heavy-duty trash bag and it was black. It started swaying.

Trembling, Cherri saw *it*. The blood was coming from Timmy's eviscerated stomach. A wave of red doused her, entirely. She screamed. Timmy's corpse landed on top of her. Before her head was pinned to the floor, she saw something else on the ceiling. Something else was holding Timmy to the ceiling. It also fell on her.

Timmy's blood created a pool on the tile floor. His guts spilled on her head. She lost her footing and slipped backward, smashing her head against the floor.

Peering to the right, Timmy's innards spread out toward the bathroom door, waving through the blood puddle.

Whiteness flashed before her.

She fainted.

3

Garth and Winny stood, silent, in the back office. They slowly slid through another door, past the office. The next room was more of a closet. Garth grabbed the cordless phone. Winny locked the second door. Space was limited, each able to hear the other's breathing.

The cordless phone sat on the desk near the filing cabinets. A terrifying realization struck Garth after he'd punched 9-1-1 into the keypad. Only silence came from the other end. He set the lifeless phone down and grabbed the back of Winny's shirt.

"We need to get out of here, now. Screw it, let's just get as far away as we can, and fast."

Winny stood with his ear pressed against the office door. He turned toward Garth. He was squinting. He was annoyed as he asked, "What do you mean?"

"Take a wild guess. I want to take a walk, get some exercise," he replied sarcastically. "Winny…the fucking phone is dead. I say we shift into *holy-shit-mode* and get the hell out of here."

"Okay." He was unfazed by Garth's snide remarks and frantic plan. But it was true, they needed to get out.

He reopened the office door and slid into the backroom. He stood next to the cooler entrance, the refrigerated room where they stored beer and soft drinks. The cooler stretched all the way to the back of the store. They headed through the cold dark tunnel. The frigid air oddly soothed them.

They moved past the chilling rows of bottled beer. There were no more screams. Shadows danced in front of the frosted glass doors. They hurried forward. Whatever was going on in the store had gotten worse. Nothing about this night or the last customers was good.

When they reached the back, Winny pumped the latch up and swung the door open. A quick breeze of humid air snuck in from outside. They were ever-so-silent as they exited. They halted. A deep voice spoke to them.

"You're not leaving now, are you? The party just started." It was the psycho blonde. She cackled in a childish, maniacal fashion.

Disturbed, wanting to run, Garth took a quick glimpse at the woman. It was Jezebeth. The strange blonde lady who'd come in with the psycho guy, Sammael.

Hadn't she been shot?

There was a hole in her stomach. The outer ridges of the hole were peeled back. Her shirt was burned. Dry blood crusted around the hole, but no blood flowed out. Somehow, she'd stopped the bleeding.

Who the hell are these people? Garth wondered as he shoved the back door open.

Winny ran outside.

Jezebeth wrapped her cold hands around Garth's neck. She pulled him backward. Her fingernails dug into the soft skin of his neck. Her grip was intense. He'd be bleeding soon. Watching in horrified silence, Garth witnessed Winny round the corner of the store. He took off into the parking lot. *Garth was alone.*

Winny stopped. Garth wanted Winny to keep going. To run until his legs quit. Winny's life would be endangered if he came back to help. As much as Winny annoyed Garth, the thought of harm coming to his brother was devastating.

The last thing Garth witnessed before he was snatched through the door, with superhuman strength, was Winny's face. Winny had spun around. He was running back toward the rear entrance. But it was too late. The door didn't open from the outside.

4

Crickets chirped. Loons cried. The night was alive. The cornfields held the night's critters. Breathing heavy, heart pounding, Winny skidded to a halt near the rear entrance. He was sweating. The night air was warm, humid. He grabbed the metal door handle and attempted to pull it open.

He yanked hard, but the door didn't budge. It was locked, impossible to open from the outside, and he didn't have his keys. The latch locked from the inside. Still, he made an attempt—and failed.

Without hesitation, he sprinted to the front of the store. He slowed when he got to the corner. He didn't know who or what would be on the other side of the store. It might be an armed robber, or it might be a sadistic freak. He didn't care to meet either, but he needed to get his brother out of trouble. Adrenaline controlled his thoughts. Scared as he was, he wouldn't let his brother fight alone, even if it meant dying.

The confusion as to *what* these people were and *why* they were here had diminished. Survival was all that mattered and not just for him. Winny and Garth would leave this hell together, or not at all.

When he rounded the corner into the parking lot, Winny's first sight was Terrance, crouched behind the wheel-well of the pick-up truck, near the back of the lot. The truck had to belong to the armed robbers.

On bent knees, he held his pistol between his legs. He was scouting the area. When he saw Winny, he raised the gun, aimed it, but didn't shoot.

"I need to help my brother!" Winny called out. Winny could tell Terrance was contemplating a return into the store, too. His friends were still in there. Whether they were alive or not: Winny didn't think it looked good. But still, *wouldn't he want to know?*

Terrance lowered his gun. He shuffled toward the front doors, gun-in-hand. His strides were hesitant, legs shaky. Without saying a word, the past—the robbery—*was let go.* Winny harbored no anger toward Terrance and was relieved he was joining him. They weren't alone, they had each other. Terrance had a gun. And two were better than one. There was strength in numbers.

Terrance and Winny shared a quick glance. They entered the store. There were no words said. There didn't need to be. Both Terrance and Winny understood that what they needed required partnership. It amazed Winny how quickly two people who had wanted each other dead less than twenty minutes ago could so quickly unite in the face of adversity.

They entered the dark store.

Chapter 9

1

Garth flailed tirelessly at the amazingly strong hold around his neck. He was being pulled through the cooler between the store area and the office. He fought with all his strength. Kicking and thrashing, he pried at the blonde woman's fingers. Her fingernails finally ripped through the skin of his throat. Cold streams of blood trickled down his neck and soaked the collar of his shirt. It was cold, the pain intense, and it was uncomfortable. This woman's strength was unbelievable. If she applied anymore strength, she'd rip his head off.

She dragged him through the large wooden office door and into the store area. His feet slid on the rubber heels of his shoes. She began laughing while she pulled him, effortlessly, toward the front entrance. Garth saw his brother, and Terrance, enter together through the glass doors.

He couldn't believe it.

How stupid could Winny be?

"Run! Get the hell out of here!" Garth screamed before the woman clamped down on his throat. His screams were cut short, turned into muffled winces, gags. She was going to crush his larynx. Her strength was unimaginable.

Garth watched Terrance raise his pistol, with shaky hands. Garth closed his eyes. The gun fired. The blonde woman's grip loosened. Her hand fell from his neck.

Garth dropped to the floor. He scrambled forward, darting away from her. Glancing back, he saw she'd been shot in the shoulder. Her hips swayed in a fluid manner. *Was she having a seizure?* She looked like a snake as she slithered down the fourth aisle. She rounded the corner near the cooler like a fish in a freshwater stream.

Then she was gone again.

Terrance fired his weapon at her until the chamber was dry.

"What the fuck is going on! I shot that bitch. She can't be moving," Terrance screamed. In a fit of rage, he threw his gun into the back aisle. *As if hitting her with his pistol would stop her.* The gun arched upward. It fell from sight. It didn't hit the ground. There was no crash. The gun didn't hit the floor. There was only silence. It was as if it was suspended in air.

Everyone stood silent. They continued to anticipate the crash of metal on tile. It didn't happen.

Scrambling backward, Winny, Garth, and Terrance attempted to run. They stopped when Sammael lurched up from behind the last aisle. He lunged across the store. Sammael leapt nearly twenty feet and landed on his feet in front of Terrance.

Sammael stood, smiling at the three of them. They tried to back up, and reached for the front door. A shuffling sound emerged from in back. Barely visible from behind

Sammael, Cherri emerged, sliding, belly down, across the tile. Judging by how fast she'd slid, Garth assumed someone had thrown her. She was covered in blood. Terrance stepped forward, his gaze locked on her.

"Cherri?"

"Help. He killed Timmy. They'll kill us, too," she sobbed while prying herself off the floor. "We need to get out." She'd gotten to her feet quick enough, but her balance was off. Her whole body quaked. Her feet slid on the blood-soaked tiling. She slipped then caught her balance. Her knees knocked. She didn't see Sammael standing in front of her.

Sammael turned, laughing, while he watched Cherri stumble forward. He winked at Winny, shook his head, and slowly stepped toward Cherri.

"I'm sorry, was that your boyfriend I split in half? Don't worry, you'll get over him soon enough." He turned, smiled, and winked at Terrance, Winny, and Garth. Then, he swung back toward Cherri. "You're too good for him. He was a loser, and you knew that. You've known that for a long time. Hell, you're kind of a loser, too.

Technically, I shouldn't kill you. I'm going to…but that's beside the point. You're a dumbass, a loser, and a guy like me…likes a gal like you…to make the world a shittier place. So, actually, I'm doing a good deed here, by killing you. I should be rewarded somehow…you know what I mean?"

Garth couldn't move. He was frozen, yet disturbingly intrigued by Sammael's maniacally deranged charm as he spoke to Cherri. His humor was offsetting.

Garth turned. He was about to slam the front door open. He stopped, stared in the reflection of the glass. His mouth drooped into an O-shape. He was terrified. Jezebeth was crawling across the ceiling. She moved fast and fluidly.

The ceiling tile broke and fell as she pumped her arms and legs forward. Garth spun around.

Before he could look up, Sammael smiled at him and said, "Her name is Jezebeth. Isn't that a pretty name? Almost as pretty as the girl whose body she took. Ha!" He broke into a fit of mad laughter.

Garth took off. He dove behind aisle one. When he came up, he was holding a can of baked beans. He drew his arm back and lobbed the can at Jezebeth. It soared toward her as she crawled toward the window, then down it. The can smashed into her face. There was a hollow thump. She fell forward, smacking the top of her head on the floor.

She jumped to her feet. Her face bled profusely from a long, jagged tear down the middle of her forehead. Her eye twitched, but she was smiling; laughing sadistically.

Garth was distracted when Terrance expelled a guttural scream. The agonizing yelp stabbed Garth's ears. It sounded like a dog having its hind legs run over by a pickup truck.

Peering past Jezebeth, toward the front of the store, Garth watched on amazed, confused, as a long snake-like arm punched out from Sammael's chest. It shot nearly four feet forward. It ripped through Terrance's neck.

Blood flung everywhere like a bloody sprinkler system. The snake whipped through his flesh and Terrance's head jumped from his neck and spun in circles. It thumped onto the floor. Blood sprayed in every direction. The head looked unreal, as though it was made of wax. Tiny veins shot gore in all directions.

Jezebeth stood in front of Garth, smiling. She was probably going to kill him. Garth couldn't turn his eyes away from Terrance's head. It wobbled onto its side and settled on the cold tile floor. A pool of slick black blood formed around the neck. Terrance's eyes blinked wildly. His mouth dropped open. He looked like he was going to say something. His teeth were chattering as his mouth involuntarily opened and closed successively.

The snake-like vine retracted back into Sammael's chest. He was laughing again, slapping his knee and saying, "Excuse me." Then he turned to Cherri. He cocked his head to the side. "I'll make this quick, okay." The snake slithered out from the gaping hole in Sammael's chest, where he'd been shot. It wiggled slowly like an attacking viper. Spikes poked out from the end of it.

Garth took a step back. He turned, attempted to run. His feet stopped moving. He felt something hot, wet, and strong wrap around his ankles. He fell to the floor. The skin of his right forearm squeaked. Jezebeth dragged him forward. Another snake-like vine shot out from the hole in her stomach, where she'd been shot.

"Help me!" Garth shouted, knowing there was nothing that could save him. These people weren't human. They were something supernatural. *Maybe they were devils?* Whatever they may be, they were stronger than anyone in the store.

Hope diminished.

Garth closed his eyes. His time had come to an end. In a matter of seconds, this woman would kill him, painfully. Those vines that shot out of her body would rip him to shreds. He only hoped it wouldn't be agonizing, that he would die quickly.

Then the wall trembled. It sounded like someone hit it with a boulder. The window shattered. Tiny particles of broken glass popped and exploded everywhere. Garth's thoughts of death were put on hold. A figure emerged behind the broken glass doors.

It was Father Gardner. He stood outside wearing gray cargo pants and a dark blue T-shirt. His attention was locked on Sammael.

"Let them go. Now!" Gardner demanded.

Sammael disregarded Cherri. He sauntered forward toward Gardner, a smile etched upon his face. He stepped slow-foot over slow-foot.

"I was wondering when you'd show up. Welcome, buddy."

Part 3: The Reunion

Chapter 10

1

Gardner stepped into the store. The broken glass crunched beneath his boots. His ears rang, the explosive force of the breaking glass was incredible. A sudden realization struck. He was jumping into this fight cold. He hadn't combated an evil like this in many years.

His nerves refused to settle and his heart hammered in his chest. His palms were sweating profusely. Forcing himself to do so, he inhaled deeply. His breathing needed to settle. Eyes locked on Sammael's, he held his ground. He was scared but stood tall. He hadn't seen evil like this in decades and didn't know if he could fight it anymore.

"Why now?" Gardner was amazed that he'd asked. As nervous and scared as he was, he wanted answers. He felt entitled to them. Even though a demon stood before him, he demanded logic. Sammael stared at him behind the eyes of the young body he inhabited. He easily recognized the demon.

How could he forget?

He'd chosen to pack the memory of this demon deep within the storage locker of his mind. He braced himself for the lies.

Demons lied, it was their nature.

"What better time than now, Gardner? What better place?"

Sammael looked Gardner over. "Wow, you have gotten old." Sammael cocked his head, as if in thought. "I'm surprised. I was hoping to see the fearless young man I saw thirty years ago. I forget that *you people* age quickly. It's kind of disappointing. Anyway, I've come back to say hello is all. But you don't look excited. And oh, before I forget, how's your wife?" Sammael finished. His lips quivered. He was on the verge of laughter, again.

Gardner was certain he was dealing with the demon he'd exorcised from Donna. It was Sammael. He knew the specificity of this demon. He could sense its unique evil. He'd researched it, studied it, and prayed for the answers decades ago, when he battled Sammael the first time.

After conducting as much research as he could, the answer had been given to him in a vision. Sammael had been brought up from hell more than once. He came at the Unholy One's request. But he could never come without permission from the Divine. That was the rule. There was no evil sent amongst the living without holy consent. There was never consent without reason. However, the mystery of the Divine remained unclear.

Scared and uncertain, Gardner commanded, "I cast you out of this body, the body of human flesh that you have stolen." He appeared confident. But he knew his faith was weak. Not that his faith hadn't remained intact, but it was much less defined than it once was.

Sammael raised his eyebrows. He winked. "I don't think I will. I'm really enjoying this body." Laughing heartily now. "You should have seen the sick things this boy did." Eye contact ensued. Sammael whistled.

Gardner's vision brightened. In the back of his mind, he was able to see what the young man, Rod Barton, standing before him, had done. Rod had slaughtered the innocent—children, lovers, elderly and youth. The body Sammael now possessed belonged to the evilest of humans. Rod was a believer in the great power of evil.

Gardner had never battled a demon in the body of anyone *this* evil. Three decades of retirement wasn't going to help him in this fight, either. He was out of practice and out of shape.

Gardner's belief in Goodness was the only strength he possessed.

The stomping of shoes thundered across the floor. The Gasper brothers and Cherri—covered in blood—ran outside.

Good.

Gardner wanted them as far away from here as possible. They raced through the back entrance. Gardner heard the door slam shut.

They'd left.

He was relieved.

"Looks like your helpers abandoned you?" Sammael asked calmly.

"They have no part in this. This battle is between you and me."

It was an accurate answer. He didn't feel like explaining that he cared for the two boys who owned the store. His concern would only act as a weakness for the demon to exploit. Gardner was relieved they had gone. They had been spared, for now.

Gardner lifted his head. He turned to the right and saw movement. Another woman stood in the aisle, a blond woman. Even though she was concealed by darkness, Gardner could see she was covered in blood. She stood against the broken glass door he'd broken with a large rock from the parking lot.

Again, Gardner's vision illuminated. It shined within him. He saw the evil things this woman had done. Gardner didn't know which fallen angel had nestled inside of this evil woman, but he knew she was possessed. He judged her status by the wounds inflicted to their bodies. When the possession was over, these bodies would be destroyed, and their souls would be cast into hell. Their bodily injuries were too severe. Both the boy and the girl were rattled with bullet holes.

Anger seized Gardner. Control left him. He ran forward. Raising his arms, he tackled Sammael to the ground. Sammael cackled maniacally.

Peering up, Gardner watched as the slithering snake emerged from Sammael's chest. It wiggled and heaved forward. It coiled around Gardner's waist. It fastened tight. It felt wet. Gardner's body was lifted from the ground, the small of his back screaming with a horrible ache.

Sammael threw Gardner across the store. Landing near the back, he crashed into a stack of Styrofoam coolers. The white boxes flew everywhere, creating a snowfall of small particles.

Gardner tumbled to the floor. His ribs throbbed. His back shot pain in every direction. He didn't want to get up. But he had to.

Forcing himself from the ground, he faced off with the two demons. They came together, closing in on him. They walked forward and stood shoulder to shoulder.

Gardner froze.

2

The cornstalks scraped at Garth's exposed arms, the sleeves of his shirt were torn. He moved fast. The tassels tore into his skin like papercuts. Garth led the way through the tall crops. The three of them were a good ways away from the liquor store. Winny and Cherri were in tow. Every now and again, Garth would hear one of them moan as the stalks cut into their skin. Both of them tripped a few times.

Garth was annoyed. He wanted to push Cherri down the hill. She was poison. She was only causing them grief. Each time Garth turned around to make sure Winny was all right, he saw Winny helping Cherri along.

How could he? She'd tried to rob them at gunpoint with her degenerate boyfriends.

Winny could be so weak. The girl was obviously evil, blatantly a criminal.

Garth and Winny would already be at Father Gardner's house if it weren't for her. Cherri slowed them down.

Garth hoped Donna was home. It would be easier to get around if she were home and awake. Regardless, they would be able to use the Gardner's phone. They could call the police. Garth's legs pumped forward. He was bothered. But he needed to think clearly and use his brain..

Garth's legs were fatigued. He was winded. His lungs burned and his breath was short. The uphill run had taken its toll. His feet kept getting stuck in the mud. Still, he moved at a steady pace. His adrenaline kicked in, he wanted to be as far away as he could from the psychos at the liquor store.

He turned around. He could tell Winny and Cherri were exhausted, too. They moved slowly. Hopefully she would stop. If she stopped, she could fend for herself. That's where Garth would draw the line. He would leave her. He wouldn't care if Winny came with him or not.

Then she panted, "I need to stop."

Garth smiled. "Go ahead, I wish you were stuck back at the store." He pointed to the liquor store at the bottom of the hill. "You belong with those…sick bastards."

"Come on, Garth, she needs our help. We need to work together," Winny pleaded.

Garth's eyes went wide and wild. He wanted to scream. He wanted to punch Winny in the mouth. He remained silent, shaking his head. He took off running and disappeared into the heavy cornstalks, hoping he'd lose them.

Maybe they'd get lost in the field and it would be great if they couldn't find their way out. At least Winny would be safe—if he was lost. Wandering around the vast acres of cornfield might be the best thing for him. Plus, it would buy Garth some time. He could call the police, diffuse the situation. By the time Winny found his way out of the cornfield, this nightmare would be over. And then, after the situation was settled, Winny would still give Garth grief.

Garth wanted to punch Winny, knock some sense into him.

Once Garth was far enough ahead—of Cherri and Winny—and elevated enough to see downhill, he saw they were moving forward.

How cute, they were moving hand-in-hand.

But they were okay. Garth was mad, but he didn't want them dead. Well, he didn't want Winny dead. He could care less about Cherri.

The tassels from the cornstalks shook slowly as their shoulders plowed through the greenery. They continued to jog uphill.

Facing forward, there loomed the darkened farmhouse. It opened up into a clearing. The house was only a football field's distance away.

Garth kicked up his speed.

3

Cherri hadn't run in years. Her stomach churned. Sharp pains twisted her bowels. Her lips were cracked. Timmy's blood had dried to her skin. It itched. It created a red paste when she tried to wipe away the blood mixed with her sweat. A light crimson stream ran down the contours of her face. She was exhausted—mentally and physically—not to mention confused by what had happened at the liquor store.

Who were those people?

She'd never been so scared in her life. The young couple—Sammael and Jezebeth—were freaks of nature. They were superhuman. She'd never seen anything like them. She hadn't had time to process the situation. The last hour of her life had changed her way of thinking forever.

Until an hour ago, Cherri lived a horrid existence with her abusive boyfriend. For one reason or another, she'd felt indebted to him. She had no concern for Terrance because he was a criminal acquaintance, tagging along for kicks. He would have left after they'd reached Detroit.

Maybe being dead wasn't such a bad thing.

Then why was she trying so hard to survive? She didn't know what to think. She didn't know how to react. All she knew was she wanted to live. Maybe it was because she wanted an opportunity to redeem herself, turn her life around. If she made it out of this night alive, she promised to change the way she lived.

What about these two boys she'd escaped with? They didn't care for her. The angry one had made that crystal clear. The taller one, Winny, was helping her. She didn't know why.

Maybe it was his nature to help. Or maybe he didn't have time to think about it. It could just be that he rationalized an extra set of hands as strength. But if they ran into more danger, Garth would leave her, and she would have to fend for herself. She, like Winny, would rather be with a group, whether they liked her or not.

Her legs hurt and her lungs burned. She wanted to puke. Every muscle in her body was overexerted. She felt like quitting, each breath a chore. Her stomach felt like it was full of ice. Somehow, she kept moving. She had to.

The first positive thought crossed her mind. She wanted to start over. A wave of guilt followed. She wanted to start over because she didn't have to worry about Timmy anymore. A sickening relief struck within her. She was free from Timmy, and she felt slightly liberated, despite everything that had happened. She would never see him again. He would never hit her again. She was rid of him. And it hadn't been her fault.

What an awful way to put it.

She wasn't to blame for his demise. She had to stop herself from thinking such awful thoughts, but she couldn't help it. Those two people—*things, psychos*—at the liquor store had killed him. They'd ripped his torso wide open. His insides had spilled all over her.

Guilt washed away. She peered up. Winny held out his hand. He wanted to help her. There was urgency about him. But there was no malice. He was genuine.

"Come on, you can do it. You can rest up when we get to the house," he whispered, as he splayed his fingers outward, toward her.

She grabbed his hand. He pulled, giving her momentum. They hurried up the hill. Cherri grasped Winny's shirt. He helped her along.

They reached the top of the hill. Winny pushed the final stalks to the side. They stood in the clearing. The two-story farmhouse loomed in front of them. The cream-colored brick was old. Even in the dark, it appeared chalky. It looked wore-out. Garth stood on the porch, near the front door. He tapped his foot while he rang the doorbell.

When he spotted Cherri and Winny, he stepped back, startled. Given everything that happened tonight, his reaction was expected. It was logical.

She understood why he was jumpy. First, he'd been robbed. Then he'd been attacked by superhuman freaks. *Maybe the freaks were on PCP?* She heard addicts in the midst of a PCP high were able to do superhuman things. They could lift cars and walk.

They could continue walking after being shot.

Physics could explain a few things, but still, the blonde woman had crawled across the ceiling and snakes had slithered out from her bullet wounds. Just the thought of the snakes sent shivers down her damp spine. Her shirt clung to her back.

Moving closer to the house, Cherri saw—and sensed—the anger radiating from Garth's scrunched face. His cheeks were streaked with dirt. His chest heaved in and out.

"I don't think Mrs. Gardner's home. We'll have to break in and call the cops. Got it?" Garth asked.

"Yeah. You need my help?" Winny asked.

Garth didn't answer. He kicked the wooden door open. He peeked around the corner. He nodded then stepped into the house.

The wind picked up. In unison, Garth, Cherri, and Winny glanced down to the liquor store. Red and blue lights swirled in circles.

The police had arrived at the liquor store.

Chapter 11

1

The black and white police cruiser turned left at the end of Main Street, headed away from the police station. The downtown was dead for a Saturday night. It always was when the festival in Watertown took place. The cruiser hooked a right on James Street, traveled through another sleepy neighborhood then headed toward Highway 26.

The night proved to be a bore for Officers Brad Zoelick and Jake Zastrow; two of the ten officers assigned to the township of Dodge Junction. Their shift had started at ten and nothing had happened. There were no speeders to pull over, no reckless teens causing havoc. The night had been mundane. Zoelick and Zastrow forced small talk and drank too much coffee. The coffee was free, of course. Shelly, the clerk at the all-night gas station was happy to serve them. The gas station sat at the edge of Maple Street.

It was just another boring night until Zoelick noticed the shattered window and door of Buggy's Liquor as they drove past. The broken glass sparkled in the moonlight as it spilled down the cement curb and onto the blacktop of the parking lot.

With his peripheral vision, he was able to glimpse into the dark void that was blasted through the front window. The twinkling glass shot quick sparkles of light into the night. His gut instinct was that a couple of seniors from the high school had broken in, stolen a few cases of beer, and took it to the Benson farm party.

The Benson farm was out on Route 8, past town limits, headed toward Watertown. Richard Benson, a Dodge Junction high school senior was hosting a keg party tonight. Small town cops like Zoelick and Zastrow could easily find out where the local farm parties were being held.

Kids like to talk. Even to cops. It made them feel important and somewhat superior. The police could always shake down some dumbass kid for information. Kids broke easily. Zoelick had busted enough teenagers for underage drinking that he was owed many favors. A few weeks ago, he pulled over Tom Delkamp for drunk driving. The seventeen-year-old had been so razzed he'd given up every underage drinking event occurring over the next few months. The Benson party included.

And in turn, Zoelick let Delkamp park his car and walk home without a fine. And if for some reason the police couldn't shake down a teen, concerned parents sometimes informed them of the parties. Parents were fearful that one of their teens might kill themselves while driving drunk. Sometimes, a scorned teen would rat on the party, out of spite.

The unfortunate obstacle about the Benson farm was that because of the new zoning ordinance, the property was located outside of town limits, but *also* outside of the county sheriff's district. The kids knew this. The local newspaper had run it as a front-page story. It had been a very slight miscalculation by the alderman. It wouldn't be corrected until next month. For now, the police could only patrol outside the perimeter.

They were able to pull over vehicles that were speeding or appeared to be driving erratically. A good cop could always pull over *whoever* they wanted and they could use *whatever* excuse they might think of.

Pulling into the parking lot of Buggy's Liquor, Zoelick's partner, Officer Jake Zastrow—a high strung rookie with blond hair and puffy baby cheeks, who looked too young to be a cop, sat up straight and slapped the back of his own head. He'd been fighting sleep the entire shift. The six cups of strong coffee he'd drunk wasn't enough.

Zastrow was given the previous three nights off, and he liked to party. He still reeked of alcohol. Zastrow, along with the rest of the younger officers, liked to *let loose* during their off days. Zastrow was rowdier than most. He probably kept the party going until early this morning.

"You think we got a breaking and entering in progress?" Zastrow asked, shaking off his sleepiness. He blinked successively and adjusted in his seat.

Zoelick ignored Zastrow. "That ain't Winny or Garth Gasper's pick-up truck parked at the end of the lot. I know that for fact."

He was right. The window was broken and the truck in the parking lot didn't belong; it was out of place. Zoelick felt a rush of excitement. His blood pumped fast.

They might get a little action tonight.

A breaking and entering would look good on both of their records.

Parking near the side of the brick building, Zoelick and Zastrow exited the police cruiser and crept, cautiously, toward the broken glass door.

Zoelick pulled his standard issue nine millimeter from its holster. He held it trained in front of him.

Zastrow did the same.

Zoelick's nerves ran wild. About to enter through the broken door, he heard something rustle in the blackness of the store. It sounded like footsteps. It was probably some punk kid. Given their geography, *kids* were the logical answer. Or it might be the Gasper brothers assessing the store damage. Maybe they'd purchased a new truck. Zoelick kept both ideas in mind. It was easier that way. He'd be able to cover his bases in his report.

Zoelick glanced through the broken window. He saw movement and heard a burst of laughter. He aimed his pistol toward the back. A shadow grew and then shifted across the back wall. It disappeared into the darkness of the store. He was convinced his first assumption was correct. It was teens. A serious criminal wouldn't be laughing nor running around the store.

"Officers Zoelick and Zastrow! Coming in!" Zoelick yelled into the dark liquor store. "You have about a heartbeat to identify yourselves!"

"Help! This crazy old man shot me and my wife! He's still in here!" A voice rang out. It echoed like it had come from the back. And there was something mockery about tone of his voice.

Zoelick held his position. He didn't want Zastrow to see his hands shaking. He was the senior officer and needed to display confidence. His pistol grip was slick from his sweating palms. There was something sarcastic about the way this man sounded, like he was joking. There was a jovial tone in his call of distress.

Was this some kind of joke?

Whoever was inside had better hope not.

A young man ran out of the store. He clutched his bloody chest with both hands as he ran forward. Zastrow popped out from behind Zoelick and raised his gun to chest level. His stomach heaved like he was going to throw up. There was blood all-over the young man, not to mention a nice sized hole ripped through his chest.

"He's got a gun! Help us, officer, please. My wife's still in there!" the young man screamed.

The young man ran beside Zastrow. Zoelick turned to him. The kid was lucky he hadn't been shot again, running out the way he did, all erratically.

"Get over here, now!" Zoelick commanded while pointing at the wall nearest the end of the front wall. "Take cover."

The man stumbled toward the brick wall.

Zastrow accompanied him.

"Hey Zoelick, you want me to stay with the kid, or go with you?"

Zoelick thought fast, turned to the man with the chest wound and then said, "Stay with him. Assess the injury…call for backup." He looked to the injured man and asked, "Where's the gunman?"

The wounded man stuttered, "He…he…he's in the back, left, corner. He's got my wife, please don't hurt my wife. Please don't let *him* hurt my wife," the young man cried. His pleas came out like a bad performance in a horror film. There was something very artificial about his demeanor.

Zoelick felt like he was stumbling into a war zone. Something was *off*. He'd never been in combat. The only battle he'd ever encountered, during his fifteen years as a small-town cop, was a few bar brawls. He was scared shitless even then.

In hindsight, the thought of his fellow townsfolk seeing him act cowardly was more frightening than the actual fight. He didn't want the community thinking he was incompetent. Obviously, this situation seemed more dangerous—life threatening. There was someone in the store with a gun and they'd obviously used it. Plus, he was going into the building blind. Someone inside had a weapon and a better line of sight. The young man with Zastrow was shot in the chest.

It troubled Zoelick that the kid was so mobile. He was curious as to how he was still alive. How was he able to function after that kind of trauma? If the bullet hit him in the chest, then he should be dead.

Rounding the corner, Zoelick entered the liquor store. He stepped on a large pile of broken glass. It crunched beneath his combat boots. He ducked down as he moved forward. He crept across the tile floor, toward the oil cans, which were stacked in neat rows on the bottom shelf.

He knelt on a small piece of glass. It ripped through his pants and carved deep into his knee. He bit his tongue. He wanted to scream. Warm blood gushed out of the wound. It soaked into the dark blue fabric of his trousers. Zoelick pulled the sliver of blood stained glass from his knee. It was long, almost an inch.

"Officer! You need to arrest the man who ran outside! This is Father Gardner speaking! He's dangerous. He's the one behind all of this!"

It was Father Leslie Gardner. Zoelick knew the voice well. He and Gardner had coached a little league together. That was years ago, but they'd remained friends.

Gardner wouldn't lie.

He also wouldn't break into a liquor store in the middle of the night. Zoelick remembered Gardner lived in the house up the hill.

Maybe he'd witnessed a disturbance and came to help. That was something Gardner would do.

"What's going on in here, Gardner?" Zoelick yelled out.

"I don't know how to explain it. You need to arrest the kid who just ran out of here! He's a criminal and extremely dangerous."

The sting of reality bit hard. Zoelick thought of his partner.

Zastrow was in danger.

The reality bite dissipated.

Fear took over. As he prepared to leave the store, something caught his eye.

Blood dripped from the ceiling.

2

Zastrow walked two steps behind the wounded young man who grabbed at his bloody chest and moaned. Even though the guy was severely injured, Zastrow remained skeptical. Small puddles of blood dribbled along the blacktop as they walked across the parking lot.

The kid tripped, lost his feet. Zastrow stepped forward and cupped his right hand beneath the kid's armpit. The kid was strong. His arms were solid muscular.

Zastrow and the kid hobbled to the police cruiser. Zastrow placed the kid's hand on the hood. He hunched over, supporting himself. He took quick shallow breaths and continued grabbing at his chest wound.

Zastrow needed a rest too, but only for a moment. All this sudden action was making him dizzy. It also wasn't helping his hangover. Shaking his head, he moved toward the back car door and unlocked it.

The door slid open. Zastrow stopped it with the palm of his hand. "Have a seat, sir. Try to relax. Real quick, what's your name? Are you able to tell me?"

The wounded kid peered up. His eyes were demeaning, they laughed at him. For a moment, Zastrow wondered if the kid was faking his injuries. The convincing agony of pain was absent. There was something insincere about his facial expression. The kid's dramatics were strange, like this was all a joke. Although, the hole in his chest suggested otherwise.

"Sammael. Call me Sam," he said, staring up at Zastrow.

"Okay Sam, what happened?" Zastrow asked. He reached into the front seat of the cruiser and retrieved his radio set. He placed the receiver to his mouth but didn't speak. He expected an answer from Sam. Instead, something wet and muscular shot from Sam's chest and slid around Zastrow's neck.

It clamped down tight. It squeezed. Zastrow dropped the radio, fumbling for it as it fell to the blacktop. He turned to the store and tried to call out for Zoelick. He couldn't. His airway was cut off. Panic seized him. The sudden pressure to his head made his eyes feel like they were going to pop out of his head.

Zastrow's knees hit the pavement. With both hands, he pried at the slimy vine wrapped around his neck. He attempted to spin. Again, he tried to yell. His mouth opened, but nothing came out. His throat was clamped shut. His cheeks burned. He swallowed, trying to breathe.

What the hell was wrapped around his neck? It felt like a skinned snake.

Whatever it was, Zastrow couldn't get a solid hold on it. He felt faint and his head ached. His finger slid along the length of the snake. It felt like it was lined with silicon. He lost his grip. His hand slid off. Grabbing this *vine-thing* was like trying to pin down a ball of mercury. He lowered his right hand to his belt. He grabbed his nine millimeter. He aimed it at the slimy vine and then twisted his hand upward, beneath the wet-thing.

He fired.

The vine snapped and let go.

Zastrow fell backward. He wrapped his hands around the pistol grip. Quickly, he aimed at Sam. The snake wiggled back and forth from his chest wound. It looked like a third arm as it snaked in and out of his wound. The tip of the vine branched out into four sharp ends that looked like thick silver fishing hooks.

Another gunshot rang out.

"What the hell?" Zastrow screamed. The slimy thing whipped Zastrow's hand as he pulled the trigger.

The gun powder felt hot against his face. It burned. His right eye stung, and felt wet.

With his left hand, he touched the tender spot near his temple.

"Holy shit! "

Zastrow had shot himself in the head. It didn't seem real. It couldn't be fatal. It didn't hurt, yet. He was fully conscious.

Maybe he just grazed himself?

He prodded his fingers at the jaggedly torn skin. Blood spat out in thin streams. It splattered across his lap. Some of it painted the pavement.

Sammael laughed.

"You bring new meaning to the word misfire. I was gonna take your head off, but this is much more amusing!"

Another shot rang out. This one slammed into Sam's shoulder. Pink mist erupted in a cloud behind his head. Sammael fell to the ground. He overdramatically screamed, still laughing, while grabbing his fresh bullet wound. "Oh my lord…you hit me. Ouch, ouchy," he roared. His laughter was hard and guttural. He started to gurgle like an infant in the depths of a temper tantrum.

Zastrow watched, terrified. Sammael crawled toward him. He swatted the gun from Zastrow's hand and jumped on top of him.

Sammael straddled Zastrow. He dug his knees into Zastrow's torso.

Zastrow felt cold all over. His limbs became numb. He was scared, trembling. The only warmth he felt was his urine when his bladder let loose.

Sammael smiled.

He wrapped his hands around Zastrow's neck. His elongated fingernails dug deep into the soft flesh above Zastrow's Adam's apple. He was tearing into his throat. The pain was intense. Time slowed. He couldn't scream, only gargled and choked. His skin peeled back from around his throat.

Sammael's fingers sunk into Zastrow's neck, wrapped around his spine, and twisted. His neck snapped.

Sammael tugged Zastrow's head from side to side. After a short struggle, his head uprooted from his neck. Blood gushed heavy and quick from the stump. A smug grin washed over Sammael's face as he stood and stared at the eight-pound head of Officer Zastrow.

He liked taking heads. They were a wonderful souvenir.

Sammael turned to the store. A smile pulled his cheeks taught.

He strolled toward the shattered doors.

3

The store was dark. The only illumination was the moonlight as it danced off the white walls. Everything was too quiet, unnerving.

Click. Click.

Confused, Zoelick turned from left to right then tilted his head up to the ceiling. The click of tiles slipping from their grooves floated into his ears. He heard something crawling, but it was coming from the ceiling. His eyes locked on *her* face.

It was a woman, a strikingly good-looking woman. She peered down at him with blue eyes that twinkled in the reflective light. As awkward as the situation was, he couldn't deny this woman's beauty. She appeared flawless, like an airbrushed model. The moonlight casted a cold spotlight upon her. The back of her silky blonde hair was highlighted, making her appear angelic. He'd never seen a prettier woman.

Somehow—scared as he was—the woman's physical perfection stole his focus. A slithering vine shot forward from her stomach. It curled around Zoelick's neck, clutched his throat, and tightened. It happened so fast he didn't have time to react. He paid no attention to his service revolver as it dropped to the floor. Within seconds, the gorgeous woman's beautiful face burned into his memory. His hands shot to his throat. He pried at the snaky vine. It was slimy.

The beautiful woman wrapped her legs around his waist. Her thighs felt like iron. Her feet locked near his pelvis. She crushed his torso and pushed his femur bones outward. Her strength was amazingly intense. His hips popped out of place. His guts churned and compressed. His bowels weakened and let loose, the odor putrid.

Zoelick's body strained, he couldn't hold himself. Blood filled his face. His eyes bulged. They were popping from their sockets. His vision went hazy. Tears streamed down his face. Something indefinable moved into his view. The beautiful woman's head swiveled forward.

Her neck stretched and elongated to unrealistic proportions. Her skin cracked as it stretched. There was crunching and popping noises emanating beneath the skin of her neck. The sight was frightening. Zoelick's heart wasn't just pounding, it was bursting. Her head continued stretching—nearly a foot in front of his—yet her body remained clamped on his back. A sick smile pulled her mouth taut.

This wasn't possible.

He was going to faint. Distant echoes floated into his ears. Someone was yelling.

It was Gardner.

But it was too late.

Zoelick's head lifted, tore, and fell from his neck. It hit the tile at the exact moment his intestines dropped through his rectum. A mass of guts, blood, feces, and gore piled on the floor beneath him. His eyes hemorrhaged and fell from his head. The blonde woman shot forward, lunging like a panther.

She ran outside.

4

Officer Zoelick's head rolled across the tile floor, thick brown hair soaking up the blood puddle there. His oval-shaped head, slick, lubricated in dark red fluid, stopped when his nose nudged the bottom portion of a dusty rack. It tilted backward, lolled, and stopped.

Gardner was in shock. He wanted to scream. He started forward, but then froze. His sight flashed white. He was given a vision.

In the vision, Sammael's jaw opened. His teeth jutted forward, and he smiled, exposing his razor-sharp teeth. He entered the police cruiser and drove off into the night.

The vision was quick.

The police car, belonged to Officer Zoelick.

Dizzy, Gardner's thoughts swam back to the present.

What did the vision mean?

Gardner glanced around the store. Shelves were broken and merchandise was scattered across the floor. The window and door were shattered. Glass peppered the tile, and even more terrifying, Gardner was alone and vulnerable. He stood amongst the carnage and gore of four dead bodies.

Where did the demon go?

He stood on shaky legs. He stumbled toward the back of the store. He was lost. He was too weak to fight this battle. A sick depression set as he acknowledged that he was in over his head. His faith was frail. There were people who needed his help. But he was incompetent—helpless.

Where were the Gasper boys?

They must have gone to his house to call the police.

The girl, she must be on her way to the house, too.

He had to help, didn't have a choice.

Standing, he lowered his head. He prayed for the answers.

Why was his strength so weak? His visions wouldn't answer. *His intuition did.* God was angry with him. He'd neglected his duty. He disregarded the gift he'd been given, and he felt void. He'd been blessed with the gift to serve the greater good and he hadn't used it.

Over the years, his gift had exhausted him. His exhaustion reformed his idea of what the gift was. His tired mind convinced him it was a curse. Because of this, he'd retired. He hung up his fight.

That was wrong.

He knew it.

A rush of excitement and adrenaline seized him. He ran out the broken door, sprinted through the parking lot, and chugged up the gravel driveway toward his house.

He would fight the unholy. He had to.

And then he remembered…

Donna.

Chapter 12

1

Donna Gardner's charcoal colored Jeep strolled down Main Street. The night breeze whistled through the open driver's side window. The spinning wheels created a pleasant distraction. It didn't sooth Donna's troubled mind, but it was refreshing; the cool summer night air.

The blinking lights of Main Street found Donna. They made her head ache. She continued forward, cruising along the downtown stretch. The stop-and-go-lights stopped switching colors at exactly midnight. Now, they only flashed red.

She came to a halt and cranked her neck from left to right. Life within the town had diminished. There was nothing, dark stores and streetlights. The townsfolk rested. There were no other cars in her path or nearing. Everything was silent. She rolled down the passenger side window. A tunnel of air circulated through her Jeep.

She took deep breaths and ran her hand through her hair. She peered toward downtown, straining her eyes to see. The shops which lined the main strip were dark windows, some held "Closed" signs. The town would be lifeless until Monday morning.

Donna pressed her foot on the accelerator. The Jeep sped forward, past Shuett's Hot Dog stand; a small hole-in-the-wall eatery, which was very popular on warm summer nights. The fresh dogs and cool ice cream treats served as a social outpost for the townsfolk. For now, the stand and parking lot were deserted.

In that moment, fear encompassed Donna Gardner. *What had Leslie seen in his visions?* She knew something bad was amidst their sleepy town. He wouldn't have told her to leave in the middle of the night if his worries hadn't been life threatening. Given the past, Donna knew questioning her husband was a waste of time.

She trusted him with every fiber of her being. He was a good man. He knew things most others couldn't fathom. Just the look on his face let her know something awful was happening. She could feel it grating her insides and chilling her nerves. Fear penetrated her, all the way to her core. Terror permeated in her bones. She would drive until Leslie called her. She couldn't go to the police station, yet. There was nothing to report. Leslie hadn't told her to go there.

She only hoped there was nothing to report.

If she went to the police station, what she had to report wouldn't fly well. Logical law enforcement would find her statements silly. They'd probably take her to the hospital for drug testing. She would only embarrass herself. Nothing would come of it. The danger lurked in another plain of existence.

Again, looking both ways, she proceeded down Main Street. The town limits ended in two miles. After that, she'd be engulfed by the back country.

At night, the dark hills, forest, and cornfields frightened her. The countryside was beautiful in the day. This part of the country—the Midwest—was picturesque. That was putting it modestly. The rolling hills, forest and scattered towns were breathtaking.

She could drive from sun-up to sun-down. But at night, the darkness served as a nest for evil dwellers. Evil took pleasure in the night's blackness. The ugliness of the world could walk amongst the living, at night, while the innocent rested in a vulnerable state.

For many years, Donna walked with the dark. Her youth had passed her by. She had nothing to show for it except bad memories. Memories she'd forgiven herself for many years ago. Sure, there were days when she wished she could have her youth again.

There were a million things she wanted to say to her young, stupid, self. Once in a while, she fantasized about how life could have been if she'd chosen a different path. She could have been a better student, a better daughter, a better person. One of the most difficult hurtles in her life had been forgiving herself for what she'd done to her parents.

In her late teens, she'd dropped out of school. She was addicted to drugs: cocaine, crystal methamphetamine, and heroin. If you could name it, she was doing it. Her friends were into wicked things. They took pleasure in the pain of others and found it humorous. Their behavior was demonic.

If she were to guess, most of her youthful associates had probably ended up in jail, or they were dead. It took an act of God to bring Donna into the light. For a time, the darkness had consumed her.

Ronald and Denise Shaney were wonderful parents. Donna was an only child due to pregnancy complications. Her mother had only been able to produce one. Donna was *it*. Together, Denise and Ronald spent countless hours loving, educating, and being *real* parents to Donna.

They'd have done anything to ensure she turned out good. But Donna's curiosity for new experiences got the best of her, at a young age. She'd lied about her addictions and hid them well. Her parents believed her lies throughout most of her high school years. But around the end of her junior year, the wall of lies began to crack. Her parents were smart people.

They intuited that there was a problem and they'd sent Donna to rehab. She'd been willing. But it didn't help. She was sober for a few months, but the temptations and the outright fun and romance of the drug culture rediscovered her fancy. She indulged in drugs again—a lot of them, enough to make up for lost time. Her parents turned to tough love.

They kicked her out of the house. The decision was a gamble. And as it were, throwing her out allowed her the freedom to live amongst the underworld. Soon, she was homeless. She didn't even know she was a transient. She traded certain *favors* to support her habit.

In trade, she was able to reserve a spot on the ratty couch of a drug den, in an unfavorable part of town. She didn't leave the couch. She would smoke methamphetamine and snort cocaine, day and night. She performed her duties with the owner of the house. On a few occasions, she had had to perform with the landlord's friends. As long as she had her drugs—her reason for living—she was okay with giving her body away.

Her soul had diminished into the darkness and her body became an empty vessel— empty space that something most unsavory found as a vehicle for destruction. With her body, the demon entered the plain of physical existence.

When the demon possessed her, she thought she was dying. At first, it felt like she'd overdosed. Her skin began to burn. Inside the eye of her mind, she saw herself falling down a dark hole. She tried to grab on to something, anything, but found nothing. Her grip was slippery. There was no net, nothing to catch her. Although her skin burned, her guts felt icy.

Every organ in her body was hard and frozen, which hurt worse than the burning. Her screams went nowhere. For days, she remained in a constant state of pain. The owner of the house she'd been staying at threw her into a dumpster in the back alleyway with the help of a few friends. They'd had enough of her babbling and her fits. The rage that she displayed didn't flow well with her cohorts. They had to get rid of her.

She had no recollection of how she'd gotten out or how she'd made it to her grandmother's house. After the exorcism, her grandmother explained how she'd been discovered. But it didn't matter. She remembered nothing and nothing clicked.

Her grandmother barely recognized her. Apparently, she'd gotten out of the dumpster and was wandering the streets when an old acquaintance—of her grandmother's—from church saw her. He'd contacted Silvia, who took her home.

At one point, when her cousin had come to visit, she'd nearly devoured her baby. There was no recollection of that, either. It wasn't until Gardner exorcised the demon that the pain stopped. And when she emerged from her dark hole, she was sober. For the first time in years, she thought clearly.

Thinking soberly, she received clarity to many things. Like the fact that she hadn't talked to her parents in four years. She got a hold of her father and he'd explained that her mother had passed away three years prior.

Denise Shaney had suffered a massive heart attack. Given her father's distant tone and subtle anger, it was clear he placed the blame on Donna. She accepted it. She put the people she loved in a state of emotional hell for her own selfish desires. Now, she had to live with it. And she did.

Eventually, she forgave herself and moved on to a more fulfilling life, with Leslie Gardner.

Now, coming to the end of Main Street, headlights emerged in the distance. They loomed like two small flashlights waving in the dark. The car moved fast. It barreled past the red stop lights. Donna was shocked by how fast the car was coming. It traveled at the velocity of a machine gun bullet.

Focused, she squinted in the rear-view mirror, trying to make out the vehicle. Red and blue lights flashed on top. She was relieved. It was the police. They must have been headed to the scene of an accident. The flashing lights swirled across the Main Street buildings.

She pulled off to the side of the road in order for the squad car to pass. But it didn't. It pulled off to the shoulder and slammed into the back of her jeep.

She was jolted, violently, forward. She smacked her head on the steering wheel. Her forehead took the blunt force, and a blinding white light seized her. She wasn't rendered unconscious, but she was dazed. The skin below her hairline tore down the center and stopped at the bridge of her nose. She bled. And immediately, the tear in her skin spewed dark red fluid. It stung when it seeped into her eyes. It blinded her. It dripped onto her T-shirt, painting it crimson.

Shaking badly, she fumbled for the door handle. He fingers slipped from it. Her grip was weak; she couldn't bend her fingers. Finally, she was able to grab on. She shoved the car door open and spilled out onto the gravel.

With trembling knees, she crawled toward the road. Besides the pounding headache, pain, and disorientation, confusion now set in.

Why had this police car crashed into her?

Donna Gardner slowly lifted her head. A man stood before her. He was young, but something about him was beyond his years. Then she realized she was staring into the face of evil.

2

The demon stood beside the police cruiser door, his feet set firmly on the gravel. He turned from the desolate fields back to the downtown area, a short distance away, and then walked toward the smashed Jeep. Excitedly, Sammael rubbed his hands together in succession. He wanted to desecrate this woman before him. He'd waited a long time for this. He didn't know what atrocity he wanted to commit first.

It was breathtaking, casting his eyes on the woman who he'd returned from the pit of eternity to torment. He wanted to pick her up, smile at her, hold her, desecrate her, and then tear the skin from her flesh. He imagined her, skinless. The eyes of a human wearing no skin was a treasure— *maybe later.* He'd waited decades for this moment. He would remain patient.

Thirty years ago, Gardner had forced Sammael out of Donna's body.

He'd been *sent back.*

He didn't like being *sent back.* It had happened on a few occasions. With Donna it was different. He'd been so close to killing her. If he'd spent another few seconds in her body, she would have met death at his hands. Then Sammael would have gone back to his thrown of despair, triumphant, forced to watch Donna burn in the lake of fire.

Sammael had come back from the *dark place* many times. He'd tortured many people and many souls. But with the Gardner's it was personal. There was a special kind of discomfort he wanted them to feel.

Possessing Donna's body had been pleasant, evilly satisfying. He'd enjoyed molesting her insides. Before he was exorcised, he'd begun grinding Donna's flesh into eternal pain. Her body had screamed in searing agony. Then he'd been ripped away, sent back to the *dark place*. It was unexpected and it had hurt. Being cast out of Donna brought Sammael deep despair. It angered him. Now, he wanted to eat her flesh while she watched.

Grabbing her arm, he dragged her toward the police cruiser. She fought him, digging her fingernails into the soft flesh of his wrist. Her other hand shot forward and hit his mouth. She grabbed his lower lip and pulled. Sammael felt warm blood trickle down his chin like juice after biting into fresh fruit. The skin inside his mouth tore sideways. He didn't care. He would be inside Donna's body soon. The body that he wore now would be dead. Its owner would burn for eternity.

Donna had been an easy target thirty years back. But now, she was different. She was hitting him, defending herself. She was placing value on her life, something she hadn't done all those years ago. She continued ripping his lip open. She had spirit, which had been absent in the past.

Her human strength was no comparison to the supernatural ability he possessed, but it was impressive. Lifting her arm upward, her body followed, and her feet dangled in the air, nearly a foot off the ground.

"What's going to happen is going to happen, Donna. *You* fighting *me* won't get you anywhere. And you tearing my lip off will only hurt the poor degenerate I stole this body from. You of all people should know that."

Sammael laughed while shaking his head. "Jee-whiz, Donna." He launched her against the car. The side of her head crashed, hard, against the rear quarter panel. The metal dented. A streak of blood remained above the wheel-well. Donna dropped to the ground like a heap of bricks. She was out cold. The top half of her body slumped over her legs as if she were stretching. Blood and saliva dribbled from her mouth.

Sammael went back to the police car, opened the back door, picked Donna up by the arms, dragged her forward, and tossed her into the back seat.

The fight in her had been impressive.

Sammael placed the palm of his hand on Donna's forehead. He closed his eyes and gritted his teeth. He wanted in. He needed in. Now was the time. He pushed with all his might. Trying to penetrate the pores of her skin, he hit a wall. He was blocked. Something was wrong. He couldn't possess her.

A sorrow sunk in. The Unholy One wasn't allowing Sammael to *take* her. He continued trying to sink into her flesh. He failed. Sammael wasn't often denied possession.

Maybe he should just torture her and then kill her.

Obviously, he'd been able to harm her, physically. He'd knocked her unconscious, but he wanted to live in her skin. Living in her body was the only subjection that would suffice.

Killing her wasn't enough. He wanted to possess her, but he couldn't. Sometimes he was allowed to harm the host and sometimes he wasn't. The forces at work determined the outcome, not he. He didn't like to think about the two forces making the rules because he had no control over the choice. He only enjoyed carrying out the work he was tasked with.

Right now, he wanted to work.

Sammael jumped into the driver's seat, turned the key in the ignition and punched the gas. The cruiser spat gravel in every direction. Pebbles and small rocks kicked up beneath the car undercarriage. The small rocks pattered against the chassis like a hailstorm. Turning the radio dial to what the human's called *Hard Rock, Sammael* wondered what sinfully pleasant things Jezebeth was conducting with the others—with Gardner.

All of this was for Gardner. Sammael wanted to seek his revenge, and rake havoc on the living. He could taste his vengeance. The taste was sweet, but it tormented him. He hadn't been able to take Donna. Sammael couldn't think of anything more rewarding than confronting Gardner while wearing his wife as a costume. The best way to antagonize Gardner was to take his wife's body. And he couldn't. Not yet, anyway. He would try again.

Looking into the rearview mirror, he saw oncoming headlights. More blue and red lights twirled brightly in the darkness.

More fun!

Chapter 13

1

Cherri, Winny, and Garth entered the Gardner's house. It was dark inside. The floor creaked as they entered. There wasn't much comfort that came from being inside. The layout was foreign. Even the Gasper's were disoriented. They'd never been to the house. Silently, Winny closed the broken front door. He didn't know who was in the house. For all he knew, the psychos had somehow made it here. He hoped not.

"Mrs. Gardner!" Garth shouted. But there was no answer, no noises from upstairs.

"I'll check," Winny said as he bolted up the staircase.

Once upstairs, Winny flung each door open. The last door led to the master bedroom; he could tell by the size of the unmade king-size bed. Donna had to be gone.

Winny went back downstairs.

They had to assume Donna had left. She hadn't answered the door, and she wasn't in the bedroom. *There had to be a phone here, of course there was.* They needed to call the police.

Winny inched the front door until it closed. The hinges creaked as he brought the door to the frame. Peering to the side, he grabbed a small stool, took the flower vase off of the round platform, and set it under the doorknob. It wouldn't cause much resistance, but the door would remain closed. It wouldn't be hanging open to where anyone outside would think the house was open for business.

Worst case scenario, if the stool broke, they would be warned by the noise of the vase being knocked over. It would shatter and alert the group—they would know someone was inside.

Winny turned and walked into the kitchen. Garth and Cherri searched opposite ends of the homey room, looking for the phone.

Upon entering, Winny looked to Garth who stood near the sink. He searched the side of the cabinet with the palm of his hand.

Winny turned to the back wall, near the screen door, saw a light switch, and flipped it on. Cherri's eyes squinted when the fluorescent bulbs infiltrated the room. The light was bright and uncomfortable. Winny adjusted his eyes. He saw the phone. It was set near the back door, resting on a recharging phone port. He pointed to it as Garth's wide eyes met his.

"Turn that light off, dumbass. We don't want those crazy assholes knowing we're in here," Garth whispered angrily.

Winny felt stupid. He should've known better. He flipped the light off.

Garth punched his fingers into the keypad of the cordless phone: 9-1-1.

A white tablecloth with blue stripes rested across the sink faucet. It was folded in thirds. Winny grabbed the cloth, wet it down, and handed it to Cherri. She smiled, took it, and wiped off her bloody face.

"Are you all right?" Winny asked her.

She looked up. She was surprised. Her lips trembled as though she didn't know what to say. And after a short silence, she finally answered, "I don't know. Everyone I know is dead. I feel lost. I don't know what I'm doing. I'm scared. I'm sure you two don't care to have me here. Sooner or later you're going to leave me."

From across the kitchen, Garth lowered the cordless phone. He turned a hairy eye toward Cherri and said, "You got that right. You can go back to the store if you like. Go be with your friends."

"Don't be a jerk, Garth," Winny barked.

Garth wasn't concerned with Cherri's wellbeing. And he definitely didn't care about her feelings. He banged the cordless phone against his hand and shouting, "What the hell! The damn phone doesn't work. There's no dial tone."

"What do you mean? Is it plugged in?" Winny asked.

Garth, again, looked at Winny like he was an idiot. He shook his head and let out a long sigh. He whispered angrily, "It's cordless, ass-wipe."

"I meant the charger. The charger has to be plugged in, too, otherwise the phone won't work," Winny said, calmly.

"Aha!" Garth cried. He was hunched over the floor, near an electric outlet. He plugged in the phone charger. He tilted his head toward Winny, smiled and said, "Sorry bro, you were right. It wasn't plugged in."

The face of the cordless phone lit up green. Garth punched in the numbers. He put his ear to the receiver. A frown formed on his face. He lowered the phone. Something crashed against the side of the house. The wall rumbled and shook. It felt like a boulder had hit the wall. The green light on the phone died, as did the digital time on the microwave above the stove.

There was silence.
Someone cut the power.

2

Sparks shot between her fingers, charring her flesh. The twisted metal tore into her skin. Burning blood oozed from her new wounds. Jezebeth stepped back from the electric meter. She held a snake of aluminum coil in her mangled hands. The sparks shocked her, sending heavy volts of electricity through her stolen body. She'd ripped the outlet loose from the side of the house.

More sparks shot in quick bursts from the jagged and twisted aluminum. They looked like speeding fireflies and burned her skin black all the way up to her forearms. She didn't mind. The body she wore would be finished soon. A smile stretched across her face. She gazed up at the old brick farmhouse and admired how dark it was.

Her excitement grew. Her prey was nestled inside, scared. She liked it when they played hard-to-get. It made the kill more exciting. She would kill all of them. She wanted to tear their insides into a thousand pieces and bathe in their blood.

She moved through the backyard. Her feet left deep imprints in the dew glazed grass. She stared forward, watching for movement in the house. Thin streaks of smoke billowed from her hands.

Peering into the Gradners' small kitchen window that sat above the sink, she saw slight movement. The room was dark. She saw a shadow bounce across the window. It was her prey. The dark form danced across the darkened kitchen.

Still smiling, Jezebeth strolled up the back stairs. She wrapped her burned hand around the small aluminum door handle while her excitement grew. She could taste the blood of the innocent watering her mouth. It was good.

She opened the screen door.

3

Every breath Gardner took was a feat. This was the toughest battle he'd fought, and it was far from over. He didn't want to think about the challenge ahead. He huffed with burning lungs while he ran up the gravel driveway.

Normally, he was in good shape. But tonight, he was fatigued. He hadn't prepared for this, hadn't seen it coming. He shook it off. It didn't matter. He would continue fighting until he couldn't go any further. His knees, back, and chest hurt. But he was determined. He had to do this. He slowed down as he neared the house. Defensively, he needed to think about his method of entry. The demon waited for him inside.

What was the best avenue of attack?

The moonlight kicked a white glow on the cream-colored brick. But overall, the house was darker than usual. He couldn't explain it. It held a dark life force. The porch lights were off. The electricity was out. He could only imagine who had maneuvered the blackout. The silence was unsettling.

He crept toward the back door. Staring down at the damp grass—that he'd intended on cutting tomorrow—he saw footprints spread between his broken electric meter and the back screen door. The meter was a tangle of twisted metal. Tangled aluminum tubing rested in the wet grass. He followed the footsteps with growing concern. He hoped he wasn't walking into a bloodbath.

He would enter from the back door with caution. Hopefully, entering through the back was less expected. Also, he noticed as he walked across the front yard, the front door was cracked, probably broken. Long splinters of cracked wood lay scattered across the porch. The wooden particles stretched down to the cobblestone walkway.

He would go through the back door. Maybe it was a good idea, maybe it wasn't. Regardless, it was the best idea he could come up with.

Images of Donna consumed his thoughts. He prayed she was all right. His longing for her was unsettling. His anxiety had peaked.

He stepped around the corner of his house. His feet stopped. His eyes rolled to the back of his head. He was being given a vision. It was of Donna. She was in the back seat of a car. Someone was whistling.

Sammael.

He was taking his wife somewhere. He could see the car moving toward a blinking light. The light was red. *They were on Main Street.* They were coming back to the house. They didn't want Donna, but they would get to him through her. He was slightly relieved Donna was alive. That was something.

They had already hurt her. Thoughts of Donna—in pain—infuriated Gardner. His anger grew.

Closing his eyes tight, he fell to his knees and prayed. It was all he could do, and he needed to do something. His hands clapped together. He raised them to the night sky. "Show me the answer. I'll do as you ask. Please keep Donna safe. I'll accept anything as long as you keep her safe."

As he prayed, he felt the disappointment of God fall upon him. He knew God's anger. He'd neglected the incredible gift he'd been blessed with. He ignored his destiny, for a very long time.

It was true—he could have saved many lives throughout the years. He started to feel he was responsible for many great losses. But he wasn't young anymore. He couldn't handle the fight. And maybe he didn't need to be fighting evil spirits and exorcising demons, but he needed to be conducting goodwill for the better of mankind.

That was something he hadn't done in many years. Sure, there were little league games, and he'd gotten through to a few teens, but he was capable of so much more. He was capable of inspiring others.

His visions guided his thoughts. He was shown the many opportunities he had had to help others but had chosen not to act upon them.

"Forgive me," he cried while tears ran down his face. The wet drops settled above his upper lip. Annoyingly, the sweat tickled. He wiped his face with the back of his hand. He felt like sneezing.

Inhaling deep, his thoughts began to come together. He felt better. He'd needed this release. The euphoria coursing though him felt like warm shining light. It radiated within his soul. His powers had been restored.

He stood.

Feeling strong now, he ran around the side of his house. He sprinted into the backyard. He jumped up the small set of cement stairs that led to the back door. One of demons might be on the other side of the door, but he didn't care. He was determined. And it felt right.

One demon at a time.

4

"We need to get into town. Maybe Father Gardner's truck is in the garage. We can take it, he'll understand," Garth said while shaking his head at the lifeless telephone. Their cell phones were smashed, the power was out. The only way to get help was to get away from here.

His eye-line traveled upward toward Winny, *and that piece of trash Cherri*. His head stopped moving. His eyes locked on what stood behind Winny. A disturbing presence was among them. Garth stepped backward and began to shake. His feet shifted.

Standing among them—nearly undetected—was the crazy woman from the store. *Jezebeth*. Her face was caked with dry and wet blood. Her arms were black, like they'd been burned. Her smile had stretched so wide the corners of her lips had torn. Her jutting teeth and upper gums were exposed. Her right cheek had begun to droop where the skin was peeling.

His hands fumbled with the telephone. His slick fingers bobbled across the buttons. He didn't know why he bothered. The phone was obviously dead. Maybe he was hoping for a miracle. Finally, the phone fell from his hand. It broke when it hit the floor. The battery slid across the kitchen floor. Cherri and Winny stood at the far end, near the table. They were scared. They trembled.

"Run! For Christ's sake, run!" Garth screamed. Then he was sprinting toward the back of the kitchen.

Halted in place, Jezebeth's arm stretched outward, beyond what was humanly possible. It wrapped around Garth's waist. Her arm, from the bicep to the forearm stretched five feet. The skin tore along her triceps. The charred skin of her arms flaked off and looked like burning embers. Blood pelted the kitchen floor from the jagged tears. Her arm retracted. She pulled Garth with her. He tried to run, but his strength was useless in comparison.

Winny turned to Cherri with wide eyes and screamed, "Go, run like hell and get help!"

She nodded. He gave her a push. She fled out the front door, throwing the small stool aside as she ran. The vase toppled over and shattered on the wooden floor.

Winny rushed toward Garth. He stopped and glanced at the countertop.

The butchers block.

He stretched his free hand toward it. His fingers fumbled across the handle of the big knife. He pulled it free from its wooden sheath. The moonlight glared off the edge of it as he slashed it through the air. Blindly, he swung the blade at the demon. It hit, slashing Jezebeth. He stabbed at her repeatedly.

Blood shot from her arms and neck. It sprayed in all directions. It looked like pink mist as it splattered the floor, cupboards, counter, and Garth. Jezebeth never removed her focus from Garth. The metal blade ripping her flesh to shreds didn't faze her. She didn't flinch. She continued pulling him toward her. Finally, the knife plunged deep into her neck. She launched herself at Garth.

Garth shot across the kitchen and crashed into the stained wood hutch. Rows of knick-knacks and antique china fell to the floor; some rolled, some shattered. A strange doll that looked like a drunken leprechaun tumbled and pelted Garth on the back of his head. It hurt.

He peered up. Jezebeth held Winny off the ground. Her hand was clamped around his throat. His legs kicked. His free hand swooped up and ripped the knife from her neck. He jabbed the blade at the wiggling snake that emerged from her stomach. This time, the end of the snake had split out into smaller snakes that extracted what looked like silver hooks that protruded from the fleshy ends. They were rattling and punching at Winny. He yelped as the sharpness snipped at him.

With each strike, Garth watched a small piece of Winny's flesh tear from his face.

"Help!" Winny screamed.

Garth jumped to his feet. He sprinted toward Jezebeth. Hatred, anger, and adrenaline fueled his rage. He jumped at her, tackling her to the ground. The snakes continued shooting out of her body, striking Winny.

The back door blasted open. Garth thought, for sure, it was Sammael. *This is it,* he thought. His life was going to end.

Jezebeth was ripped through the back door. She howled in a deep demonic tone as she went.

5

Sweating and frantic, Cherri opened the side door of Gardner's garage. The truck was parked against the far-right side. The walls were lined with benches. Tools and aged boxes were stacked semi-neatly.

She grabbed the door handle and tried to open it. Locked. She pulled and twisted, nothing. She peered into the cab. Her eyes tilted to the ignition. No keys. Gardner probably had them. She had no time to think or devise a plan. She exited the garage and ran down the driveway.

Dust kicked up from the gravel. She coughed. Her throat was full of dirt. She made it to the bottom of the hill. Though she was fatigued, tired, and exhausted, her legs kept pumping one after the other. She thought of nothing else but getting help for Winny and Garth. Especially Winny, she found herself taken by him. In the short two-hour span she'd spent with him, in this hellish nightmare, she'd developed a sense of care for him.

It wasn't lust or a girly crush. It was genuine care and concern. Unfortunately, she'd aided in robbing his store. That would complicate what he thought of her, later. If they survived this night, he might not think so highly of her. For now, it didn't matter. He wanted to help her out of this mess. If she could get to the store, she could get Timmy's truck, go to town, and find a cop. Never in her life had she wanted to find the police as badly as she did now. The thought was almost comical.

Screaming, grunting, and heavy breath infiltrated the night air from the distance. Her throat felt hot, inflamed with oncoming tears. She hoped Jezebeth hadn't gotten to Winny. But also, she was beginning to think her efforts would ultimately lead to nothing.

As she reached the bottom of the driveway, she took a quick glance back at the house. The screams emanated from the backyard. Something bad was happening. She had to get help, fast. She wanted to survive—in one piece would be nice. If she could get help, maybe she could save someone's life.

The thought of helping someone other than herself strangely fulfilled her. It felt good to be exerting her energy for no other reason than to help another. She kicked up her speed. She reached the parking lot. If she remembered correctly, the keys were in the ignition. During robberies, Timmy left the keys in the ignition. That way, if they got into a jam, they didn't have to worry about searching for the keys or possibly misplacing them. They could simply jump in the truck and go.

That's what Cherri did. She jumped in the truck, started the engine, and drove to the edge of the parking lot. She stared forward, to the highway. She looked to the farmhouse on the hill. Her gaze was stuck on Gardner's house.

Maybe there wasn't enough time to go into town and find a cop. How long could Winny and his Garth, honestly, hold that thing off? Plus, a cop might think her mad if she started screaming about murderous creatures that could crawl across ceilings and shot snakes from bullet holes.

Maybe another set of hands was better than wasting however long it might take to find a police station. Or flag down a random patrol car. She cranked the wheel to the right, hoping she'd made the right decision.

She headed back to the farmhouse.

6

With all his strength, Gardner wrapped his aching arms around Jezebeth's neck and pulled her down the cement steps. Her head tilted backward. She strained. Together, they fell to the ground. Anger, adrenaline, and rage coursed through him. He felt the presence of *good* working through him—using him as a tool.

Jezebeth's skin was incredibly hot beneath his palm. She growled. She was spitting, trying to shuck free of him. He pushed her onto the ground. He straddled her. Her hips thrust upward. She bucked him like a rodeo horse. He clamped down and forced her arms back down. Her wrists shook violently with the rest of her body.

Gardner dug his knees into the soft portion of her arms, where the biceps met her forearms. Her wiggling continued, violently. Her eyes shot forward, bulging from their sockets. They locked on his. He felt the fire of hell in her stare. A thin ring of hazy white-fire danced around her pupils. She looked like a viscous wolf.

"I shall see you in hell," she hissed. Then, her convulsing stopped.

Gardner closed his eyes. He leaned forward and whispered.

Jezebeth's mouth heaved open. Sickly yellow foam spilled out. It burned her lips as it trickled out. The putrid substance slid across her cheeks. It was scalding hot against Gardner's hands as it seeped between his fingers. Her voice became deep, almost harmonic.

She was chanting.

Gardner couldn't make out the words, but knew they were Latin.

"In the name of all that is good, I command you out of this vessel," Gardner hollered.

When he opened his eyes, he experienced deep sorrow. He watched the girl beneath him die.

The demon had left. The girl's body was no longer possessed of Jezebeth. She expelled her last demonic breath. Her chest rose, fell, and stopped. A mist of vapor escaped her mouth. The final pocket of life escaped this body.

Gardner turned toward the field when a snake slithered past him. He didn't know if he was imagining the snake or if it existed. It seemed to have slithered from the sickly fluid expelled from the girl's mouth.

Maybe it was Jezebeth slithering through the grass?

Everything became silent. Gardner sat up, still straddling the girl's body.

Patty was dead.

Gardner felt strong again. The Lord had used him. God breathed life into him. His body shook. Beads of sweat formed on his forehead, soaking between the creases of his aging skin. The drops detached from his pores and ran down his face, over his jawline, then fell to the grass. He closed his eyes. His shoulders slumped. He inhaled deep.

Before he stood, he thought about the girl beneath him. A vision took hold. He saw the awful things she'd done. This girl—Patty King—had taken lives from the innocent and the damned alike. In his vision, he was shown images of Patty and Rod Barton—killing *her* parents. They had tied them to a pole in the basement. They'd desecrated them.

Gardner didn't want to see this vision, but if he was being shown, then it was necessary. Patty's mother and father had been tortured for days while she and Rod laughed and sought pleasure in their misery. Their murder was a cruel joke.

Patty was evil. Still, Gardner shed a tear for her. She hadn't been born evil, she'd been taught evil. Now, she would endure torment for eternity. It was the consequence of her cruelty.

The vision stopped.

A pair of headlights emerged from the driveway. It was a truck.

It must be the girl, Cherri.

The dead girl began breathing.

7

Patty King awoke from her nightmare and faced hell. Fully alert now, she was locked in some kind of dungeon. It was dark, almost black and the walls were lined with black sludge. The last thing Patty could remember was torturing Judy, the young professional, she and Rod had tortured. She had been in her basement. Rod had cut her throat.

Patty's memory started to flow. She remembered being sick. Her stomach had twisted in knots. She'd become faint. A sensation had sizzled inside of her and her organs had felt like they were burning.

That was the last she remembered before opening her eyes to this dark place. She wanted out. Her insides were sour and rotten. A bitter stench arose in the room, emanating from all around her.

Looking to her left, she saw Rod plastered to the wall. But she could only see a glimpse as he was propped against it. The wall was wet and slimy with running ooze. There was a thin layer of clear skin blanketing him with suction. It was wrapped tightly to him like shrink-wrap. His eyes were pried wide open and pinned back. His expression reflected great horror.

Light shined into the room, a fiery glow. The bright rays danced in the dark behind Rod. For a moment, Patty's attention was drawn away from him. Someone had opened the door to this dark place. Depression set in as she sensed something worse than death behind the door.

Or maybe she could go now? She hoped, but didn't believe.

She promised herself she would be back for Rod.

Her slimy restraints ceased, and she could move. She turned. When her body twisted, she saw the light led to a brick house. The world opened to her. It was someone's house on a hill.

The light ceased and it was dark. It was a farmhouse. The cool air surrounded her. Her lungs filled with heaviness. She was drowning. And she was removed from the dark place. It no longer surrounded her. Her sight became filled with the night. Millions of stars lined the sky. To her right, she saw the moon. It was fully engorged and luminescent.

Pain seized her. She was lying on the ground and the grass beneath her was wet. She gazed up and saw an aging man, probably sixty years old. He stared down upon her. His eyes were intense, and he was sweating profusely. She wanted him to help. She tried to scream. Wetness erupted from within her. Pain seared through her body like wildfire. For all the atrocities she'd committed—torture, sorrow, agony—she felt regret. Regret so deep it peeled her apart from the core outward.

Then it was dark again.

She was falling, burning.

She was scared.

Chapter 14

1

The truck Timmy, Terrance, and Cherri had arrived in sped up Gardner's driveway. Cherri hit the brakes, put the truck in park, and hopped out. Her feet hit the ground, and she ran, sprinting. Her desire to help—to fight—was incredible. She peered into the backyard. Gardner was leaning over the blonde woman from the store.

Hesitant at first, Cherri continued toward Gardner. She slowed to a shuffle. Fear encompassed her. She didn't know what evils lurked in the darkness. Also, she didn't know Gardner, or what he would do to her, *what he thought of her*. But right then, she wanted to help him. She needed to trust him. Her intuition insisted he was good.

"Are Winny and Garth all right?" she asked, searching the backyard. Nothing crawled from the shadows. Genuine concern accented her voice, and she hoped both Gasper brothers were okay.

Her anxiety created a twist in her stomach. She wished it would loosen so she could think clearly.

"Let's check," Gardner said after quickly inspecting Cherri. He stood and they ran toward the back door of Gardner's house.

Before they could enter the house, Garth and Winny blasted out the screen door, nearly knocking Gardner and Cherri to the ground.

"Father Gardner, what the hell are these people? I'm freaked out and I need answers," Garth demanded.

Gardner turned and walked with Garth, Winny, and Cherri. He was struggling for breath but managed to say, "They're unholy, demonic spirits. The bodies they wear are stolen. I know that's hard to believe, but it's real and it's happening. And if we don't come together and unite, we'll be picked apart."

"What do they want with us? What did we do to…the demons?" Winny asked, humbly.

"I don't know, but it isn't good. You might not have done anything. They want me. I think the two of you were used as bait. There's a reason *he* sent this upon you. Part of it was that they used you and your store to lure me in. They knew I'd come.

"And the three of you were just pawns to hook me. They'll enjoy killing anything they're permitted to in the process." Gardner cocked an eyebrow. "Which means we're all in danger—the both of you…me." Then he turned to Cherri. "I don't know who you are. But I know that you…"

Garth cut Gardner off and said, "Her and her boyfriends were in the middle of robbing us when those two showed up—the *unholy* or whatever you say they are. As far as I'm concerned, she can go anytime."

Gardner shook his head. "There's meaning to everything about this night, Garth. Right now, we need to stick together. There's strength in numbers."

Cherri stood near Winny, hoping Garth would listen to Gardner.

Cherri lightly grabbed Garth's shirt. He shrugged her off and frowned at her. She stepped forward and said, "I didn't want to rob your store. I didn't know what else to do. I'm sorry. My…" She couldn't say the word boyfriend in front of Winny. It would turn him off to her. But, right now, she needed to be honest. "I was in a bad relationship, and I felt stuck. They robbed stores like yours for traveling money. We were on our way to Detroit. They needed more money. They've never killed anyone before…and I guess I've always been too weak to turn away from them."

Gardner turned to Cherri and took her hand. It was warm and comforting.

He smiled. "There's good in you. You are not weak. You can be strong, but you need to choose your strengths. Staying with us is a good start."

She was ashamed, vulnerable. She couldn't help but agree with everything Gardener said.

"Right now, I need to find my wife," Gardner continued.

"Why does he want you?" Garth asked.

"He is the demon Sammael. I exorcised him from my wife, Donna, many years ago. He wants to kill us both, but mostly he wants to torment me. I took what he was intent on taking. The demon holds grudges; Donna is in danger."

"What kind of a priest were you?" Garth asked.

"The kind who deals with the vilest of evils imaginable; there's a supernatural realm living all around us. We don't see it unless it slips out, as it has tonight. I was born with the gift to see *it* and to fight *it*. I gave up my fight decades ago, which is why I believe this night is happening. I don't know the level of your involvement in this fight, between Sammael and me, but you have been chosen, for one reason or another."

Garth looked to Winny and then down at Cherri and said, "I don't trust her. For all I know, she's one of those *devil-things,* too."

"You're going to have to trust her, or you'll weaken our strength," Gardner said.

"Why can't I just get the hell out of here, find the cops, and let them take care of this?" Garth asked.

"It's not that simple. If you must you must, but I'll tell you this, I believe the result of bringing more people into this fight…is going to be the rise in body count. I don't want anyone else to be hurt at my expense. Garth, there's been too much death tonight. We need to find my wife and Sammael. I will fight him. I can beat him. I have before. I will do my best to protect you from him." He shook his head. "But if you want to go your own way, there's no one stopping you. I'm saving my fight for the demon."

With total disregard for Gardner, Garth turned toward Winny. "Are you coming with me?" he asked and then walked toward the cornfields.

"Wait. We need to stick together. If you leave—" Winny started.

"If I leave, I'll get help, moron. You can stay here if you like. Get ripped apart by whatever the hell those things are."

Cherri stepped toward Garth but stopped when he locked angry eyes on her. "Garth, I know you don't care for me. You have no reason to, but we need to stick together. It's like Gardner said, there's strength in numbers."

"Yeah, like you and your two dumbfuck boyfriends robbing my store. They had strength in numbers, too." Garth turned to Gardner. "Why is it that the bad guys always win? I'm an honest man and I can't get a fucking break!" Garth finished, stepping away toward the cornfield.

A light breeze kicked up. It flung Cherri's hair in front of her face.

The cornfield rustled.

"Let him go," Gardner said. "His anger will only tear at our group."

"I can't." Winny pleaded while walking toward his brother. "Garth, wait up."

Cherri could no longer hear what they were saying. Garth pushed Winny away from him and then darted into the concealment of the corn.

Winny didn't attempt to run after him. He came back, looked from Gardner to Cherri and asked, "What do we do now?"

Chapter 15

1

Pain stabbed at every joint in her body. The pounding in Donna Gardner's head brought her back to consciousness. She hoped that when she opened her eyes, this would have all been a dream.

It wasn't.

She forced her eyes open. Dry blood crusted her eyelashes shut. Her muscles ached. Hot burning sensations exploded from her every extremity.

Shakily, she sat up straight and adjusted to see. She peered out the front windshield. She was in the squad car. Her stomach felt like it was filled with twisted metal. The outline of the man in the driver's seat was overwhelming.

It was the demon, her demon.

The night's canvas whipped passed as she looked out the window of the speeding squad car. The man sitting behind the steering wheel looked young. His body was beaten, rotting, and foul, but appeared young.

The demon inside of him was old, ancient, and powerful. There was something familiar about this demon. She knew him. It wasn't his physical appearance she recognized. It was *his presence*. She knew what this evil man was, what was inside of him. She'd felt the same evil three decades ago.

How could she forget?

Never again would she allow herself to become so weak that her soul would allow her body to be taken by a foul thing like the demon sitting in front of her. She didn't care if he killed her—she would fight until her body quit. She would die before she became a victim of possession, again. Staring out the back windshield, she saw more headlights in the distance. Red and blue swirled above the headlights. The colorful illumination should have been reassuring, but Donna knew what the demon was capable of.

"What are you going to do?" she asked.

When he turned his head toward her—this time—his face appeared pale, almost green. His eyes were pure white, and his smile stretched upward. His lips were torn in the corners. Dried blood was caked to his chin. It fell like flaking rust.

"I'm going to take your body…"

When he smiled, his face peeled back around the jagged tears on his mouth. Donna could see his teeth and gums. He looked viscous, like a rabid dog. His comically perverted demeanor was put on hold. "…and tear you to pieces from the inside out. You'll beg for death while I rip your limbs to pieces and eat them in front of you."

His white, fiery eyes settled. He smiled as if pretending to be sweet-natured. "And, of course, that will be right after I take care of our little problem back there." He nodded toward the approaching police car. "It's your fault the officer driving behind us is going to…you know. If you'd only let me have you thirty years ago, this could have all been avoided."

There was an awful screeching noise. The squad car felt like it was lifting forward. Donna was thrown into the passenger seat. Sammael had slammed on the brakes. He spun the steering wheel left. The rubber tires burned on the pavement, and she was jolted forward. She closed her eyes when her head smacked the glass window. For a moment, she was certain the car would flip.

The cruiser stopped. They were moving forward again, picking up speed. Donna was slammed over the back seat and landed in the front passenger side.

She was blinded. The police cruiser heading straight for them had hit the high beams.

Laughing, Sammael stomped on the gas pedal, hammering it to the floor.

2

For the last few hours, Officer Fred Thompson had been searching for Officer's Zastrow and Zoelick. He'd been patrolling the small town for nearly forty-five minutes. Finally, he saw their squad car. He attempted to call them on his radio, but he got nothing. The squad should have stopped when Thompson hit the red and blue lights. Instead, it zipped past him. The cruiser headed down Route 26, headed outside of Dodge Junction. For a moment, Thompson wondered if he was imagining all of this.

What were they thinking?

If they were in pursuit, they would have checked-in with dispatch. Dispatch would have alerted all officers on duty. That hadn't happened. Zoelick and Zastrow had been missing for over two hours.

Maybe this wasn't Zoelick's squad car?

But he was sure it was. Thompson knew exactly how many squad cars were on patrol; three. There was *his*, there was the squad sitting in the parking lot at the small station, two blocks from the edge of Main Street, and there was Zoelick's. And there were two spare cruisers in the station garage near the back entrance to the jail.

Why was Zoelick speeding?

Zoelick was the responsible-type. Normally, he checked in with dispatch every hour on the hour. He was like clockwork. He was reliable. It wasn't like him to *not* check-in after investigating a break-in, even if the call amounted to nothing.

Thompson should have gone to the break-in call.

Dispatch relayed to Thompson that Zoelick and Zastrow were inspecting a possible break in at Buggy's Liquor Store. Zastrow was a bit green, but he'd never been so irresponsible that he'd forgotten to check in with dispatch. There hadn't been a report from either officer concerning the outcome of the break-in.

Thompson began to assume the worst. He started thinking that—maybe—there had been an intruder at the liquor store. That Zoelick and Zastrow were tied up, *or worse*. Maybe they were seriously injured and stuck in a ditch. Maybe they hit a deer? The backroads were filled with them. It wouldn't have been the first time a squad car had swerved off-road because of one. Up until now, he'd been certain their disappearance was some kind of an accident.

Then why were they speeding down the highway, chasing no one?

An accident: That had to be the reason communication was delayed from Car 27, assigned to Zastrow and Zoelick.

The worst was setting-in as Car 27 continued speeding forward, past Thompson. It almost seemed like they wanted to play a game of *chicken*.

Then it struck him. Someone—somehow—had gotten control of Zoelick's squad car, and thought it was funny to play games.

Maybe a couple of drunks had stolen it from a bar? Or maybe it was a dumb kid.

There was a high school keg-party in full swing on outskirts of town. Maybe some dumbshit kid had gotten a hold of it? That type of vandalism had happened before.

The status of Thompson's fellow officers was becoming of grave concern.

Two hundred yards and counting.

Slowing down, Officer Thompson's paranoia got the best of him. He played it safe and pulled over. He would wait for the squad car to pass. Then he'd pursue. He could ram the back of Car 27 with the heavy-duty ram-bars attached to the bumper of his cruiser. That would stop them. If worse became worst, he could disable their car, push it into the ditch and hope no one was seriously injured.

"Car 32 to base, I found the missing squad car— twenty-seven—in high pursuit on Route 26, request immediate back-up." Thompson said as he pushed the call button on his radio handset.

"Car 32, I'll send Officer Buckley right away…any word on Zoelick or Zastrow? Over."

"No word. Over." Thompson parked his cruiser on the shoulder of the highway.

Nervously, he waited for car 27 to zip past again.

Squinting to see, Thompson stared forward. It was hard to see into the squad car coming at him. The headlights were too bright. He made-out the form of a woman in the back seat. She flailed her arms, erratically. The driver was laughing. His white face was frighteningly pale. It was bloody.

Fear seized Thompson. The thick black hair on his forearms stood tall. Whoever was driving the stolen squad car was roaring with laughter.

Thompson watched, frozen, while the laughing man leaned forward, gripping the steering wheel tight, bracing himself. The laughing man tilted his head back and cackled harder.

The blunt force of Thompson's car door smashing inward, and ripping his leg off from below the hip, happened so fast it took a moment for him to acknowledge the intense pain. He was thrown across the interior of his squad car and his body landed in the passenger seat. His left leg remained pinned between the driver-side door and the crushed steering wheel.

Arterial spray painted Thompson's face when the car flipped over. It rolled onto its side and then tipped onto the roof. A shower of blood dropped on Thompson, drenching his uniform.

Thompson fell to the top of the car, which was now upside down.

Screaming, his first reaction was to grab his shotgun. Normally, it sat holstered in its rack near the center counsel. Now, it was sticking halfway outside of the vehicle, through the shattered windshield, the barrel bent.

He couldn't quite reach the buttstock. His fingers fumbled against the edge of the cold metal. Each movement hurt. His wrist felt shattered. Sharp pains exploded through his forearm and shot to the tips of his fingers. He could barely apply any strength to his hand. The shotgun fell onto his chest. The loss of blood made him nauseated, faint, and woozy. The sound of footsteps outside of the car drifted in. He tilted his head backward in order to see.

The laughing man leaned down and rested his forearms across his knees. He smiled. His lips were torn up to midcheek level. His teeth jutted out from his mouth like a sick clown and his eyes were pure white, no pupils.

Gravel tore at Thompson's back when the *laughing man* dragged him out of the vehicle, onto the grass, into the ditch. Blood continued to pump from his stump.

The last thing Officer Fred Thompson saw before he blacked-out from the pain were the wet snakes slithering out of the laughing man's hands, chest, and mouth. They waved back and forth like the hair of medusa before they shot into Thompson's face.

3

When the police cars collided, Donna was thrown into the windshield. The weight of her body pushed the large glass shield forward. It didn't break-free and Donna bounced, hard, back into the seat. Her neck cracked when it slammed into the headrest. She bit into her tongue and blood seeped from her mouth. She leaned forward and grabbed her forehead. It felt hot. Blood leaked out of a long tear above her right eye. Her vision was hazy, at best. She was more disoriented than she'd been previously.

Staring out the windshield, she saw Sammael standing over the police officer from the car they'd hit.

Squinting to see, she saw the snakes waving out of Sammael. This time, they slithered out of more places than his chest. They must have ripped through every organ of the body he possessed. They swayed back and then shot forward. Torn skin hung from the holes where the snakes rattled. One of the scaly vines took the officer's head clean off, launching it high into the night sky.

Watching the decapitation, Donna brought her hand to her mouth. She was appalled, disgusted. The spinning head slammed against the road. It bobbled a few feet and then stopped next to the vehicle. Blood flung from the neck-stump and sprayed the windshield.

Reacting fast, Donna grabbed the door handle and pulled. It wouldn't open. She turned left. The side window was shattered. She kicked out the loose particles of glass jutting from the window rails. Forcing herself onto her feet, she leaned out the window. She fell from the car and hit the blacktop, before springing to her feet, and glancing right then left.

Legs pumping in stride, she ran toward the dimness of Main Street, toward the flashing red lights. She sprinted half of a mile before turning back to the tangled mess of police cars. She was amazed. Sammael hadn't caught up to her.

As quick as her relief set in, it diminished. An obnoxious creak pierced the silence. Metal twisted with metal. Donna watched, horrified, as the police cruiser drove out of the ditch. Steam hissed from beneath the hood. The headlights illuminated the steam, making it appear foggy.

The engine revved, hard. The wheels spun. Rubber burned.

Sammael was going to run her down.

4

Minutes earlier, Sammael's boots crunched while he stepped across the gravel that lined the shoulder of the highway. Whistling while he strolled, he calmly approached the cruiser he'd *borrowed* from Officer Zoelick. He wrapped his elongated fingers under the door handle and pulled.

The bones beneath his fingers were lengthening. They threatened to rip through the tips of his fingers. The skin he wore was dying. It looked like cheap leather that had been bleached. It was splitting and peeling.

Sammael pulled the crinkled driver's side door open and sat behind the wheel. He cranked the key in the ignition. A maniacal smile stretched wide across his face. He laughed heartily.

The squad car started easily enough. Separating his squad car from the second squad car—the one he'd slammed into the ditch—was another story. The bumper wouldn't untangle from the smashed in door panel, where Officer Thompson's leg remained clamped between the door and steering wheel. Meat spilled from the stump. It stewed in the steady flow of erupting blood.

Sammael revved the engine, slammed the car in reverse, then drive, and then shot into the street. Tires screeching, he was free.

With a grin and a wink, he turned to Officer Fred Thompson's decapitated head. It rested in the middle of the seat, where he'd placed it. Sammael glanced down at the waxy bulb of Thompson's head, smiled, and asked, "That wasn't so hard. Was it?"

Sammael bent forward. He placed his thumb and index finger between Thompson's lips and pushed them open. He spoke for Thompson: "No, that wasn't so hard. Thanks for ripping my head off…it was too heavy for my neck anyway." Sammael cackled as he patted the abandoned head.

Thompson's neck stopped bleeding. There was a thick pool of blood beneath it soaking into the seat cover. It looked thick like black syrup.

Sammael lifted his head toward the road ahead of him. He'd given Donna a good head start. Now, he would have fun with her. She was only a short ways ahead and it would take less than a few moments to catch up.

He didn't want to kill her, that wasn't enough. He wanted to torment her body while she burned. She was running into town, hoping someone would see her, help her. He smiled at the thought. If she found someone, then he would have another body to play with. She would feel the sting of guilt, knowing she'd caused another human life to end, tragically. That and the body he wore had worn out significantly.

Maybe she would lead him to a new one.

Shining the police cruiser's headlights at Donna's back, he smiled big.

He slammed the car into drive.

He floored it.

5

Donna felt the warmth of the headlights shining on her back. Her shadow elongated on the ground in front of the heavy splash of fluorescent light. Looking forward, she lengthened her stride. Frightened as she was, she wouldn't stop. Not without a fight.

God helped those who helped themselves.

Donna believed everything happening was part of a plan. She believed destiny was written—tonight had been written. She would fight to survive because she valued her life. Winded and hurting, she would go until her body quit, until she was unable to move.

The dim lights of the small downtown began to brighten. The stop and go lights flashed red, in unison, from street to street. She hoped no one was out walking the streets. It was a Friday night. Even so, the town's nightlife, which consisted of one small bar called "The Pub" was sure to be closed. Due to the county fair, the town was deserted.

Dodge Junction wasn't known for its night life. If one wanted a fun tavern, they would travel to places like

Jefferson or Watertown. Thank God for that; she didn't want anyone to see her. She didn't want to bring anyone else into this nightmare. She didn't want anyone to help her—that *someone* would end up getting killed. She dreaded the idea. She wouldn't let it happen.

The squad car's engine roared as the edge of Main Street emerged. She hoped to take cover before she got to First Street.

She glanced back, using her peripherals.

She would run into the cornfield. Hopefully, she would lose Sammael, and then jump back onto the street, when she passed Main.

Millen's Dairy was the first shop in sight. Behind it, there was an alleyway that veered into another alley, through the back. If she could get to the slim, brick corridor, she might be able to lose Sammael. That was being hopeful. God only knew what kind of vision and senses Sammael possessed.

He might be reading her thoughts right now.

She didn't know. Still, escaping through the alley was a plan and she went with it.

Bolting left, she twisted her ankle. A sharp sting ran up her leg. She stumbled but didn't fall. Her arms flew out in front of her. She quickly kicked off her shoes so she could run faster.

She hit the grass and darted into the cornfield. If her feet got cut-up, *oh well*. Cuts and bruises were worth the price of survival.

The mud felt cold as it seeped between her toes. She sprinted down the first row of corn and ducked through the stalks and hit the third row from the road. She continued forward, into the darkness. The moonlight shed a hazy glow between the swaying cornstalks, and she followed the illuminated tassels. The field held a cold blue hue in the moon-filled night.

The high beams from the police cruiser startled her when they shined brightly through the dancing corn. She heard the tires spinning in the mud, tearing up the crops.

She didn't stop.

If she could make it another four hundred feet, she could turn right and hit the downtown area. She could make it to the alleyway. The police cruiser wouldn't fit through the slim brick path, even if forced. It was too narrow. She hoped she wasn't wrong. She hadn't been in that alleyway for a long time. Her memory might be serving her incorrectly.

The squad car moved faster. The front bumper was so close it kicked-up mud onto the back of her legs. It sped forward, threatening to run her down. If the bumper caught her calves, she'd be ripped under and spit out the back.

With no time to think, she spun right. Scared, she wanted to scream. Her foot landed on a jagged rock. It ripped through her skin, shredding the bottom of her foot. The pain was excruciating. With each step, the tear lengthened, messily. The sensation of blood running from the wound sickened her.

In the distance, were the red stop and go lights. Her arms pumped hard, and her lungs burned fiercely when she kicked legs forward. She jumped out of the cornfield as the squad car slid sideways. It nearly clipped Donna's legs out from under her.

She ran up the side of the ditch. Her feet fumbled when she hit asphalt. The cold road was soothing—for a quick second. The headlights blinded her. The police cruiser leapt out of the ditch. The front wheels hovered above the lip of the road and then the front end dipped down. The cruiser lurched toward her.

To Donna, the cruiser looked like a giant metal shark with its jaws opened, preparing to attack. When the cruiser landed, it was as if the jaws had snapped, barely missing her.

She ran across Millen's parking lot and ducked around back, nearly running into the dumpster. It was set crooked and it blocked the entrance into the alleyway.

In the near distance, Donna heard the cruiser's engine revving, harder. There was a metal cough and the engine sputtered. She was no mechanic, but it sounded like something vital had broken.

The second story of the brick structure above Donna displayed three windows; the one above her creaked open. The dirty glass slid upward, and a pudgy-faced woman grunted as she forced her pasty head into the alley.

Donna jumped back and leaned against the dumpster. She didn't want the pudgy woman to see her. She was in a vulnerable position. From where she stood, the cruiser could run her down, easily. She peered up.

"What the hell is going on down there?" The pudgy woman hollered. "People gotta work in the morning." Her chubby face poked further out the window.

Donna remained silent. She didn't want the woman to see her. She wanted her to stick her fat face back inside her apartment and close the window.

If Sammael saw the chubby woman, he'd be tempted to possess her, kill her, or both. Donna didn't want to drag anyone else into this nightmare.

"Sorry. Please, close the window." Donna called up to the woman.

Her round face glared down. She was frowning. A puzzled look spread across her pasty, dough-face. *Donna recognized her.*

"Is that you, Donna?" the woman called. She seemed calm now, almost friendly.

Donna silently sobbed. She feared the danger of this woman. All she could think to say was, "Yes, but please, close your window and go back to bed. You don't need to come down here."

The sound of the cruiser's engine revved again. Donna turned to see where it was.

It was parked across the street, facing forward. Donna could see Sammael's silhouette. He was a black figure, behind the windshield. Wild snakes coiled around the form of his body.

Something sliced through the air. Wind shot past Donna's ear. A second later, the heavy woman fell on top of her. The heavy woman was Frida Carmen, the nice waitress from Senor Vasquez's Mexican Restaurant. She was driven from the window.

The weight of her body slammed Donna to the ground, and she twisted her ankle. Sharp pain shot up her leg. She cried out.

Frida moaned.

Donna couldn't hear her, at first, because the police cruiser's tires were screeching, smoking, and spinning. Sammael was getting ready to charge.

Donna planted her hand into something wet and mushy. It was blood and muscle. Frida's head was spilt open, and her left leg had a compound fracture, below the knee. The bone protruded like a broken twig. Donna's heart cried out. There was nothing she could do. She felt helpless and enraged.

Donna grabbed Frida. She wanted to help her. And then she realized how Frida had fallen from of the window. One of Sammael's snakes was pinned to her head. The snake had to be twenty feet long—at least. It had shot out from Sammael's chest.

It ran, straight, from the police cruiser. The slithering vine was crammed down Frida's throat. It was going to rip her entrails out, through her mouth. The heavy woman's stomach was bouncing beneath her skin. The bubble of her belly waved back and forth, and her heavy-set body was dragged forward. She slid into plain sight, near the mouth of the alley.

The cruiser came blasting forward as Frida lay helpless between the dumpster and the alley entrance. Donna pulled Frida's arm with all her strength, but it was too late. Sammael crashed into Frida's bulging stomach. The cruiser pinned Frida to the dumpster.

The black plastic lid flew off and spun to the ground. Blood exploded from where the car had ripped Frida's stomach wide open. The maroon liquid painted Donna's already bloodied and bruised body with wet-red. Frida's eyes bulged out from their bloody sockets.

Donna wanted to cry. An overwhelming wave of guilt pierced through her gentle soul. But her sorrow didn't stop her, it couldn't. She stood and ran down the alley, as planned.

The alley forked into another passageway twenty feet forward, splitting off to the right.

Donna stumbled to the right then rounded the corner. The cruiser crashed into the wall beside her. The red brick building shook as though it were in the midst of a California earthquake.

Donna saw Main Street. She hustled forward. She could hear the tenants in the apartments above as they were waking, wondering what all the fuss was.

Behind Donna—and above—she heard Sammael's evil laughter. The guttural screeching rumbled in unison with the cruiser's broken fan belt.

Sammael forced the cruiser forward.

Chapter 16

1

The early morning hours had grown cold. Gardner, Winny, and Cherri stood, shivering, in the backyard. Silently, they stared at the dead woman lying on the lawn. Her face wore a mask of horror. Her body was used. It looked haggard, abused, and torn.

The woman had been in her twenties, but the abuse over the last few hours had made her look ancient. Tiny blades of grass sparkled around her bloodied corpse where the moonlight struck the dark green tips that swayed in the cool night breeze.

"We can't just leave her." Winny broke the silence.

"I think we're going to have to. When this is all over, there will be an investigation. We shouldn't move anything. If we move her, they will ask why," Gardner said, not looking too concerned.

"How will the police investigate this? Isn't this going to look pretty bad if it gets *investigated?* Won't the police think we killed her? And I'm assuming we aren't going to tell them demons from hell did this, either," Cherri asked, looking over the dead girl. Her lips trembled and her teeth chattered. She rubbed her hands up and down her shoulders.

Winny wished Garth hadn't run off. He was alone.

And who knew what kind of danger he might be in.

Collectively, they didn't know where Sammael was. For all they knew, he was on his way back.

Maybe he was among them, hidden?

He may have already taken or possessed or killed Garth, for that matter. Winny found it best not to let his paranoia get the best of him.

Winny couldn't continue to think awful thoughts about Garth. He had to believe Garth was okay, that he would remain unharmed.

"What do we do, Father Gardner? I mean, we can't just stand here and do nothing," Winny asked.

Gardner closed his eyes. He shook while he stumbled backward. At first, it looked like he might fall over. His balance tilted. Grabbing his elbow, Winny felt warmth beneath Gardner's skin. It felt good, comforting, like he was touching sunlight on a nice summer day. He didn't want to remove his hand. But Cherri gently slid her fingers over Winny's hand and pulled him away.

"He's having one of his visions," she said.

Winny and Cherri watched-on, as Gardner experienced his vision.

"Do you think we're going to be all right?" she asked him.

Winny didn't know how to respond.

He took a deep breath.

"I'll try my best to protect you," he finally said.

"Me too."

Gardner stepped forward, opened his eyes, and said, "We'll stay here. They'll be here soon. The fight will commence here."

With a trembling voice, Cherri asked, "How do you know?"

"I saw them. My wife is in great danger, and we need to stay here. This is where the fight will take place. Sammael is bringing her here." He stared, blankly, into the cornfield.

Two things scared Winny in that moment. One: he didn't know where Garth was, and that was bad. If anything were to happen to Garth, he didn't think he could handle the grief and guilt that would follow. And two: how were they going to fight an evil so strong? Sammael was too much for them to handle. Apparently, he was too much for Gardner, too. Winny became angered. Gardner didn't seem too concerned—for Garth, or the welfare of his own wife, Donna. This frustrated Winny.

Winny knew Mrs. Gardner fairly well. She was a wonderful woman. She was always a pleasure to be around. She had a wonderful smile and when she talked with you, she was genuinely interested. No matter what the topic. If she was *his* wife, Winny would have been out looking for her a long time ago.

"Shouldn't we try to find them?" Winny asked.

Gardner's eyes fixed on Winny.

Winny saw an intensity he didn't want to challenge. He reminded himself Gardner was experienced with this, not he.

"They're coming here."

Chapter 17

1

Garth's anger had begun to shed. He was still frustrated. He didn't like being alone. He felt vulnerable. But he felt guilty for having left his brother and Gardner. They needed him. He was being stubborn, he knew it. His stubbornness had gotten him in trouble before. But now, as he thought about the severity of what had gone down tonight, he came to the conclusion that he needed to return because his brother needed him.

And he needed them.

Trudging down the dark path in the corn, he was paranoid. It was too quiet. He didn't know what was lurking in the night. The wind rustled the corn stalks, and he could hear them sway. Each time a stalk flailed, he thought Sammael would step out from behind a row of corn. Garth jumped every time a tassel whistled in the wind.

For a moment, he stopped walking, glanced back, scratched the back of his head and asked himself, "Shit. What do I do?"

A gust of wind blew an opening in the cornfield to left of him. For a brief second, he could see Gardner's farmhouse. It looked tiny from this distance, but he could see it resting on the hill.

More than anything, Garth wanted to turn around and walk back. But he didn't want that thief, Cherri, to be with them. That stupid bitch had robbed their store, and now Winny was drooling over her. Garth could see the crush his brother had developed in the way he looked at her.

Garth continued toward the store. His car was parked around back. He would go to the office, grab his car keys from the desk, and drive to the police station. He wished he could just call 911, but his cell phone had been crushed during the robbery and the land line, at the store, had been ripped in half.

His frustration grew just thinking about it. He was angry with himself, partly because he couldn't shake his stubborn nature. It was a part of him. All he had to do was turn around and go back to the farmhouse. No one would say a word to him about changing his mind. They'd be glad to have him back. There would be no judgment set upon him. But for personal reasons, Garth had it in his head they would see his weakness. They would silently belittle him.

He wouldn't let them see his weakness.

In the back of his mind, he remembered being stubborn was his weakness.

Well, nobody's perfect.

The parking lot came into sight. He pushed the remaining cornstalks to the side and walked beyond the edge of the cornfield. He stepped onto the cracked blacktop that he and Winny planned to repave next summer. They held an account for small maintenance savings. The funds had matured along with the long cracks in the parking lot.

Broken glass crunched underneath Garth's Sketchers. He kicked the sparkling pieces as he stalked through the broken door frame. He really didn't want to go in the store.

Garth's nerves were shooting out of control. It didn't matter that the store was dark. He knew his way around in the dark just as well as he did with the lights on. He'd grown up in this liquor store. Sure, he was sick of it. But he knew the layout, inside and out. The building came as second nature to him.

The small liquor outlet was like a dead marriage to him. Still, he held many fond memories of this place. It had served as a means for their family to live comfortably. He and Winny had spent countless hours playing cops-and-robbers, hide-and-go-seek, kick-the-can, and many other childhood games in or around this place.

But that was then. His heart wasn't into it anymore. He wanted to move on. After what had happened tonight, he was almost relieved. He now had an excuse—*a sign*—to shut down shop. He could work something out with Winny. He could collect a small share of the profits in return for his share of the store. It probably wouldn't amount to much, but it would get him out of Dodge Junction, out of Wisconsin.

Glancing at the bloody corpses of Timmy and Terrance was enough to make his stomach roar. The bodies smelled like raw sewage. Their bowels and intestines were ripped apart and strewn across the floor. The tile was glazed with their dark wetness. Their innards looked like a disgusting splash-art mural. And smelled like an outhouse.

Garth slipped in Terrance's blood as he crossed the store room floor. He caught his balance and quickened his pace. He wanted his key, and he wanted to get out of here.

Taking a deep breath, he wrapped his hand around the doorknob and pushed the office door open. His heart was beating fast. He thought he was going to hyperventilate. It occurred to him that, given the oddity of this night, there might be someone or something on the other side of this door waiting to rip him apart. Again, he wished he was back at Gardner's place. Maybe not safe, but he could take comfort in the company of others.

Except for that twit Cherri.

Without turning the light on, he shuffled to the metal desk.

The *gray clunker* hadn't been moved in more than three decades. He pulled the first drawer open. It screeched at first, as it always did. The hinges had been *jimmy-rigged,* the screws forced in. He dug his hand inside, retrieved his keys, threw them up in the air, caught them, and then jogged out the back door.

His blue Ford Tempo sat adjacent to the store. It sat in his parking spot. If the power hadn't been killed, his car would have been sitting beneath a halo of light the large lamppost normally provided.

Opening the door, he hopped inside, cranked the engine, and drove toward the front of the store. When he got to the mouth of the parking lot, he looked left—up the hill, to the Gardner place. With each passing second, his desire to go back and get Winny grew stronger.

That was the right thing to do.

He wondered why they hadn't left yet, either. He would have gone nuts, just sitting up there, waiting.

I hope they're all right.

He didn't know which way to turn. If he went left, he'd be doing the right thing and if he went right, he'd be doing the right thing. Logic set in.

They needed the police.

Garth turned left.

Chapter 18

1

Donna's raw, bleeding feet slapped against the sidewalk. She nearly toppled over. The pain was incredible. But she dug deep, bit down, and continued forward. After a few strides, she finally caught her breath. She sprinted down Main Street. The sharp sting in her feet was growing intolerable, but she continued on pure adrenaline. She was still two miles from the farmhouse.

Gardner told her not to come home, but she didn't have anywhere else to go. Things had changed. For the first time, she considered that she might not make it. Maybe not even past the edge of town. She might die out here like a wounded animal. She had to try and go home.

The crash of bricks exploding rang-out behind her. The nose of the squad car—smashed and scraped—poked out from the alleyway. The grill stopped moving forward and steam rose in the form of chalky mist. Rock particles danced in front of the headlights. The squad car was stuck. The front quarter-panels were wedged-in tight at the slim mouth of the alleyway. The door panels peeled back when the car moved forward.

The brick wall imprisoned Sammael. He was stuck.

Although it was dark, Donna could see Sammael laughing. He cackled like a drunkard who had innocently fallen in the street.

Donna jumped back startled. The driver's side window shattered and the glass blew outward. It allowed her to see him more clearly. His skin was pale and flaking off. His lips were dark red, like they'd been done-up with black lipstick. The torn edges of his mouth were purple. Laughing his sinister head off, he looked like a decomposing corpse. He trained his eyes on Donna.

"Excuse me, young lady, could you help-out an officer of the law!" Sammael shouted. He was laughing and it sounded like he was gargling. His neck was bent at an awkward angle and his head dangled out the window. He tried to squeeze out of the small space. His eyes winced as the jagged glass tore his skin, above his temples.

Donna made it, almost, to the edge of Main Street. Her legs were fatigued, and she thought her body might simply stop working. Her vision was hazy, at best. Her lungs felt heavy, swollen. She wanted her husband. He could help her.

Before she hit Amber Lane, which bisected Main Street, she glanced back and saw Sammael forcing himself out of the police car. From this distance, it looked like every bone in his body was crushed and snapping. He crammed his body through the broken window and the brick wall. Every hinge and joint of Sammael's body was contorted at obtuse angles.

The last image Donna witnessed, before turning around and focusing on her escape, was when Sammael fell to the ground. His face planted itself into the cracked sidewalk. She heard it thump. His neck cranked upward and to the left. It lolled one hundred and eighty degrees. His right eye slowly opened and adjusted on her.

She wiped her shaky hand across her face. A heavy layer of sweat and blood ran down her cheeks and neck. She was tired. Her lungs needed to recuperate. Her legs stiffened, hard as boards. She couldn't bend her knees. Wanting to cry, she fumbled forward, fell to the ground, looked behind her and saw Sammael was free.

He'd gotten out of the car. He skittered along the street. The snake-like arms ripped through the skin of his back and wrapped around his torso, like they were holding his body together.

The wavy ends folded and planted on the road. The snakes carried him across the blacktop. He looked like a giant tarantula. His head displaced another ninety degrees, the wrong way. Blood dribbled, in thick streams, from his torn mouth. There were jagged holes where the snakes ripped through his skin. His bottom lip hung by threads of shredded skin. The drooping skin looked like melted white cheddar.

And he was moving fast, skittering across the pavement.

Donna took a deep breath. She tried to swallow, but she couldn't. Her throat was too dry. The lining of her esophagus was arid, cracked, and felt like it was about to bleed. There was nothing wet to lubricate her mouth. No saliva. Her tongue stuck to the roof of her mouth.

She nearly gagged. It wouldn't move. It was unable to retract. It frightened her when, after a few seconds, she couldn't cluck her tongue. For a quick second, she thought this night would end with her suffocating.

Sammael reached her. His snakes slithered around her body. They squeezed hard. Not tight, uncomfortable. She wanted to scream, but all that escaped her mouth was a dry woofing sound. Her mouth was so hot her gums ached and her teeth throbbed.

She cried.

2

Sammael treasured Donna's increasing amount of pain. He wanted her to *let go*. He wanted her to die. But she had spirit. She wouldn't let this *vile thing* beat her. And that was fine. Her tears encouraged Sammael. He squeezed harder and howled into the warm night air. His eyes rolled over white as he prepared for the pleasure of taking her soul.

He'd taken many souls during the many centuries he'd existed, but he would savor Donna's soul the most. The suffering he would make this woman endure excited him.

Tiny claws sprung from the ends of his tentacles. They shot at the tender skin of Donna's neck. He hoped they would cut her, peel the skin from her jaw to her collar bone. The thought of blood drenching her sweet skin was tantalizing. Sammael was a fiend for death.

His excitement halted. The sharp hooks stopped. So did his tentacles, less than centimeters, before they struck her skin. They'd hit an invisible wall. Donna held some kind of a protective shield. Despair struck Sammael. He looked to the yellow moon and screamed, "Give her to me!"

Why had the Unholy One stopped him? He'd been the most loyal of dark servants—the bearer of pain, to those the Master deemed supreme torment upon. All he wanted was to take this soul. He'd, nearly, done the job years ago. To Sammael, it meant everything to destroy Donna. He wanted to eat her heart and torture her forever. He was promised these pleasures. Now, he was on the brink of experiencing them.

Again, he'd been stopped before he received her.

The Holy One had stopped him. He could. He commanded *all*, including the Dark Master. There had been very few times Sammael had been halted—stalled—from his sinful deeds. But it *had* happened. This is what it felt like. *He* was protecting her. It was the only explanation.

The snakes slithered back into the body and Sammael was paralyzed. Donna was being let free. Her face was that of confusion, but also of strength. Sammael saw, in her face, that she understood what had happened. He wanted to turn from her, ashamed. The body he possessed was giving out under the stresses of what he'd done to it. He didn't have much more time with this body. It would be useless, soon.

Suddenly, he could move again. With his remaining strength, he groveled to his feet. He swayed, watching Donna walk, unharmed, toward the streets of this forsaken town.

3

Donna's lungs opened. Her muscles relaxed and she could breathe again. Her body shook horribly, but she kept moving. Nearly hyperventilating, she inhaled huge gulps of air.

She caught her breath and she ran harder than her body's limit permitted. She needed to regain her rhythm. The tendons in the arches of her feet stretched. They ached badly. Every pain receptor peaked. Still, she was relieved. She'd witnessed the divine at work.

Her life was spared.

Jogging now, she turned her stiff neck around. Sammael stood beneath the halo of a wooden streetlight.

He wobbled on weak legs. He looked like he would fall over if the night breeze kept at him.

A sigh of relief escaped Donna. She continued toward her house. Did being spared mean she was immune to the dark powers that these creatures possessed?

Maybe.

She wouldn't stick around to find out. She wanted to be with her companion, her husband, Leslie Gardner. He had the answers, to all of this.

Chapter 19

1

Father Gardner led Winny and Cherri into the farmhouse through the back screen door. They'd left the young woman's body lying in the grass, where the demon departed from her. The decision to leave her body hadn't sat well with Winny or Cherri, but Gardner insisted. He'd been through this before. Sure, this was the worst of his demonic experiences, but still, he had the only experience. It wouldn't be wise to move the girl.

Reaching the backdoor, Gardner noticed the hinges were ripped away from the door frame. It didn't matter. All that mattered was that they were alive. With a little elbow grease, the door could be fixed. It was their lives that needed to be maintained.

Beyond the back screen door was another, smaller, door. It led into the basement. The smaller door was heavy, made of solid wood. Gardner turned the knob and descended down the stained wooden stairs. He turned back, once, making sure Winny and Cherri were following.

They were.

At the bottom of the staircase, Gardner flipped the light switch and a small light bulb buzzed. It slowly came to life. It wasn't bright, but it was enough to illuminate the basement. It was enough that they could see.

"What do we do now?" Winny asked.

Gardner found himself lost for a moment.

Why had he brought them down here?

It was a safe place.

At least, down here, they would have a place to hide if Sammael came back.

And he would.

Gardner could sense the battle. It would arrive soon. The thought of what might happen frightened him. Not because he could be harmed, but because someone could be killed. He'd become weak in his faith. For this battle, he needed to be strong. The ache in his heart intensified. He couldn't sense Donna right now.

No visions came to him. It was frustrating. More than anything, he wanted to see his wife. He wanted to hold her and to know she was all right. After that, he could deal with the fight. The *unknown* was intruding on his confidence.

"I want you two to stay down here until I come back. It's a lot safer here than it is out there in plain sight. Now that you're here, don't leave. I don't want to come back and find out you've left."

"But what if that...*thing* comes back?" Winny asked, taking a step forward. "Won't you need our help?"

Gardner was touched by Winny's passion. He admired the fight within him.

"Sammael. His name is Sammael, and he will surely be back. I can feel the fight ahead. For now, I need you to be as safe as possible. This is the only place I can think of, right now. So stay down here and be quiet. Rest. You'll know when you're needed. Hopefully that won't be at all."

"I don't get it, how will we know?"

"Because I'll tell you," Gardner answered. The look of confusion and doubt planted within Winny's facial expression. That was fine, as long as he did what Gardner asked.

As Gardner ascended the stairs, he stopped and said, "I need you to trust me."

2

Winny's thoughts raced, creating a tornado of doubt, denial, and questions. He even questioned his sanity. After everything that had happened tonight, he didn't know what to believe anymore. Thinking logically wouldn't work now. There was nothing logical about anything that had happened tonight.

The only logic was that he trusted Gardner. He would listen to him and follow his orders. Gardner had experience dealing with supernatural evil. Sure, Winny believed in God, but he'd always thought religion was more of an organized set of guidelines, a way of life that was followed in order to be a good person.

Never in Winny's lifetime did he imagine he'd see these awful things. The horrible creatures and acts he'd witnessed tonight were insane. The worst was that he'd never be able to talk about it. No one would believe a word of what he'd say.

He never imagined these things were possible. Demons: possessing people, coming after people, trying to kill them. It was farfetched, ridiculous.

Yet here he was, frightened for his life having witnessed this evil. The idea that he'd *lost his marbles* was resting on the table. But he was quite certain this was *really* happening.

He was concerned about Garth. Where could he be?

Standing in the dark basement, Cherri huddled close to him. The warmth of her body was comforting. She grabbed his arm, tight, after Gardner closed the basement door. When the deadbolt slammed home, Winny became even more skeptical. He hoped Gardner was right about the basement being safe.

But, given their predicament, he didn't trust that anywhere was safe. Not up there, and not down here. For the time being, he would just have to have faith in Gardner.

"Why did he lock us down here?" Cherri asked. She was shaking. Her damp clothing caused friction.

"He's trying to protect us. He wants us down here to keep us away from those…demons. If we're down here, then maybe he thinks he can defeat the demons up there, without us. He'll let us out when he's finished. Whatever the reason is, he's looking out for us. He doesn't want any harm to come to us."

"I'm still scared. What if it beats Gardner? What if it finds us down here?"

"I'm scared too, but all we can do is wait. I hope Garth is all right. I'm worried about him."

Cherri lowered her head. She sniffled and then mumbled, "I'm so sorry. I feel like this is my fault. We robbed your store. Your brother left because of me. And now you don't know where he is…or if he's all right."

Winny should have been mad, but he wasn't. Garth left of his own free will. He should have stayed. Sure, there was a logical reason for him to leave, but he hadn't digested their situation. He was being selfish. He should have stayed and helped them. *Leaving* only put him in danger and caused others to worry. Garth was stubborn.

Even though Winny was upset with his brother, he hoped he was safe—and that he'd found help. If Winny knew Garth, he was headed to the police station. That worried Winny, too. If more police showed up, more people would get hurt, probably killed.

Curiously, Winny turned to his surroundings. Lined along the basement floor were stacks of assorted flowerpots. They were flush tight against the cold cement wall and neatly aligned in stacks of three and four. The back wall rounded out beneath the staircase and set as a background for the numerous bags of soils and fertilizers. They were for Donna's greenery.

Everyone in town knew Donna was a florist. Winny often saw her downtown and at the farmer's market. She sold neat and beautiful flowers. Her flowers were designed in interesting and creative arrangements. Even Winny— who couldn't have cared less about flowers—found Donna's displays intriguing. He openly acknowledged her talent.

Continuing his look around the basement, he found the laundry machine and dryer near the last plastic bag of soil. The large white appliances were spread out toward the back wall.

Peering up, Winny saw another light bulb screwed into a fixture on the ceiling. There was a two-foot piece of white string dangling from a row of metal bearings beneath it. He went to it. Cherri followed him.

"Where are you going?"

"The laundry machine, we can sit on it."

"Sounds like fun," she joked.

He pulled the string. The light bulb flickered and sprung to life. This bulb was no brighter than the other.

"What do you want to do?" he asked.

3

For the first time tonight, they had a moment to settle. Cherri thought it would be impossible to relax, but they could at least rest. Just the fact that their bodies were able to stop moving, stop exerting energy, was comforting. They could collect their thoughts and catch their breath.

Cherri was worn out, but she was amped at the same time. The charge of adrenaline held her alertness. She was gross, sweaty, and fatigued. Her stomach growled. There was nothing in her belly. She wasn't hungry. The last thing on her mind was food. The thought of eating made her feel sick. The only relief was Winny. His presence was comforting.

"I don't know," Cherri answered. She sat. "My legs are achy. So is my back."

"Yeah, mine, too."

He sat down next to her and she felt the warmth of his body. He wasn't touching her, but his body temperature radiated upon her. It felt good.

"Why are you so quiet?" he asked.

Snapping out of her daze, she glanced at him, caught his face, and realized how close he was. He must have seen the frightened look in her eyes. She tried to hide it. He suddenly slid back a few inches.

"I'm sorry. I didn't mean to get in your space."

"No, I'm sorry. Please, sit closer. I'm cold." she said.

She slid nearer to him. She wrapped her arms around his shoulder and leaned into his chest. She felt warm again. She focused on the comfort that he gave her.

"So, before tonight, where did you think you'd be right now? You know, before life threw us this curve ball."

Cherri sat up. She stared down at the cold cement floor. She could feel the dust beneath her. It felt chalky. "We were on our way to Detroit. Timmy has a brother there. He was going to give him a job…I guess you'd call it a job.

They were going to steal cars and sell them. You know. A chop-shop."

"If you don't mind me asking, why would someone like *you* end up with someone like him? I hope I'm not upsetting you."

She didn't know if she minded. That was the truth. But she wasn't angry, either. She thought it might be comforting to talk with Winny. He didn't seem like the type of person who would judge her. "I guess because he was the only guy who cared about me. He never judged me. He accepted me for who I am. That and he saved me from the life I was living. But, in hindsight, that life might not have been so bad. We just seemed to make sense at the time. We were both damaged."

She could tell Winny was curious about the details of what she'd just said. He was staring at the floor and fidgeting. His thumbs twirled in circles.

"I'm sorry."

She believed him. He was sorry. She appreciated that he didn't pity her.

"I should be apologizing. We robbed your store, held a gun to you…I know I didn't do it directly, but I was there…I guess…I just hope you're okay."

She felt horrible. She'd robbed him. And it mattered how he felt.

"Does it feel weird that he's…you know…*gone?*

"I don't know. I mean I was with him for a long time. It seems like forever. I cared about him. But to be honest, I don't think I ever really loved him. I'm sad that he's…gone, but…oh, I'm a horrible person…"

"No you're not. Tell me what you were going to say. Come on, we're talking here."

She wanted to tell him, but what would he think of her?

"I feel relieved that I'm not with him anymore. But I'm not glad he's dead. I'm not that cruel, I swear." And now she was crying. She pulled her bloody shirt collar up to her face and wiped away her tears.

Winny leaned back. He grabbed a small blue rag off the top of the laundry machine. He held it to his nose, smelling it, making sure it was clean. She nodded, took it from him, and wiped her face. When she was done, he took the rag from her.

"I don't think less of you. No one could have predicted what happened tonight. Forgive me for saying this, but maybe tonight happened for a reason. Actually, I'm sure there's a reason for all of this. I'm sure Father Gardner would say the same. I don't want to glorify what happened, but it did and now we are where we are. Does that make any sense?" His brown eyes glinted in the low brightness.

"I get it, but I still feel horrible. Like some part of all this is directly my fault," Cherri responded.

"If you think that this is your fault…then you're going to be stuck in your bad thoughts. They'll spiral out of control. Just let it go. That was then. I know it hasn't been very long at all. But put in perspective, a lot has happened since the robbery. We're past it. If you don't let it go, you won't be able to move forward with your life. I know that we're just sitting here talking, but I can feel you have a life ahead of you."

"I can't even think about how this is all going to end up. I mean those cops are probably dead. We still need to find your brother. God only knows what Gardner's doing upstairs," Cherri finished.

Part 4: The Gathering

Chapter 20

1

Gardner stood in the kitchen near the sink, leaning against the countertop. His forearms flexed, holding him steady. He didn't know what to do. His mind was racing.

What was his next move?

He needed to be patient. He gazed out the back window. His eyes were drawn to the dead woman lying in his backyard. Guilt struck him. She was just lying there, displayed, and out of place. She had been discarded. As evil as she was, she was a person. For a moment, he thought she looked like a sick decoy.

Who knew, maybe she was. Maybe Sammael would be drawn to her corpse. He hoped the evil which possessed the girl was gone and descended back to the hell—her home.

And then he saw *her*.

Donna.

She jogged up the small gravel driveway. Lurching forward, she limped, forcing herself up the rocky path. She looked tired, weak, and exhausted. Gardner wanted to run to her, take her hand and help her.

Maybe she was Sammael's bait? Did Sammael want Gardner to go to her?

Gardner didn't care.

He needed to be with his wife.

Pushing off the kitchen sink, Gardner ran to the back screen door—not even thinking about Winny and Cherri. He left them downstairs. He would run outside and get Donna. Then, they could come back and regroup. Donna should have been far away by now. She wouldn't be this distressed unless the demon had gotten to her. Gardner was sure, now, the demon had. His wife had obviously been through hell since he'd told her to leave.

The night air was cold, and the moonlight grew in luminescence. He could see her form, haloed by the chalky light. She acknowledged him and began to run faster, her damp hair flailing behind her. She needed to hold him, and he needed to hold her. They would comfort each other. That was their companionship.

The gravel beneath Gardner's boots caused him to slip. He almost fell, but he quickly regained his footing. He heard Donna's breath pumping hard. She was whining, forcing herself to breathe.

The air around her swirled. Then they were holding each other. She smelled of sweat and had a metallic odor about her. He couldn't quite place the smell. Her legs gave out and she leaned forward onto him, for support. Lifting her up, he kissed her forehead and pulled her in.

"What happened?" He looked her over. "Let's get you to the house."

She didn't respond; he simply nodded in agreement. She was tired. Her face had sunk in, and her skin looked ragged. She looked like she'd aged ten years.

She wrapped her arm around his shoulders, and they stumbled up the driveway, toward the house. When they reached the backyard, Gardner watched as a growing sense of horror gravely lit Donna's features. Her mouth fell open. Her eyes went wide.

She'd seen the dead girl in the backyard.

She tried to speak but only raised her hand in the direction of the corpse.

"The evil has left her. I expelled the demon from the girl," he said while bringing her body around, so that he could face her. "Is Sammael on his way?"

Donna nodded her head. Yes.

Chapter 21

1

Garth drove in silence along the tree covered streets of Dodge Junction. The night breeze licked his face and fussed his hair. He was halfway through town. He drove fast. The dark homes slowly dispersed when he neared downtown.

The space between the residential homes began to widen. He entered Lincoln Park and drove near the small baseball field, where the little leaguers played their summer and spring sports. Main Street was a mile away.

Across from Main Street, near McCoy's Bakery, was the police station. It was a small station house and Garth doubted there were many officers on duty. Still, police officers would be more equipped to handle these *criminals*. He couldn't for the life of him logically identify what those people were.

What he did know was that more cops would be needed. Seeing what the young couple had been capable of was enough to know an aging, retired, priest, a criminal, and his naïve brother would not be able to handle this unique situation. Law enforcement was the logical answer.

If the local law couldn't handle the problem, then maybe the National Guard, State Police, or whoever had the biggest guns would be able to. Gardner and his merry little band of idiots were going to get nowhere, staying cooped up at the farmhouse. Still, as pissed off as Garth was, he didn't want any harm to come to them.

He finished driving through the park, hit Lincoln Street, and rounded the corner toward Main Street. Staring down the long narrow street, he could see, in the distance, the flickering red lights from the stop-and-go signals of the downtown area. They were tucked behind the draping Birch trees that lined the downtown sidewalks.

The police station wasn't far. Everything was silent. There were no crickets chirping. The only noises came from the calm sway of rustling leaves as the night breeze whistled through the branches.

Garth wanted to leave this stupid place and move on to a better life. It was Winny who wanted to remain a prisoner in this Podunk town.

Garth stared forward. He watched the silhouette of a drunken man stumbling from the left portion of the sidewalk to the right. The drunkard sidestepped into the street. Garth slowed down. The last thing he needed right now was to run over a drunk.

He drove his car to the other side of the street, making safe passage for himself. There was no traffic at this time of night, and a confrontation was out of the question. Before he drove to the other side, he heard the man yell, "Garth!"

He stopped the car. Maybe this guy would have a cell phone? He exited the car and strode toward the man. The bottom of his pants became damp as he walked through the dew glazed grass. Frowning, Garth wondered who this guy was.

The local bars had been closed for hours. It wasn't out of the ordinary for someone to recognize him. He'd spent his whole life in this town, and he knew more than one obnoxious drunk. The town was full of them. He squinted to see. The man was covered in dark shadows, cast from the streetlights, above the trees.

The man looked bloodied and bruised. He stepped into a patch of light.

Maybe he needed help?

Garth walked toward him and stopped.

Could this be the guy from the liquor store, the one with snakes spilling out of the bullet hole in his chest?

No way.

Fear encompassed Garth. He contemplated going back to the car and driving to the police station, as he'd planned.

The man stumbled closer. He waved his arms like an excited child at a baseball game.

It was him. Sammael.

The police station was only a few more blocks.

He could make it back to his car.

Garth broke into a dead sprint. His legs pumped. He darted across the street. He turned to see where Sammael was. The sight was shocking. He was unable to turn away from the grotesque picture behind him.

About one hundred feet away now, Sammael had fallen to his knees. The snakes shot through the skin of his back. They curled around his chest and planted themselves, solidly, on the sidewalk. He looked like a giant spider. A smile was ripped across his face and blood oozed from every wound, causing little puddles of blood to form behind him as he scurried toward Garth.

Garth froze. His legs stiffened. His run began to break. It was no use. Sammael was mere feet away and lunging at him.

Tackling Garth to the ground, Sammael wrapped his arms around him. He slammed him into the front lawn of an old Victorian house. Garth tried to squeeze away, but Sammael dug Garth's face into the lawn. He smelled the pungent odor of freshly cut grass, marinated in the night's dew. Under other circumstances this smell might have been pleasant.

Sammael's tentacles were strong, wet, and slimy. They lifted Garth. He was helpless and his movement was restricted.

This was the end.

Peering down at the maniacal monster beneath him, Garth wanted to scream. There was no life behind the face that peered at him, only death. The monster's skin was ashen, almost gray. At the corners of his mouth were long jagged lacerations. His skin looked purple. If this man had been alive, the wounds would be red, flowing with blood.

"Garth, what do you say I set you down. You and me can have a chat? Man to man."

Garth couldn't believe what was said. He was dazed. He wanted to know what was happening. Sammael set him down, gently, on the grass. Garth tried to roll away, but Sammael grabbed him, lightly, and pulled him back.

Sammael sat beside him and rolled over. The vines disappeared into Sammael's back, beneath his shoulder blades, into the skin.

Hardly able to speak, Garth asked, "What are you? What do you want?"

"Funny you should ask. I can be a friend or an enemy. That's up to you. I recommend being my friend. You've seen what I can do to my enemies. Besides that, I don't want to hurt you, or your brother."

Bullshit, Garth was smarter than that. He'd seen what this guy did back at the store. He wanted to kill everything that lived.

"If those people hadn't gotten in my way, they wouldn't have died. I only want Gardner. If you stay out of my way, you'll be fine. So will your brother. And that redhead."

Garth could care less about the redhead. But this was starting to make sense. He didn't want Gardner to be hurt, but if it came down to it, he cared more for his brother. And if he had to make a decision, he'd choose to stay out of this guy's way and let him do what needed to be done, in order to save Winny and himself.

As maniacal as Sammael was, Garth had to believe there was some semblance of truth to what he was saying. He needed truth. He wanted to live. Plus, what he said was making sense. If doing as—whatever this thing was—said enabled his brother and him to stay breathing, then he'd do it.

Plus, on the off chance Sammael was telling the truth, maybe he could calm him down. A glimmer of hope set in. Garth relaxed a bit.

"I'll be a friend as long as you…you don't hurt me or my brother," Garth found himself saying. He knew he sounded lame and easy. But he didn't want to die. Survival mode kicked in. Still, what he'd just revealed made him an easy target. He hoped he wasn't being used, but the thought was very prevalent.

"Was that so hard? That's all I ask. All I want is Gardner," Sammael said while trying to smile.

Sammael's skin, which now looked like wet paper, drooped. It wasn't stuck to his face anymore. The skin had separated from the muscles beneath it and his cheeks hung down. Sammael's face dangled from his skull. It swung in Garth's face.

Garth realized the snakes had reappeared. They were sliding around his body and restraining him. Fear seized his thoughts. Then the pain began.

"Oh, I need one more favor from you. Your body." The demon smiled as the skin fell from his face.

Turning away from Sammael, Garth moaned. He was nauseated. Cackling erupted. The snakes pushed further through Sammael's skin. Garth knew this was the end.

His day had come.

He should have stayed with his family, and Gardner. He shouldn't have bought into what Sammael had said. If he'd only stayed at Gardner's, this wouldn't be happening.

His body froze. He couldn't move.

Eyes locked on Sammael's, he watched as the white flame behind Sammael's eyes peered down at him. His pupils flickered and spread to pure white. The snakes wrapped around Garth's torso. They squeezed. The ends danced across his skin. They were slimy, uncomfortable. Sharp hooks scraped his skin.

The moist vines slid up Garth's chest. They tickled across his nipples, but he wouldn't laugh. This tickle tortured his senses. He wanted to scream. His voice didn't work. Beneath his skin, he felt his blood boil, as if it were in a kettle.

The wet slimy snake touched his lips, pried them open, and then massaged his gums, above his front teeth. Garth wouldn't open his mouth. He knew what was happening. Sammael was taking his body, possessing him.

The idea mortified him. He couldn't fight it. His jaws loosened. The snake ran down his throat. It wiggled through his insides. It moved down, like a breathing tube, nesting in his organs. Nauseated and dizzy, the last sight Garth saw was the serrated teeth erupting from Sammael's dead mouth.

A burning sensation traveled beneath Garth's skin. He was in the dark, now. Blackness encompassed him. Unpleasant, it smelled like rotting meat. He was paralyzed. He felt the awfulness of where he was.

2

Garth's body convulsed as Sammael's presence filled it with sinister life. Garth was almost gone. Soon, it would only be Sammael.

Energized and rejuvenated, Sammael felt the power of Garth's youthful body. He was a strong boy. The sensations of the fingers, arms, legs, and neck fell into place, followed by his feet and toes. It was refreshing.

Garth's stomach muscles flexed when Sammael sat up. He looked at the murderer, Rod, whose body he'd just left as it laid on the cold earth like a stray dog that'd been hit by a passing semi-truck. The corpse looked like something no one would want to touch without the aid of a shovel.

Sammael had destroyed Rod's body. The skin hanging from Rod was papery and thin. It slid off the skeleton and muscles. It was dead. Rod looked like a melted wax sculpture in a horror museum. Sammael had put this man through the ringer.

Laughing, Sammael leaned over and touched the dead man lying at his side. Rod's corpse stewed in the dew glazed grass.

Sammael squeezed Rod's fragile head. It broke apart in his hand. The skull was weak. It broke apart as if it were made of wet Styrofoam. Blood, bone, and fleshy ooze spilled between Sammael's fingers.

Standing and inhaling a gust of fresh air, Sammael admired his new senses. Humanity held such wonderful sensations. The warm night air was pleasant, something to be experienced. His skin tingled. Blood rushed through his organs.

This young man, Garth, was fresh. It felt good to wear his body. Garth was, now, Sammael's mask to the outside world. The muscles in his legs were strong. There was a lot to be experienced with this body, before he destroyed it. Mouth forming into a smile, Sammael acknowledged the awful things he would do with Garth's body.

The porch light of the Victorian house shined. Sammael turned around. Light splashed across the brown hair of his head. Smiling, he strutted up the walkway. There was an older woman of about seventy-five standing at the top of the white wooden stairs. She wore a shower cap firmly over her silver hair. A pink bathrobe was draped over her large figure, and it looked as old as she was— judging by the small holes and ratty cloth it was made of.

The old woman put her hand above her eyes to shield out the fluorescent porch light and she asked, "Who's out there? I'll call the police."

Sammael, now dressed in Garth's body, continued confidently up the cement walkway toward the porch steps. He stepped upward and stopped near the old woman. Her bulbous figure stretched the cloth of her robe. She was still, silent, and her droopy lips quivered. She wanted to speak but didn't have the words.

When Sammael smiled, the older woman eased up. She was charmed. "I think calling the police would have been a good idea about five minutes ago. That man on your lawn over there…" Sammael stepped to the side. The old woman leaned over to see, "He's a killer. In fact, he killed a young woman not too far from here."

"Really? Is he still alive?" the older woman asked, morbidly curious.

Laughing outright, Sammael held his belly and turned to the body of Rodney Barton. He said, "No ma'am, I'm afraid I killed him good. I turned every organ in his body to stewed shit. If he were to get up and walk I'd be…well…that just ain't gonna happen, if you know what I mean."

The old woman took a step backward. Her right hand reached behind, and she fumbled for the door. Her fingers clawed at the air in search of the screen. Her fingers danced to the small plastic knob. She twisted it.

Sammael stepped in toward her.

The old woman's eyes squinted. Her face pushed forward, toward Sammael. She asked, "Say, ain't you the boy from the liquor store?"

"Yes ma'am. Garth Gasper."

"I just bought a bottle of Khalua from you a few days ago."

"Well, I hope you drank a bunch, ma'am, cause what I'm gonna do next isn't going to feel very good, at all."

The woman didn't have a chance to look scared or to scream. Sammael grabbed her robe. He shucked her through the front door, and she spun so fast she became a pink blur. The screen door unhinged.

Sammael stepped through the broken door. He gently closed it behind him.

Once inside the house, he stood at the base of the staircase. At the bottom of the last step, the older woman lay crumpled and bleeding. Crimson fluid trickled from her bulbous nose. Sammael had thrown her so hard she'd tripped, slammed her head on the stairs, and snapped her neck. Her head was crunched. It stretched sideways at a horrible angle, set perpendicular to her shoulders.

Laughing, Sammael knelt beside the woman. He placed one hand on top of her head, the other under her jaw. Gritting his teeth, he cranked her neck to the right. Her skin stretched and tore. The bone in her neck cracked and snapped and broke.

He pulled her head off and then held it in front of his face while blood spat in all directions. The wood floor became drenched. A lake of blood pooled at Sammael's feet. The old woman's dying nerves operated her mouth. Her livery lips opened and closed successively. It looked like she was saying, "yah, yah, yah, yah," but there was no sound until her teeth began to clack.

There was a tumbling noise from above. It sounded like feet stomping down the hardwood floor of the second story. Sammael glanced up.

"Jean! What's all that racket going on down there?" an old man cried. The stairs creaked, loud, when he came down them. His legs were shaky, and his eyes shot wide with terror. He met Sammael's stare as he stared at his wife's decapitated head in his hand. He held it up to show her. A sly grin etched onto his face. He dropped the head onto the stairs.

The old man's sock covered feet shuffled fast. They shot out from under his legs. He reached for the railing. Unable to catch the wooden beam, he fell onto his back and slid down the hardwood stairs, thumping and wincing as he went. He landed near his wife's head.

He tried to lean over and inspect her—*as if he could help*.

"Impressive," Sammael said as he made his way toward the injured old man, whose heart was broken at the sight of his dead wife. "Your turn."

Sammael raised his leg and stomped down on the old man's stomach. There was a cracking noise and the old man lurched forward. A woofing sound escaped his thin lips. Urine fled from his bladder and pooled with his wife's blood.

With shaky hands, he tried to grab his stomach but couldn't. His head fell backward onto the stairs. Sammael split the old man's head wide open with the boots that Garth Gasper had chosen to wear that day.

The slimy gray matter that erupted from the old man's blood-soaked skull—which was spilt in half beneath his aging skin—fell to the stained wood stairs and *rested* on his wife's neck. Blood soaked into the old woman's pink bathrobe. Sammael savored his newest image of desecration.

Looking to the front door of the house, Sammael stopped smiling. He had much left to do.

He saw red.

He saw Gardner.

Chapter 22

1

The sobering crash of the back screen door slamming sounded above Cherri's dizzy head snapped back to the moment. She and Winny stood and quickly made their way toward the bottom of the staircase.

"What if it's Sammael?" Cherri asked. Her hand was shaking. Winny grabbed her by the wrist and pulled her to her feet.

"Stay behind me, for now. If it's him, run as fast as you can. I'll fight him off as best I can. You got it?" he answered.

Cherri's heartbeat quickened. "What about you?"

They turned their heads toward the door—at the top of the stairs—when the lock clicked. The doorknob turned.

The door creaked open.

Cherri bit down on her bottom lip. Winny squeezed her hand. Judging by the look on Winny's face, he was unaware he'd squeezed so hard.

A shimmer of moonlight splashed down the stairs, making everything appear dark blue. The outline of two people emerged into Cherri's sight, behind Winny's shoulder. Her head began to shake—the image of Sammael, laughing at her, fluttered through her head. A gentle voice called down, "Cherri…Winny…are you all right?"

It was a familiar voice. Relief swept through Cherri. Her lungs gave way to a refreshing breath.

"We're okay, Father Gardner!" Winny hollered.

"Come on upstairs. We have work to do," Gardner returned.

Without hesitation, both Winny and Cherri hustled up the stairs.

When they reached the top, Cherri stopped. She nearly crashed into Donna Gardner. They didn't know each other, but they shared a familiarity. Without words, they both knew who each other was.

They didn't need Gardner to say, "This is my wife, Donna."

Cherri knew this was no time for mindless chit-chat. The two woman shared a nod and a once over and then they looked to their leader.

2

Gardner rummaged through the house. He gathered his flashlights and tool kit from the basement, filled up three empty milk jugs with tap water from the kitchen sink and when the last jug was filled, he led Donna, Winny, and Cherri through the living room, toward the staircase. They quickly ascended up the wooden stairs.

Gardner hurried them down the second-floor hallway. They halted a few feet in front of the master bedroom where the door stood half-open. From there, Gardner peered up at a small rectangle break in the ceiling. It was two feet wide and four feet in length. He reached up, grabbed the latch—set in the middle—and pulled it downward. A small set of stairs extended from the attic. They stopped two feet from the floor.

"Winny, you go first."

"Yes sir," Winny responded. He quickly crawled up the small staircase.

Cherri followed him. Gardner helped his exhausted wife climb next. He held her shaking calves as she mounted the stairs. She was still exhausted and in need of rest. Her legs quivered as she climbed, causing the frail stairs to shake and creak.

She was beat-up, badly. There were scrapes and tears in her skin. She was dirty and full of sweat. Gardner quickly gave thanks that she was here, alive, not too injured to carry on. When she finally disappeared into the attic, Gardner climbed up the creaky latch. Once he reached the attic, he brought the small staircase up and closed off the entryway.

They stood in darkness. The air was dust ridden. Their only guide was the moonlit night as it shined through a small circular window, covered in dust, at the front side of the room.

Gardner walked to the glass square and wiped his hand across the film of grime that blocked his vision of the small world in front of his house. From this window, he could see twinkling glimmers of shattered glass at the liquor store. The glass particles were spread out into the parking lot.

Gardner's driveway looked dark and gray as it wound up toward the house. He felt the hot breath of his wife who stood behind him. When he turned, his eyes adjusted, and he was able to see everyone. They were looking to him, silently, wanting to know what needed to happen next.

"We're going to be quiet. The lights need to stay off and we have got to stay alert," he said. He locked eyes with Winny and said, "Sammael may have your brother. That is a realization which we must face. If Garth comes walking up that driveway, you need to know it may not be him.

"It might look like him, talk like him, but it might not *be* him. We need to make sure it *is* him before we let him in. I know that's confusing, but we need to be aware. If it's not Garth, then it's Sammael, and he will destroy us, if we let him."

Winny remained speechless and fidgety. Gardner knew what he'd said was *too much to comprehend*. Winny wouldn't be able to understand what was happening. He was inexperienced. He wouldn't be able to fight what *looked* like Garth. To be told he might need to combat his brother—or who he thought was his brother—was incredibly overwhelming.

"I have a twelve gauge shotgun in the gun case…over there," Gardner said, while pointing across the room. The moon reflected off the glass encasing. "A bullet won't stop evil, but it might slow it down for a minute or two. Sammael is coming to us. He'll be here soon. I can feel it."

Gardner put his hand on his Donna's shoulder. He guided her across the attic. They stopped in front of a stack of old boxes and she sat and opened one of the water jugs. She took the plastic container eagerly, breathed in deep, and guzzled the clear fluid. Gardner pulled the jug away from her. She was holding her breath. He said, "Breathe, honey."

Nodding, she took a few more breaths and then drank a third of the water. The sound of feet shuffling across the dusty attic floor drew Gardner's attention back to Winny and Cherri.

Gardner instructed, "Drink some water. You'll need to build your strength."

Winny, staring wildly as if he hadn't listened to what had been said, suddenly turned to the water jugs. Gardner had set them near the attic opening.

Winny walked cautiously across the floor, leaned down, and picked up one of the jugs. Before taking a drink, he made his way to Cherri, popping the top as he walked. He held the jug in front of her.

"Take a drink."

"Thanks." She fumbled with the jug when Winny set it in her hands. She quickly regained control and held the plastic container to her lips.

Gardner rubbed Donna's shoulders while she leaned forward and caught her breath. Startled, he quickly spun around when Winny stepped behind him.

"You scared me. I'm quite jumpy, tonight," Gardner explained.

"I think we all are," Winny returned. "Can I talk to you for a minute?" He motioned his head toward the back of the attic.

Gardner nodded to his wife. Donna's eyes granted approval. His wife was the most important thing. And he would check with her on everything.

Standing on creaky knees, Gardner walked with Winny toward the back of the attic. They stopped near an old desk. An upside-down wooden chair rested on top. In the moonlight, Gardner saw a myriad of spider webs draped across the open spaces between the chair and the musty desk.

The smell of old newsprint was pungent. Gardner had stored memorable old newspapers in these desk drawers. Long ago, it had been in his study, when he was still with the church. The newspapers were index markers from his life. Tales of strange occurrences he'd been involved with;

none of the stories had been able to print the truth. The façade that had been written was enough for the masses. Still, the false news served as a staple of Gardener's journeys. He found nostalgia in these musty pages.

Gardner's head rose. He found Winny's silhouette near the wall. Even in the dark, with limited visibility, Gardner could sense Winny's glance was grim. His topic was grave. He needed answers and he would want them quick.

3

Winny didn't know what to say. He was confused and angry. He needed answers. He didn't know if he was upset with Father Gardner or not. The things Gardner said about Garth—that Sammael might have possessed Garth's body—were terrifying. Winny guts churned. The very idea of his brother being possessed knocked, hard, at his bones. A sick feeling pined within the depths of Winny's stomach and gnawed at his soul.

"What you said earlier…about Garth, you're not telling me everything. You think we'll have to kill him?" Winny asked. He stared at his hands. He was digging his fingernails into the fleshy parts of his palms, repeatedly. Winny stopped kneading his hands when he thought Gardner might think he was getting ready to punch him.

"*We* are not going to kill Garth. We don't even know if he's possessed yet. I just want you to understand the worst-case scenario. For the record, I had a vision of Garth. It wasn't good. I think he's made contact with Sammael. And yes, I believe you will be tested tonight. I believe you might fail," Gardner explained. There was no emotion in his voice.

"What is this? That's pretty vague, don't you think? I don't understand what's happening. Are you trying to trigger me or is this just some kind of…I don't know…joke? You know I can't…won't…kill my brother."

"If a fight goes down, you might believe you're fighting Garth, but it's not your brother, it's the demon Sammael. If we can defeat the demon without physically hurting your brother, then that's what we'll do. But it will be extremely difficult." Gardner said but was cut-off.

"So what you're saying is that, by fighting Sammael, I'll be destroying my brother. His body will pay the price. We'll probably kill him? That's assuming Sammael doesn't rip me to shreds before I even have a shot."

"Winny, this isn't easy. But these are the facts. This is the ultimate test of your faith. If you choose not to fight, then you will die and both you and your brother will be destroyed. Do you understand? I'm not going to sugar coat it. I know what it is, and it is very ugly. You will be tasked with doing things that will cause harm to the ones you love. Unfortunately, it's for the right reasons. And it's necessary."

"It's just too much, Father Gardner. Isn't there another way? There has to be another way."

Leaning against the desk, Father Gardner rubbed the top of his head, scrunching the loose skin of his scalp, obviously lost in deep thought. And then, slowly, his eyes met Winny and he said, "I will fight my hardest—do everything in my power to avoid the physical nature of this fight. I can't promise anything. If it is written, then it is written. I cannot do anything about what has been predetermined. That's my best, Winny."

Winny's stomach filled with burning bile. He began to massage the muscles below his chest. The pain was quick and sharp. The stress of this night had probably given him an ulcer.

He respected Gardner, liked him, and looked up to him. But right now, he was angry with him. Why couldn't he come up with a better answer than saying he'd do the *best that he could*? That wasn't good enough. For their leader in this mess—in all actuality, the man who'd gotten them all into this mess—he should have a better answer than *his best*.

"I guess we'll see what happens, then," Winny responded.

Winny moved back to Cherri. She sat near the circular window, at the front of the attic. She peered out at the dark night sky with a blank look on her face. She shifted in her seat, slightly jumping when Winny placed his hands on her shoulders.

She held his hands as they rested there. He cupped them, lightly squeezed them.

"I just want this night to be over with," she said.

It took Winny a moment to rationalize what she'd said. But then logic set in, and he answered her, "I'm scared of what's going to come out of the darkness." And then he nudged his chin toward the window. They peered down at the driveway.

An evil, far from fathomable, was very near.

Part 5: The Battle

Chapter 23

1

Sammael basked in the night air. He walked freely down the center of the darkened highway. Bloodlust and murder swam in his sick mind.

The neon sign reading "Buggy's Liquor" glowed brightly, a few hundred yards in the distance. He wanted Gardner. He could feel how close he was.

He was a hindrance.

His existence caused Sammael anguish and torment. If he'd just left the woman, the junkie girl, Donna, to Sammael, this night wouldn't be happening. It wouldn't be necessary.

And those people wouldn't be in danger. They wouldn't have had to feel his red rage. Sammael was very capable of dealing torment. He enjoyed it. Now, all he wanted to do was rip Gardner to pieces. He wanted to feast on his heart. He wanted his precious, junkie wife, Donna, to watch.

Then, afterward, he would tear her to pieces. He would torture her for days. Thoughts of what he would do to her made him skip in his step. He anxiously awaited the destruction of the Gardners. The heat of what was to come excited him.

He came to a slight turn in the road. Around the bend was Gardner's farmhouse. It rested on top of the smooth rolling hill. It wouldn't be long before Sammael unveiled his wrath upon Gardner and his group of young naïve humans. They had no idea that they were incapable of preventing the atrocities of what would happen to them. The outcome had already been written.

Ultimately, it had been decided by the Divine. But it was the culmination of two much greater powers that held the fate of these simple people. Sure, Sammael's master was the weaker of the two. But Sammael's master was good at the art of persuasion. He would not let Sammael fall. Not on this night. It had been many years in the making. The Unholy One would give Sammael what he asked for, he'd earned it. Sammael could taste the salt of his revenge.

The crickets chirped. The night air felt warm, a bit stale. The humidity surrounded him, making the flesh of his borrowed skin slick. The house was near. The scent of terror radiated from those he wished to eviscerate. He felt another presence—one he was familiar with.

It was Jezebeth.

Was it possible she was still here? When Gardner expelled Jezebeth from the girl's body, Sammael assumed she'd been sent back. Sent to the place that they'd both come from—the house of sorrow and pain.

But now, he thought differently. He could smell her presence, her anger. He could taste her rage and feel her vengeance. It was subtle, but flavorful. *But did she hold ill will? Would she get in the way?* She held no loyalty. Their kind was incapable of loyalty. Her only judgment was to torment, much like Sammael.

She wouldn't be a problem.

Standing amidst the rows of corn, Sammael stared forward. The cornstalks parted and the flames of hell opened. Through the dancing flames, Sammael was assured this was *his* night. He could destroy these people. Jezebeth was still of worth to him. She was at his disposal, a weapon in his arsenal.

He could feel it.

Sammael left the cornfield. He stood at the edge of the driveway, which led to the farmhouse. A burning energy swept through him. He felt his beautiful anger blossom. It swirled into rage. His rage would guide him in this battle.

Still, the power which Gardner possessed made him shutter.

Skirting along the driveway, Sammael braced himself for the battle.

Chapter 24

1

"I need to pee," Cherri announced as she swayed from one side of her butt to the other. She stood from the stack of boxes she'd been sitting on. She bounced from one foot to the other, her teeth chattered. Her fingers fidgeted and she had a hop to her step.

Gardner, looking annoyed, turned to the small door in the floor. He spun around toward Cherri and said, "Can it wait?"

Shaking her head, she lifted the plastic milk jug. "I drank all of it." It was empty.

Gardner raised an eyebrow. His eyes panned from the jug to Cherri's stomach.

"I guess I could go in this." Cherri held out the jug.

Hesitantly, Gardner returned, "That might be a better idea than going downstairs."

Donna stood, shook her head, and looked, sympathetically, from her husband to Cherri and said, "I'll take you downstairs."

Gardner didn't appear happy, but he nodded his approval. Donna walked to the back of the attic, grabbed the long wood handle, and pulled the door in the floor open. A shimmer of light splashed a tint of gray into the attic when the door fully opened.

Donna and Cherri descended the short retractable staircase. The steps creaked loud, causing Cherri more anxiety.

Once in the hallway, Donna led Cherri down the hall, past a few bedrooms, and then opened the last door on the left. It swung with a subtle squeak. The white tile gave off a blue tint.

Donna said, "Don't turn on the light. It might draw unwanted attention."

Cherri nodded, entered the bathroom. The last thing Cherri wanted to do was draw attention, especially while she was peeing. Again, she was in a vulnerable state.

She pulled her pants down and sat on the toilet seat. It was cold. She yelped. The chill from the porcelain held a bite. It took a second for her to get comfortable. She kept her lips pressed together and her eyes shut.

She focused on relaxing. Finally, she was able to relieve herself. About halfway through her *business* she felt the small white hairs on the back of her neck stand tall. For no reason at all—well, with good reason—she was scared. She felt alone, but not alone.

Suddenly everything became a contradiction. She felt that someone or something was in the room with her—a presence. It was nothing that could be seen, only felt. She glanced around the cold dark enclosure. Her sight was drawn toward the bathtub. It was encased in a white curtain with blue flower print that swayed slightly.

But there was no breeze.

Maybe the draft was coming from the space at the bottom of the door?

Cherri wiped, pulled her pants up, and stood from the toilet. Her shoes squeaked. There was a knock at the door. She jumped. Stepping backward, she nearly tripped over the toilet. She sat back down before she fell.

"Hurry up," Donna whispered.

Cherri turned toward the door. She opened her mouth to say she understood. Her vocal cords ceased to work. She froze, unable to answer. Fear seized her voice. The bathtub curtain slid to the side.

A bloody hand pushed the plastic divider to the edge of the tub revealing a man. He bathed in dark water. It was her dead stepfather. He was covered in blood and rotting skin. His eyes were bright white. They glowed in comparison to his blood ridden face.

It couldn't be. Her mother had shot him years ago. Blood ran from his mouth. He smiled big. His teeth were rotted and bloodstained. They looked wooden. His voice was loud and raspy.

Cherri wondered if Donna could hear him. Maybe, given all that had happened tonight, her exhausted mind was confused. She was bringing suppressed thoughts to the surface. They had manifested into visions—the cause of all this sudden stress.

She'd heard of such things.

Closing her eyes, she counted. She tried to block out the images like she did when her stepfather used to come into her bedroom at night. And then, she smelled the foulness of his breath, like she had so many years ago. It was warm, stained with beer and whiskey. It repulsed her.

It was heavy. Cherri's throat heaved. She wanted to vomit. She wanted to scream, but her mouth was frozen. She opened her eyes. Her stepfather was still in the bathtub.

The tub was filled to the rim with blood. The thick red fluid swished out of the tub and onto the floor.

He attempted to crawl out.

The gaping hole in his chest bled profusely. *Cherri imagined her mother aiming a shotgun at him.* Her stepfather clawed at the floor while pulling himself out. Heavy torrents of blood pumped from his mouth and chest. He was exerting himself. He coughed, loud and wet, with an undertone of laughter.

"We won't tell Momma about the games we like to play…will we, sweet Cherri? You know this isn't wrong…these things we do. I ain't your real daddy, you know. So it isn't sick," her stepfather explained as he exited the tub. He fell to the floor with a wet thud. He was naked. His torso was raw and torn open. His guts spilled across the tile in a tangled mess.

Cherri couldn't move. She was paralyzed with fear.

A quick burst of energy struck. She turned away from the monstrous sight of her dead stepfather crawling toward her. He left thick blood streaks along the white tile floor. The wrapping at the door grew louder. Donna pounded, hard. "Cherri, get out here now! Are you all right?"

Still unable to answer, Cherri had no choice but to look at the vile creature before her.

2

Jezebeth's presence grew along with Cherri's fear. Her strength had expanded. Soon, she would be able to possess Cherri. She just needed to feed the redhead's worst fears. At first, she seeped in like an invisible fog. Now, she concentrated on becoming the illusion of Cherri's stepfather.

Jezebeth took the image from Cherri's terror—locked away in her subconscious. Jezebeth recognized it right away. She had pried the lock and connected with the vile image of Cherri's stepfather. It wasn't hard for the demon to find Cherri's most intimate darkness. She quickly manifested into the rotting man and brought the fear into form.

Jezebeth wanted to laugh. Cherri's horror ridden face amused her. She couldn't wait to inhabit Cherri's body. She took pleasure in the terror surmounting upon Cherri's face. The illusion of Cherri's stepfather didn't consist of matter.

It was an illusion. It could scare her, but it couldn't touch her. Still, Jezebeth enjoyed the torment the illusion was causing. Cherri experienced ultimate horror as her mutilated stepfather crawled toward her. The image was working. Cherri was frozen. And in this vulnerable moment, Jezebeth could possess Cherri.

Cherri's body would make a fine suit for Jezebeth to wear, a wonderful mask.

Jezebeth's presence vacuumed into the open space. It attempted to penetrate Cherri. It was cut short. She couldn't take her body.

Cherri had more strength than she'd anticipated. Frustration seized Jezebeth. She'd seen the life Cherri had lived thus far and was certain she would be an easy target. It shouldn't have been a task for her to inhabit this body. But Cherri had hidden strengths that wouldn't allow the possession.

Jezebeth was furious.

Her anger increased when Donna pounded on the door.

Donna's insistence to help had increased Jezebeth's inordinate amount of rage.

Cherri moved toward the image of her dead stepfather. Her face filled with blood, red. Her cheeks flushed. Her fists clenched. She drew her foot back and kicked at the laughing, bloodied man, on the floor.

Cherri's feet sifted through the image.

3

Donna stood in the hallway, pounding on the bathroom door, lunging into it. She was frightened. It didn't matter how loud she was anymore. The demon had discovered Cherri, she was being attacked. Something very bad was happening behind this door. Donna didn't want anything to happen to Cherri.

It would kill her if she were hurt. Donna didn't know Cherri well, but they were fighting on the same team. She cared, but her hope was diminishing. Mentally, Donna didn't know how strong Cherri could be.

If the door were to open, Donna didn't know if Cherri would come out, or if it would be the demon. Cherri was a *good person*. Donna could sense that about her. But she'd been through a lot. Her misfortune in life was painted on her face. She wore it like a hat. She carried her defensiveness in her gaze.

She could still fall victim, if seduced or attacked in a customized way. She could be manipulated. They all could. Donna didn't know if Cherri was able to keep the vile spirit from corrupting her body.

Quick footsteps scurried down the attic stairs. Donna spun around. Her husband lurched down into the hallway. He darted toward the bathroom. Donna knew he could see the fright on her face.

"What's happened? Is Cherri all right?" he shouted.

"She's in there. She won't come out. Something is with her. I can feel it," Donna answered.

Gardner grabbed the doorknob. He twisted it. Calm at first, and then he pushed and pulled, hard.

Donna watched on. Gardner stepped back. His back was flat against the wall. He faced the door. His head bolted upward. His eyes shot to the back of his head.

He was having a vision.

4

Gardner tensed. His vision brought him into the bathroom. The image was vivid, as if he was watching the attack unfold from a close distance. He could see Cherri standing near the sink. She lunged forward repeatedly. She slammed her foot through the bloody creature as if it weren't there.

It cackled each time she kicked it. Blood erupted from the creature's mouth and chest. It spread across the floor. Gardner saw the rage in Cherri's face. Then she closed her eyes and unleashed hell on the man grabbing at her feet.

Cherri's kicks swung right through the man, like he was an illusion. He was an illusion. Gardner had seen this before. It was the demon he'd expelled from the young woman in the backyard.

Upon realizing what was happening, Gardner saw Jezebeth. Not the body she inhabited earlier, but her presence—the make-up of the demon. Beneath the surface-realm of reality, the bathroom was filled with slimy tentacles, vines, and black goo.

Her vile presence seeped from the cracks in the walls, and the spaces between the tiles. They were living vines, twisted with barbed hell. He was certain it was the demon Jezebeth. Gardner could feel her unique evil. She was trying to possess Cherri.

Hope seized Gardner when he felt Cherri's strength. It emanated in the room. It was warm. The demon wasn't able to possess her. Cherri was strong. Her anger hadn't weakened her mind yet. That was enough, for now.

The vision left Gardner. He opened his eyes. He glared at the door in front of him. The brightness he'd once known well was building within him. His strength increased and he was filled with fight. He kicked the bathroom door. A long crack ran up the center of the door as it flew open.

The gored man on the floor looked to Gardner. Anger burned in its yellow eyes. The demon hissed.

Cherri continued kicking. Jezebeth snapped her blackened snakes back, toward Cherri.

She wanted inside.

Jezebeth was not granted access.

"Cherri, stop. It can't hurt you. Walk out. Don't look back."

5

Cherri's mouth was dry. Her throat burned and her breathing was erratic. A moment's comfort came when Gardner's voice drifted in. She stopped kicking her stepfather. She was slow at first, and confused. It took a moment to catch her breath and another to open her eyes.

But when she did, her heart fluttered heavy before it slowed. Standing in the doorway, Gardner stared past Cherri. When she turned to see what was behind her, she felt the awful presence again. Her stepfather had disappeared. Frantically, her gaze searched the room.

It was empty. The blood was gone. So was her stepfather. His cackles died out. It struck her: that wasn't her stepfather. It was the demon in the form of an illusion.

"It's that thing, isn't it? I thought you killed it," Cherri asked. Her anger settled.

Gardner's attention swept toward Cherri and he said, "You can't kill this kind of evil. First, you must accept it. Then, you do your best to fight it. But it never dies. You can only suppress evil…for a short time. I thought I'd sent *it* back to Hell when I exorcised the woman in the backyard, but I was wrong. And for now, I need you to go back upstairs. I'll handle this."

Cherri ran from the bathroom.

In the hallway, she ran into Winny. He startled her. When she recognized his face, she wrapped her arms around him before they finally separated. Winny grabbed Cherri's hand and pulled her down the hallway. He practically threw her up the staircase and into the attic. The last thing Cherri saw before Winny came barreling up the stairs was Gardner walking into the bathroom.

6

Gardner stepped slowly into the dark bathroom. Once he was inside, he stopped and turned back to Donna and said, "Go with them. I'll be up in a moment."

Donna nodded. She turned and hurried down the hallway. She didn't ask any questions. Gardner continued into the bathroom. He closed the door behind him.

He saw the black ooze. It slithered along the walls. It draped across the ceiling and snapped at Gardner, threatening to tear at him. It was a living evil.

Gardner knew Jezebeth couldn't hurt him. She'd been denied of possession. The brightness within him radiated, beneath his skin. He closed his eyes. Confidently, he extended his hand toward the massive manifestation—the demon. His lips began to quiver as he prayed.

High pitched screaming rang out and stabbed at Gardner's ears. The demon felt the pain of goodness rip at its being.

Before the mass—that was Jezebeth—melted into a wave of bloody ooze, Gardner turned and stepped out of the bathroom. The destruction of Jezebeth was loud. She imploded from this plain of existence.

Gardner was satisfied. He'd been used by the divine, controlled by the goodness within him. Earlier, he'd doubted his gift. He knew he'd disappointed the Holy One. But now, his gift was fueled and renewed. He strode with confidence into the hallway. The demon Jezebeth had been sent away and was descending into the place where the foul dwelled.

Gardner walked to the dangling staircase and ascended into the attic.

Chapter 24

1

Sammael walked past the liquor store. Nothing could stop him. He was going to finish this. He would kill Gardner. The gravel crunched beneath his feet as he strolled up Gardner's driveway. He could taste the battle ahead.

He'd destroy everyone hiding at this farmhouse. Then he turned to the liquor store. The small store had only served as bait to lure Gardner in. Killing everyone else was a satisfying bonus. And he would continue to kill. He'd make the rest of them suffer. They slowed him down and that shouldn't have happened.

It irritated him and he should have destroyed these simple humans with ease. But he hadn't. They were fighting well against him. It took an enormous amount of will for a human to do that. He hadn't planned on these *simple beings* possessing such strength. They must have been given help from the Divine. That was the only way this was possible. Still, he would take what was promised to him by the Unholy One.

Earlier, he'd taken delight in killing the thieves. It had been fun eviscerating them. They weren't enough. They had been weak and no challenge at all. He wanted to kill Gardner and slay that bitch he called wife. Donna. They were a worthy battle.

Step after step, he stalked up the gravel drive. He found himself standing in front of the farmhouse staring, maliciously, at the brick structure. He sensed the fear harbored inside.

They were in the attic, and he would take them one-by-one. He paused. From a distance, he peered into each dark window. He could feel the walls breathing. The house took-on a life of its own—it was a living thing.

His plan of attack needed revision. He would need to separate each one of these filthy humans. From there he'd tear at their souls before he tore at their flesh. He would need to access their thoughts. Then, he would rip into them physically. From the inside out, he'd grind them to shreds.

Jezebeth had been *sent back*. He felt it. Earlier, he'd been able to feel her rage. Even after she'd been expelled from the body she'd taken. Jezebeth manifested her energy into something, he assumed, was powerful. That's how he could feel her. Gardner must have defeated her. Sammael could no longer sense any trace of her presence. Her rage, anger, and filth had evaporated.

Oh well, she wasn't that powerful.

He'd known all along she didn't possess the amount of power he did.

Standing at the foot of the driveway, leading to the Gardner's farmhouse, Sammael's smile stretched across the face which had once belonged to Garth Gasper. The evil cycling through him culminated into a massive energy of rage.

He hurried to the house.

2

Donna paced back and forth. When she passed the window again, her attention was drawn outside. She stopped in front of the attic window. She gazed out into the night. Tiny bumps lifted across her arms and the back of her neck. She saw *him.*

Sammael stood at the base of the driveway. Sure, it looked like Garth Gasper, but Donna knew, judging by the maniacal grin spread across his face, he was consumed by the evil demon Sammael. Even his eyes were full of evil.

They were glossy and they flickered. They weren't Garth's eyes. The way he just stood there watching the house, analyzing it, judging it, made her shudder. He looked like a snake preparing to eat a small white mouse. Then he looked up into the window and she swore he was staring into her thoughts.

Donna jumped. Her husband stepped behind her. She turned to him. He was frowning and an intense expression. It reflected the gears of thought cranking through his mind. He walked toward her and peered out the window.

Sammael walked toward the house. Immediately, Gardner turned to Winny Gasper.

A lost look of helplessness overwhelmed Gardner's face.

Donna knew her husband didn't know how to handle this. There were no words to express what needed to happen. He wouldn't be able to contain Winny. There was nothing he could do. Winny wouldn't turn against the evil *thing* that was eating away at his brother's soul.

Plain and simple, Sammael was using Garth's body. She had to shake off the awful thought of Winny dying. He wouldn't fight his brother. Sammael would manipulate

Winny and then kill him. Still, she thought, *they could make it through this night.* They could find a way. She had faith and she had hope.

"That isn't your brother," Gardner informed Winny.

Without hesitation, Winny stepped away from Cherri. He shuffled to the window and eagerly peered down at the driveway. His brother strode toward them. Garth's eyes found Winny. He smiled from below. Garth waved, innocently, and then hurried around to the back of the house.

3

Winny's breath quickened. His prayers had been answered; he was swept with relief. His brother was back, and he looked okay and in good health. Winny darted toward the door. The wooden floor bounced as he made his way. He reached down to the floor and opened the staircase leading to the hallway and then began to descend. He was halted. Gardner grabbed his arm and pulled him upward forcefully.

Too eager to care about the aching pain that shot through his shoulder from where Gardner gripped him, Winny peered up at Gardner's stern face and said, "It's Garth. He's fine. We need to let him in before those evil bastards get to him."

A frown took Winny's face when he saw the intensity of Gardner. And then Winny pulled himself free from Gardner. Quickly, he descended the small staircase. He hit the hardwood floor. His shoes squeaked. He jumped halfway down, skipping the rest of the stairs.

He ran toward the next staircase, at the far end of the hallway and sprinted to the first floor. Then he ran to the front door.

He stopped.

Knocking, drifted into his ears. The flower vase that had been set in back of the door fell over. It spilled dirt onto wood flooring. From behind, Gardner hustled down the stairs. He nearly tackled Winny before he fully opened the door.

"That's not your brother. Do not let him in. You'll be endangering us all." The authority in his voice was strong.

Reaching for the doorknob, Gardner swiped at Winny's hand.

"I just saw him. He looked up at me and smiled. I know it's hard for you to understand, but you're wrong. I swear it. You're wrong. That's Garth out there. It's okay, really."

The knocking grew louder. Garth's voice drifted in. "Winny, open the door. I don't want one of those *things* to get me."

Convinced, Winny grabbed for the door again. This time, the door flew off the hinges from the outside and Winny was knocked to the ground. His stomach cramped as though he'd been kicked. The pain was brutal. Gardner was pushing his way forward and punching at Garth.

Winny sprung to his feet. Gardner was tossed backward toward the foot of the stairs and a huffing sound pumped from his mouth when his back hit the stairs. Winny pushed Garth out the door.

"Winny, it's me. What are you trying to do? I need your help."

Winny knew then Garth had been taken. This wasn't his brother. Pain washed over him. He was devastated. He wanted to know where and when Garth had been *taken.*

How could this have happened? How would they fix it? He looked to Gardner as he stood from the floor, hunched over, and gripped his throbbing love-handle.

"Get out of this house you retched thing! I command you in the name of all that is good! Go to your distant land,"

Gardner shouted as he stood, proud, face to face, and ordered Sammael out.

Looking to Gardner for help, Winny moved toward Sammael. And when he turned to face him, Sammael grabbed at Winny's throat. He squeezed, digging his bony fingers into Winny's neck. Winny locked eyes with the monster and prayed. He hoped some semblance of his brother was alive and would help him. His airway was constricted and breath shortened. His chest pounded. He heard Gardner scurry out of the room.

Winny was frightful. The end of his life was near. Beginning to feel faint, he slumped to the floor and peered up at what used to be his brother. A tear spilled from his eye. And around the eyes of Sammael, the white fire of hell burned the radius of his pupils.

About to pass out, Winny saw colors flash before his eyes. His neck felt weak. His head bobbed and threatened to fall forward. All sound diminished and there was only silence.

Then, a sizzling noise seeped in. It sounded like water dripping onto a hot skillet. Forcing his eyes to open, with all of his might, Winny came to. The sizzle was, in fact, some kind of liquid. It bubbled on Sammael's forehead. The grip Sammael had around Winny's neck quickly fell. Winny gasped for breath, and he received it. His strength grew. Adrenaline pumped through his system and coursed though his arms and legs.

Winny rolled away from the monster who wore his brother's skin and darted behind Gardner, who now stood in front of Sammael throwing water upon him from a small vile. It resembled a flask. *It must be holy water.* Gardner was saying something, but Winny was too wound-up to understand it.

"I cast you out of this body you have wrongfully stolen," Gardner was saying over and over. Then he looked to Winny. He pointed toward the stairs. "Go to them."

Winny nodded. He ran toward the staircase. He jumped, step by step, to the second floor hallway and then sprinted to the small staircase hanging down from the attic. He pulled his way up and jumped into the attic.

He was alone. The attic was empty.

4

The enormity of thunderous footsteps struck loud and Cherri and Donna could hear the fighting coming from downstairs. They quickly nested behind the larger stacks of boxes in the darkest corner of the attic.

They crouched down low and waited in silence. The shouts, stomping, and pounding that came from downstairs had frightened them both and they anticipated the worst. Cherri wanted to go downstairs. She wanted to help the men, but Donna had prevented her and convinced her that Gardner didn't want them to go, that they'd only get in the way of what needed to be done.

Gardner was protecting them. Cherri listened to her. From what Cherri knew, Gardner was some kind of holy man and he'd dealt with the likes of these creatures and had done so for many years. Therefore, he knew best. Cherri understood. She had faith in him.

When heavy footsteps grew louder and threatened to lurch into the attic, Cherri's first reaction was to stand and get ready to fight. She would face the enemy, courageous. She had had enough, and she was mad as hell.

Maybe she'd grab a box from the back of the attic and she could throw it at whatever came into the attic. It probably wouldn't do anything except make the demon mad. But hell, the demon would probably enjoy it. Her throbbing heart slowed. The square in the floor filled with the shape of a man. *It had to be Sammael, coming to finish them off.*

It wasn't.

Winny burst from the floor and jumped into the moonlit attic. Cherri held her hand to her chest and focused on her breathing.

"Winny, what's happening?" she asked.

Winny glanced around the attic, confused. He didn't know where the voice was calling from. Cherri stood and revealed herself.

"It's Garth. Well, it's not Garth, it's that thing. He's possessed Garth…"

Cherri watched the frightened form of Winny's eyes. Grief had struck him. Cherri could sense he'd already written his brother off as dead and she was saddened.

"I don't know what to do. I'm scared for Garth, he must be in so much pain… I don't know how he let that evil piece of shit take him, but we need to help him. There's got to be a way we can help him," Winny pleaded.

Donna went to Winny. She gently touched his shoulder with her fingers. "We need to help them both. They need us. I know how my husband works. When he wants us to go, we'll know it. He'll call us."

"He needs us now!" Winny screamed at her.

Shaking her head, slowly, from side to side, Donna calmly said, "What was the last thing my husband said to you?"

Cherri could see Winny wanted to argue with Donna, but in the end he nodded and said, "He told me to come up here, that I should stay with you."

"Then he wants you to be with us, up here. Strength in numbers, remember?"

Cherri was scared by how intense Winny had become. He was angry. He couldn't sit still, and he wanted to do something. Still, he seemed to know the right thing to do was stay in the attic, with them.

"So, we should just wait here until something happens? What if he kills Garth or your husband? What then? Should we stay up here until he kills us?"

Donna closed her eyes and nodded. "We'll wait for my husband to tell us what to do." She opened her eyes and looked at Winny. There was an understanding in the way she gazed at him.

Shaking his head, obviously disappointed, Winny stepped back from Donna and said, "That's weak."

5

Gardner stood near the cracked frame of his front door. Wood splinters angled out from all sides of the rectangular doorway. He was standing above the demon, Sammael. He frowned upon the snarling beast he was defeating. Although he was *defeating* the demon, he had not *defeated* him.

The holy water had hurt the demon, dazed him, and thrown him out of commission for the moment. The demon was temporarily blinded. He hissed and growled.

"I command you...in the name of all that is good, to leave this body. Leave this house. You are not welcome. Go to your distant land."

Standing slowly, unable to look at Gardner, Sammael wobbled like a drunkard. He stumbled to his feet, frantically wiping the sizzling water from his face. The holy water left dark red lesions on his forehead and the skin on his face bubbled and burned downward and across the side of his nose.

Gardner watched on, confidently, as the demon slowly shifted his gaze. Sammael's eyes rolled over to the back of his head. They were bulbs of pure white, and they were flickering fiery white halos. They burned brightly. Stepping backward, Sammael smiled, maniacally.

"I will leave this house, but I will destroy the flesh which I wear. And it will…" he looked up, seemingly toward the ceiling. "…destroy those who you love…and they will destroy you and each other in turn."

With that, Sammael whisked out the front door.

Gardener's first instinct was to run after Sammael. The demon hadn't been concurred and the sinking despair Gardner felt in the pit of his stomach was incredible. His focus was on Winny.

He knew Winny's anger would consume him. Gardner wouldn't be able to convince Winny of otherwise. His rage would build. Sammael was right. It would turn Winny against what was good and what was right. It would turn him against the group.

Gardner quickly made his way up the stairs. His lower back groaned with each step. Sharp pains exploded from all his joints. He yelled to the girls as he hobbled stair after stair, "It's me! I'm coming up!"

He made it into the attic and Donna ran to him. She wrapped her arms around his beaten torso and held him tight. Winny stood in the corner of the room biting his nails and kicking his foot at the wooden planks that made up the floor. A thin layer of dust jumped up each time his foot landed.

Gardner looked to the dust-rumbled floor, and it reminded him of the desert during the beginning moments of an earthquake. He'd once witnessed an earthquake caused by the hand of God. That had been an angry tremor. It was a recorded six on the Richter scale.

There had been a small cult in the Arizona desert that practiced black magic and witchcraft. They'd defiled the property where they resided. They'd kidnapped children and done awful things with them. Gardner had been called in and there had been a short investigation. The spiritual battle had been brutal. The fighting took place on not only the living world, but the spiritual plain that existed beneath the surface of human acknowledgement.

Gardner feared telling Winny what he knew, but he knew he must. He needed to do it quick. He needed assurance that Winny wouldn't fight them. That he wouldn't be of risk or get in the way of what needed to be done. But if he were going to fight them, then they could deal with him by restraint. Once they knew if he was friend or foe, they could strategize their defense.

"I couldn't save your brother, Winny. He's gone. He's been taken. I know you're hurt, but we need to find the demon and destroy it before he hurts others. It's the right thing to do, Winny." He took a step toward Winny.

Winny turned pale. He looked grim. Gardner was hesitant to proceed. The need to intimidate Winny was necessary. It might win his attention. And as Gardner half expected, Winny wasn't fazed. He moved past Gardner, toward the door in the floor.

Gardner grabbed Winny's arm and twisted it backward. A look of terror took Winny's face as he was driven to his knees. Gardner wrapped his arm around Winny's neck, placing his elbow in the inner pocket of his trachea.

Gardner pulled, hard behind Winny and squeezed with all of his might. He wanted to render Winny unconscious. If Winny were out cold then he could be restrained and Gardner could hunt Sammael.

Winny swung his head backward, piling it into Gardner's face. Blood exploded across the top of Winny's head as it drained from Gardner's nose. Gardner was going to lose him. He wouldn't listen and his mind was made up. There was no stopping him. He escaped the dazed Gardner.

Winny dove down the hatch, into the hallway.

Winny tumbled down the hatch. Losing control, he fell fast and landed on his shoulder. The pain was sharp and intense, but the brunt of it fled quickly. He felt his shoulder pop out of place, but it quickly knocked back in. Without wasting a moment, he took off away from the attic.

He needed to find Garth—his brother needed him. In Winny's mind, the bond of brotherhood was stronger than any evil that could possess Garth. There was a way to get through to him—to save him and to beat the demon. *There had to be.*

Fumbling to his knees, pain shot upward through his body. His teeth chattered. Not stopping, he stood and ran toward the stairs and then down them and out the front door. He ran into the night. Realizing he didn't know where he was going or what he was going to do didn't stop his legs from pumping hard and fast. He felt as though he were being guided by something unseen.

Before he hit the mouth of the driveway, he heard a voice call to him. It sounded like Cherri's. There was a sweet tone to it. He turned and gazed out into the night. He saw she was standing near the corner of the house. She stood still, staring at him. She didn't look frightened—*as she probably should have.* She looked delighted to see him. Suddenly, he felt that he needed to go to her.

Relief washed over him. Then fear struck when he saw Garth. Garth was possessed. Still, there was something different about his appearance now. It was Garth. Not just his flesh and blood, but *his brother.* He stood behind Cherri and there was nothing evil about him. The evil presence that radiated from him was gone and his eyes were sullen. *It was really Garth.*

Maybe Gardner had somehow cast the demon out?

Garth looked sad, yet cautious, as if he didn't want anyone to see him.

Winny went to his brother and Cherri.

7

Jezebeth burned. Her existence had grown weak, and the pain was intense. It was sharp. And she savored it. She hadn't been sent back yet. For one reason or another, the matter in which her existence was consisted of was not in a solid state.

She was a presence, particles of searing pain. Each particle more intensely tormented than the other. But she remained in the world of the living. She still possessed strength. Not the level of strength she'd possessed when she arrived in this realm, but enough strength to present images to those she wished to possess.

The red hair beauty, Cherri, would be a good image to project upon Winny. Winny's optimism was Jezebeth's strength. She could make him weak, and his guard would fall and then she could wear his body while she tormented his soul. Earlier, when she inhabited the body of Patty, she'd seen the attraction Winny held for Cherri. It was unmistakable. Now, she would use this attraction— weakness—in order to take his body and destroy it.

She would possess Winny first. After she had a body, she'd destroy the others. She would be rewarded in Hell. She didn't care what happened to Sammael. Yet she acknowledged he was strong. He was better at this sick game than her.

Rightfully so, Sammael had existed for many centuries. He'd been around much longer than she had and therefore he was more experienced. But given what had happened tonight—being able to escape the power which the priest carried—she knew she could continue on her path of destruction. She could be rewarded by the Dark Master.

And now, as Winny walked toward what looked like Cherri and Garth, Jezebeth smiled. Winny looked comforted. He thought he was seeing Gath and Cherri. *Too bad it wasn't them; too bad for him.* Winny thought he'd found his brother and Cherri. He slowed down as he neared the edge of the house.

"Garth…Cherri, what are you doing?" he asked.

Jezebeth could sense his defensiveness. That he was probably contemplating whether or not she and his brother were in fact who they claimed to be.

Obviously they were not.

They were here to destroy him. Naivety was a pleasant weakness in the human race. When people want something bad enough, they're willing to justify their thinking to suit their wants.

8

Winny shivered as the cold morning air surrounded him. The temperature had dropped significantly. It had been hot in the day, warm in the evening, and was growing bitter cold in the night. He rubbed his shoulders as he walked toward his brother., but couldn't take his eyes away from Cherri.

How did she make it down here so fast? He'd just seen her in the attic a few moments ago. He didn't care. She was here and so was Garth. His faith continued to build. He didn't recognize any evil within his brother. It just wasn't there as it had been before.

Maybe Garth had been able to get rid of the demon on his own. He lacked the glazed eyes and the sinister grin. There was life behind his eyes now that reflected goodness. He looked, strangely, apologetic. The humanistic gleam in his eyes expressed his regret. *He was sorry for leaving earlier.*

"Hey bro, look, I'm sorry I took off like I did. All of this…that happened tonight…it's just too much. We shouldn't deal with this on our own. We need help. We need to get out of here.

You need to come with me. I'm not leaving without you; that's why I came back." Garth stared apologetically at Winny. "And before, at the door, that wasn't me. That thing was in me. After you took off, Gardner did something…he made it go away," Garth said. Everything he said made sense. It paralleled his assumptions.

Winny felt an overpowering sense of camaraderie forming with his brother and it was much needed for some time. He stood close to Garth. Still leery, he stepped closer. He was terrified. Garth wrapped his arms around Winny and squeezed. It was comforting. The two brothers held each other. *It really was Gath, had to be.*

Winny parted from Garth and turned toward Cherri who was smiling. She ran her hand gently down his face. It was as if she were happy to see them come together.

"I believe him, Winny. I took off right after you. Gardner and his wife are still up there. I'm not saying he's bad, but I think he's going to kill us if he gets a hold of us. He thinks we're those…demons." Cherri explained. "I heard what he was saying."

Winny wondered, *Was he being fooled? And why was Garth so sided with Cherri?* Quickly, he stepped back. He shook a flat hand in front of Cherri, looked to his brother and asked, "Why are you being so good to her? You hate her."

Without hesitation, Garth smiled and said, "If I need to play nice with her in order to get you out of this hell hole, that's what I'll do. I'm not going to be stubborn. We need to get out of here and get help. We need her." Garth was silent for a moment before lifting his head toward Gardner's garage. "Gardner's truck is in there. Maybe his keys are, too. We can go to the police station and get more help."

That seemed logical. It seemed like something Garth would do. The three of them walked toward the garage. Cherri smiled brightly at Winny while they went.

The grass was wet. It glistened in the moonlight. It soaked the bottom of his jeans. But the moonlight would pass soon. It was early morning. It had to be four o'clock by now. The sun would come out soon. With the light, Winny knew everything would be all right. In the movies, nothing bad happened in the day.

The garage door creaked as Winny pushed it open. They filed into the musty scented wooden enclosure. There were wooden shelves jutting out from the wall on all sides of the garage. Garden tools hung from large hooks and dangled from the ceiling. Father Gardner's pickup truck sat parked in the dark.

Winny went to the driver's side and tried to open the door. It wouldn't budge. It groaned when he pulled on the handle. He tilted his head to the side, staring at the steering wheel. There were no keys in the ignition. Spinning his head quickly, he found Garth and Cherri staring at him intently.

"No keys?" Garth asked, looking to Cherri. He turned and headed for the door. "I'll get them. I saw them on the kitchen counter earlier."

"Be careful," Cherri whispered.

Winny saw a smile stretch across Cherri's face, but it didn't matter. To Winny, the comfort of having his brother and the girl he'd come to grow fond of was enough that he'd stay. He needed Garth and Cherri to be all right. Garth wasn't the enemy anymore. Neither was Cherri. It was hard to believe and it was complicated, but Gardner was the problem now.

Winny watched as Garth slid out the side door. It creaked when he closed it, and it tapped against the wood frame. The room was dark again. Winny could barely see the outline of Cherri's body until his eyes adjusted. She was smiling at him, seductively. Her lips curled and her smile shifted to the right side of her mouth. Her eyes drooped and her eyelashes slowly batted. Her appearance was sexy and inquisitive, as if asking: *"Now that we're alone, what do you want to do?"*

Winny shook the fantasy. There was no way this was happening. Sure, he wanted it to be happening, but not at a time like this.

"I'm glad your brother came back. I had my doubts about Father Gardner, but I didn't think it was my place to say anything. I know he's a good man—that he's dealt with this kind of stuff before, but I think he's confused, out of practice."

"It's okay." Winny nodded. "I'm just glad we're all together."

"Can I ask you something?"

"Sure," Winny said. He swallowed hard as Cherri swayed toward him.

"In the basement…earlier…did you want to kiss me?"

Winny felt his heart rate quicken. Tiny bulbs of sweat beaded up from the skin of his forehead. He was going to sweat. His cheeks were red. The blood-flow below his navel swelled.

"Ah…I mean. Is it okay that I did?"

"It is. I wanted you to. I still want you."

Then she was pulling her shirt up, exposing her flat stomach which spread at the sides where the perfectly symmetric curves of her hips began. Her skin looked soft and flawless. It was vibrant, even in the dark.

"What are you doing?" Garth asked, struggling to catch his breath, his breathing becoming erratic.

"Giving you a sneak peak," she whispered while lifting her shirt even farther, exposing the rounded bottom of her breasts.

Winny was fully aroused. Suddenly, he was embarrassed. *She might be able to see his erection.*

Taking a step backward, Winny crouched. He peered up at Cherri. She smiled and said, "It's okay. I want that, too." And yet, Winny didn't feel at ease. He continued to back up.

His mouth was dry and he tried to swallow. She'd taken her shirt off and her breasts were completely exposed. Her nakedness was accentuated by the moonlight that shone in through the small rectangular garage window.

"This isn't the time, Cherri." Winny said, fumbling for words.

"Is there ever a right time?" she asked. Her voice had become monotone as if she were a bad actress in a horror film seducing the unsuspecting male victim. She kept moving forward.

"Stop," he said.

He stood tall, firm—as if telling her he'd take action if she took another step forward.

She smiled while tracing her index finger down the center of her chest. She traced the underside of her right breast. "You don't find me attractive?"

9

Standing in the garage seducing Winny, Jezebeth's attempts were becoming questionable. Her actions displayed too much. The seduction wasn't subtle. It was forced. Winny would soon find her actions ridiculously false.

Jezebeth's desperation was becoming apparent. The results were written in Winny's fearful expression. She sensed her seduction was failing. It had succeeded at first, but now her attempts were drowning. Still, she needed to continue. She wouldn't allow herself stop. She needed to lure him in. Cherri's beauty was the only way.

Jezebeth wouldn't be able to seduce him any other way and she needed his body. Rage boiled within the matter of her being. The possession needed to happen now, or she would be sent back. If she went back, she would live, burning in flames, for too long. It would be decades before she was permitted back to the world of the living.

She looked below Winny's stomach. Beneath his jeans, she saw he was aroused. *She held a chance.* But if he touched her, she'd be revealed as an imposter, *an illusion.* That would end her existence, and he would know she was fraudulent.

She pushed her breasts together and moaned—another feeble attempt.

He licked his lips. Jezebeth could tell he was trying to justify his arousal—make it all right—while trying to control himself. Her confidence built as she found that he wanted her but knew he couldn't. *Humans were so easy.*

Jezebeth needed Winny to believe she was Cherri.

Or at least forget that she wasn't.

10

Standing in the garage, alone with Cherri, should have been tantalizing. Being in the basement with her, earlier, was exciting. They'd almost kissed. Frustration suddenly set in. He shouldn't be feeling these things. The timing couldn't be more wrong. But she was coming on to him, seducing him.

Winny's will shattered. He moved forward to Cherri. Lustful thoughts dwelled in his mind, and in his heart. *He had to have her.* To touch her soft flesh wasn't enough. She'd exposed herself to him. Beautiful girls like Cherri never showed interest in him before.

He accepted the bait.

Garth would be back momentarily. When he returned, they would *have* to stop. For now, he only wanted a taste, just a nibble. He wrapped his arms around her. He should have felt her warm body. He anticipated the comfort and the warmth of her, but his arms sifted through her and he fell forward.

It was as if she weren't there. She was weightless. She was shaded energy, drawn in the air. That was all. No sustenance to her being. And then, he felt her trying to get in. It felt like the pores of his skin were being penetrated by fiery wind. It hurt, but he wasn't going to let her in. He closed his eyes and prayed.

Garth stepped into the garage. His feet scraped across the chalky cement floor. He was a shadow in the dark as he leaned against the doorframe and said, "If you let her take your body, she'll give you the pleasure you desire. Don't fight it. I didn't. I feel like I could crush mountains. Imagine the two of us with strength like that, Winny. Trust me. Join me."

He wanted to. To be that strong and to taste the flesh of this beautiful girl. Wanting her wasn't enough. He had to have her. In that moment, he didn't care, even if it meant giving up his soul. He wanted her badly. He could taste her in the air between them.

And for just one moment, his guard evaporated. He felt the fiery winds sink deep into his flesh like a million hot needles.

It burned horribly.

Chapter 25

1

Cherri stood in the attic staring out the window. A million thoughts raced through her head. After facing the evils of this night she'd been able to put her life into a new perspective. If she made it through this, her lifestyle would change.

For now, she waited for a sign that Winny was all right. Everyone had become silent since he'd left. At the time, Cherri wanted to run after him and she tried, but Donna had stopped her. She wanted Winny to be all right and his safety weighed on her heavily.

Her guts twisted at the thought of what those creatures could and would do to him. It saddened her to think of how vulnerable he'd made himself. She'd never had any brothers or sisters and, therefore, she couldn't, honestly, grasp the feelings Winny held for his brother.

They were enough that he'd disregarded his own safety in order to help him. She found him noble for doing so even though she would do anything to have him back in this attic where she sat near the window. Donna and Leslie Gardner stood near the hatch like guard dogs. They remained silent and seemed to be communicating on another level. Their communication wasn't of the verbal variety.

The sound of Gardner's creaky knees drew Cherri's attention. He was stumbling forward, gripping his back and wincing.

Cherri opened her mouth, "I want to find him."

Gardner glanced up at her. His mouth moved, but he didn't say anything. He turned to Donna.

"What do we need to do?" Donna asked.

Gardner answered, "He's being tested. From there we will know what to do."

Cherri was angered. It seemed like Gardner didn't care. It was like he was being lazy. Waiting wasn't the right thing to do.

Shouldn't they be trying to save Winny from being tempted by those creatures?

This thought linked her to the next. She wondered how Winny was being tempted. Had Sammael somehow convinced Winny *he* was in fact Garth? Had Winny bought into Sammael's deceit because he needed his brother to be all right? Had the demon tempted him like it had her? Like the image she'd seen of her stepfather?

The thought of Sammael tempting Winny—somehow—with thoughts of *her* hid silently at the back of her mind. What if Sammael had somehow become Cherri and seduced Winny. She knew the demon was able to conjure illusions.

She'd been fooled earlier when Jezebeth had manifested into the terrifying image of her stepfather. He appeared in the bathtub, and she'd bought into it. But Gardner and his wife had saved her. Why couldn't they save Winny?

"I think we need to help him…I need to help him," Cherri finally answered.

"For now, we need to stay together. If we separate, the demon will corner each of us and prey on our weaknesses. That is what the demon does. You know this. It tried to get you earlier and it will do the same again with you, my wife, and certainly with me. I guarantee that is what the demon is doing with Winny."

Cherri frowned. It felt like she'd been stabbed in the belly. How could Sammael tempt Gardner? It didn't make sense. He was blessed somehow. He had some kind of holy shield; a knowledge of how to fight these evil creatures.

Even though it sounded ridiculous.

But then, this whole night sounded ridiculous. Gardner had certain gifts, and his powers had enabled him to fight off the retched creatures. He possessed the strength to fight them. Cherri couldn't imagine he could be tempted. There was no way. He was too solid and he seemed to do the right thing all the time. His morality was flawless.

"That doesn't seem right, Father Gardner. How can he tempt you?"

"The demon always has its ways. It can threaten me with violence against my wife or against you. It could create threats that would force me to succumb to its demands. And he *will* do anything in his power to sway me, and you."

Gardner's argument seemed logical. Crazy as it all sounded, what he explained made sense. She almost laughed when thinking of the word *logical*. There was nothing logical about this night or anything that had happened during the course of it.

But now, listening to what Gardner said calmed her. Her eager need to be with Winny—to possibly sacrifice herself in order to gain closure was settled. Still, she wanted to abandon her safety in order to find him. She couldn't bear the thought of Winny suffering.

Cherri knew Winny was tormented by the *taking* of Garth. That was probably what Gardner meant when he said Sammael could tempt him. Horror seized Cherri. Just the mere thought of Winny being taken, possessed by Sammael, haunted her. The idea was agonizing. *And what if Jezebeth still lingered?* Gardner had fought her twice, but somehow she'd come back.

Standing, Cherri leaned forward and peered out the window. To her surprise, she saw something shift near the garage. She stared down and saw *him* standing in the front lawn.

It was Garth.

Chapter 26

1

Winny stood in the garage inhaling the rising dust as it kicked up from the dirty floor. His skin felt like it was on fire. His feet, legs and arms were tight, solid, stiff. He couldn't move. He raised his hand to his face. It felt heavy.

Each finger seemed to weigh a thousand pounds and his skin felt like it was barely hanging on. His forearm seemed to be filled with solid steel instead of flesh and blood. He fought to keep his eyes shut. He didn't want to see his arm. He was sure it was melting. He thought so, anyway. The pain was bad, and he knew he was being disfigured.

Jezebeth's heat was reforming his body. *This was it.* The thought of opening his eyes and seeing his skin had melted away from the bone was haunting and images of his bones covered in bloody muscle flooded in. His stomach crumpled. When he finally opened his eyes, he saw his arm was fine and completely intact.

It felt like it was on fire, but it looked as it always had. His thoughts had gotten the best of him. The demon had tricked him. Then he looked ahead toward Cherri. Her entire body flickered like she was being erased, and she was still shirtless. She was convulsing and shaking heavily.

She vibrated at a high velocity and her appearance changed. The woman he saw before him, now, looked as though her skin was charred and blackened. Her eyes were white; without color or pupils. She quickly turned into Cherri again. Abruptly, Winny realized what was happening.

The demon was trying to seduce him.

She was trying to break down his guard. Jezebeth wanted to possess him and take his body. A blood churning sickness twisted in his stomach. He was sure Garth had been taken, and it killed him to think that his brother was enduring intense pain and torment. And he assumed he was.

Sammael had possessed Garth. Gardner was right. Still, he had needed to be sure. *He couldn't be faulted for his doubts.* Now, he needed to get away from this evil thing before he too was possessed. Slowly, the sensation of the burning wind cooled. His skin no longer felt the flames and his awareness blocked the demon's attack.

Winny was angry. He wanted to get back to the attic and see Gardner and his wife. The last time he'd seen Cherri—not the vision of her—was in the attic. The sweet girl who had come into his life on this fate-filled night and now he wanted to feel the comfort of being with her.

He was ashamed for having bought into the demon's seduction. Jezebeth used Winny's feelings for Cherri, to lure him in.

Standing now in front of Jezebeth, he was able to see the demon for what she was—a retched beast. Her skin was black, charred, and scaley. Her eyes opened and they flickered at him. His anger trumped his fear.

Her pure white eyes gazed into his. She was still trying to force her way in, but he wouldn't let her. It was obvious, from the flickering, fiery, glow of her eyes she felt rage. She was losing the fight. Intuitively, Winny knew she couldn't continue this battle.

If she could have, she'd have done it already, but for one reason or another she was unable to hurt him. *Maybe she didn't have enough power?* He could only speculate when it came to the unknown. Jezebeth wasn't fulfilled. And she wasn't getting in.

Good.

The fiery sensation subsided, and Winny no longer felt like he was being held captive in a furnace. The muscles in his legs loosened and his arms swayed at ease. He stepped forward. Heart racing, he inched past the demon. It snarled and hissed at him, but it didn't move, and it didn't strike. It only stood there, vibrating, and flickering. Heat radiated from where Jezebeth stood. Winny moved past her and left the garage. Still scared, he felt the slightest hint of relief.

He had passed this test.

He made it out of the garage. Smelling the cool morning air felt good. It was refreshing. A new fear set in. *Where was his brother? Where was the demon?* His brother wouldn't have allowed Jezebeth to do this. The demon encouraged Winny to believe what Garth had said, but it wasn't Garth. No matter how mad Garth was, he wouldn't wish harm upon his brother. A faint chuckle rippled down from the roof of the garage.

Winny looked up. Above him, Garth stood smiling. His skin was pale. He cackled his head off. At first, Winny thought he was choking, but he was only laughing too hard.

He hoped Garth was somehow fighting the demon. Winny wished he could help, but the only help was Gardner.

"Hey buddy. Didn't quite like her, did you?" Sammael called down as he sat on the roof. His feet dangled off the side.

"Leave my brother alone," Winny growled at the demon. For a quick second, Winny could sense his brother. The feeling was vague and almost unnoticeable, but it was present. A stammer of Garth's soul escaped the demon's eyes. The look was sad. He looked frightened. Sammael quickly returned, with his maniacal chatter.

"Join us, Winny." He cocked his head to the side. "And what kind of a name is Winny? Your parents must be pricks. Do you have a friend named "Piglet?"

Anger brewed and suddenly Winny's fear subsided. He could help his brother. The fear of the unknown, supernatural being, sitting above the garage wasn't going to stop him from trying. He yelled at the top of his lungs, "Let my brother go!"

Then the snide sarcasm, the belligerently sinister nature of the demon dissipated into something that restored fear within Winny. The demon opened its mouth and a snake shot forward. Just before it snapped at Winny's face, a small bony hook poked through the end of it. The hook tore, jaggedly, through Winny's right cheek about three inches, and it was deep. It hurt. Winny immediately put his hand to the wound. When he pulled his fingers away, he found they were streaked with blood.

He felt the warm red fluid running down his chin and under his jaw. It dribbled down his neck. He peered up. Frightened, yet too upset to turn away, he screamed, "Let my brother go!"

For the second time, Winny felt his brother's presence. *Sammael couldn't stop Garth from breaking through from wherever the demon was holding him captive.*

"Help me, Winny, go get Father Gardner before he kills me," Garth screamed. Then, as quickly as Garth had come, he was gone. The angered white eyes of the demon were gleaming down at him with treacherous intensity.

Turning to run, another snake snapped from Sammael's mouth. It whipped through the air and snatched a small patch of skin from Winny's shoulder. It tore his shirt open. The pain didn't stop Winny from running fast toward the front door of the house.

As he ran, the padded drop of Sammael jumping from the roof of the garage and landing on the lawn drifted through the early morning air.

The demon stood still, watching.

Winny rounded the house and entered the front door. He slipped when his wet shoes hit the hardwood and then he dashed upstairs. His mind was clouded.

What would he say to Gardner when he reached the attic?

He wasn't able to hide the warmth that flowed within him when the image of Cherri erupted into his mind.

2

In the garage, the wooden planks that made up the walls began to shake. Dust kicked up. Jezebeth, still vibrating and exposed to the world, shuffled into the early morning darkness. She was being vacuumed from the garage. Depression and sorrow encompassed her.

Sammael stood in front of her as she exited through the side door. His arms were crossed and he was smiling. A curl of sarcasm dangled from his face. He shook his head.

"I think I'll take it from here. You're just not that good. I sure hope you had a good time, though. And don't worry, you'll only get better," he said, crooning his neck toward the cornfield. The surface plain of existence opened and the corn parted. The long stalks looked like they had been stretched into an oval of black.

A white haze flowed forward, and the flames of searing hell opened. The heat blasted into the world as it beckoned Jezebeth.

She was a swarm of ash. Each particle of her being began to blacken into flakes of charred matter. The flakes broke off and sifted through the air into the opening in the cornfield. Rage filled her heart. Sorrow glazed her thoughts. She didn't want to go. There was no reward for her failure. The Dark Master wouldn't be pleased, and she would be punished. There would be ridicule and laughter.

As if hooks had sunk into her flesh, she was pulled toward the opening. Her charred skin shedding as she went. Her voice lowered to a growl, and she hissed. She resisted, but there was nothing to grab onto. She was unable to stop. She was dragged forward, like a child being dragged to the dentist's office. Not wanting to go but knowing there was no other option.

She turned, once, to watch as Sammael smiled. He waved while laughing in his sinister way. The flames engulfed her and then she erupted into a fiery cluster. She was gone. The porthole was closed and the corn peeled back into place as though it had never been touched. .

Then, silence.

3

Sammael stared at the cornfield for a moment. He knew the Unholy One demanded the slaughter of these people. Of Gardner. He wouldn't let him down. He couldn't.

Sammael turned toward the farmhouse. His arms fell to the side and his hands bunched into fists while his shoulders shrugged. He watched the house. He sized it up like a boxer studying his opponent while looking for the perfect weakness, the right spot to strike.

Stepping forward, Sammael vowed the games were over. There was no more time to play. He could feel the Unholy One's anxiousness. It wasn't wise to disappoint the Unholy One. The torment would be infinite. He didn't have much time to destroy Gardner, and he certainly wouldn't be able to possess Donna anymore. That would take too much time. Killing them would suffice.

He could taste Gardner's blood.

He strode to the front of the house, peeked up to the attic window. He knew *they* had gathered up there. He could feel it. *They* were probably watching him, too. He smiled up at the window as he visualized the attic.

He painted a picture of what it would look like when he finished ripping them to pieces. He imagined blood covering every inch of the room. He would litter the floor with rolling heads and shredded body parts while he would dance in their innards. In the middle of the room, he imagined himself standing before his masterpiece. He would bathe in their blood.

Chapter 27

1

Donna stood near the attic window. Although she was tired, she stood alert. She trembled at the sight of Sammael as she watched him move across the lawn, staring up into the window, wearing a maniacal grin. His glare held awful intent. His eyes gleamed like white globes.

It seemed like he was staring into the dark future; enjoying what he saw. He was going to attack, soon. The time had come. She stepped back from the window. The sound of hammering feet thundered across the hardwood floor and continued up the staircase. Her attention drifted toward the small door in the attic. She shifted her gaze toward her husband. He opened the hatch. He was calm. There was no immediate danger.

"It's Winny." Cherri announced.

Cherri stepped forward, excitedly. She looked anxiously from Donna to Gardner and asked, "Are you sure?"

Gardner nodded slowly. "I saw it. He's seen the darkness and escaped it. He will fight with us."

Winny's head peered into the attic.

"It's me. I swear it's really me. Sammael is coming."

Gardner helped Winny up the stairs. He leapt up from the hatch and then closed the retractable staircase. A cloud of dust powdered Winny's face when the hatch slammed shut. Donna watched as Winny's eager eyes drifted toward Cherri.

Donna could see the relief and comfort on Winny's face when he laid eyes on Cherri. In turn, Cherri's smile lifted from her face. Her teeth jutted forward, and she leaned forward as if to lunge at him.

Within seconds, they were holding each other. Donna was familiar with the emotions they were feeling. It was the comfort that stemmed from longing. *These two had been thinking about each other.* They took refuge in each other's presence. She'd experienced these feelings many times with her husband. She was glad Winny and Cherri had found a moment's joy even though it would not last long.

And it didn't.

Winny parted from Cherri. He turned his attention to Gardner.

"They tried to take me," Winny explained. "It felt like I was being lit on fire. That's the best way I can explain it."

Gardner was unfazed. He'd heard it all before.

"The battle is going to unfold. We're either going to concur the demon, or we'll fall prey to it," Gardner said. He stared straight into Donna's eyes. He looked as though he was looking for the right words to describe what needed to be said. Everyone's blood curdled when he spoke. The time was now, and they would fight and be triumphant. Or they would die, horribly.

Everyone was silent, terrified.

2

Gardner's lips moved, but nothing came out. He didn't know how to say what he needed to say. Normally, he was good with words, but not now. He didn't know how to tell everyone that this was *it*, that their lives depended on what would happen in the next few moments.

Minutes earlier, Gardner was given a vision. The vision had been dark, and he'd seen the future battle from a distance. It was uncertain and hazy. The vision concluded with a dark cloud over his house. What he'd seen was vague, but it left him mortified.

He heard the screams of the innocent. But the demon would not win this battle. This he knew. That should have been reassuring, but it wasn't. The demon would lose, but it would take something from this group, something dear. Sadness washed over Gardner as he realized the loss would be great. Greater than it had already been.

He thought about the loss of Garth and how heart wrenching it had been. Worse yet, Gardner's despair would dig much deeper before the end of this awful night. The possession of Garth was terrible, but it was just the beginning. For a moment, he'd accepted that Garth was dead, at least his human self even though Garth could still be alive, but he doubted it. Sammael would destroy Garth from the inside out.

Gardner snapped back to his reality. His vision had been hazy—as to what would be lost—but he knew more carnage was ahead.

He had to warn the group of what was in store.

"This battle we are about to fight., I believe we will succeed…but at the price of a great travesty. I haven't been given a clear vision as to what the outcome will be in its entirety. I know the conclusion, how this night will end. Everything that is going to happen has already been written. First of all…" Gardner looked directly at Winny. "You *must* fight the demon…and win at any cost. No matter what shape it comes in. Do you know what that means, Winny?"

Winny's eyebrows sprung upward. His eyes moistened. A crazed excitement illuminated his face. "When I escaped from the first demon, I walked out of the garage and saw Sammael. I became so angry I wasn't afraid anymore. It didn't matter what the demon did because I wouldn't give in to him. I told him to leave my brother alone…and for a minute Garth came back, and he begged me to help him. I have faith it was him."

Gardner believed him. It was the truth, and he also believed Winny was capable of fighting the demon. His fight might be enough to bring Garth out of the hell he was captured in. If Winny had faith, and believed in it, then it could happen. Only pure goodness could bring out the living. Gardner felt—for the first time—that there was a chance for Garth.

"Do you believe we can save him?" Gardner asked.

Bobbing his head successively, Winny answered, "Yes. I *know* we can. I believe it."

"Then we will," Gardner returned. "But be prepared for the attack upon us…"

He wanted to say more, but suddenly the hatch in the floor sprung forward. It crashed into the floor, hard. The wood square broke into pieces. The hinges spat across the attic, and the tiny splinters of wood created a cloud. A snake shot forward from the hole in the attic floor.

One of the demon's snakes slithered into the attic like an attacking cobra. It retracted its hooks. Quickly, it shot behind Donna. She didn't have time to react. She didn't even see it. It coiled around Donna's neck and tugged her backward. Sammael emerged from the hatch. He stood, digging his razor-sharp daggers into Donna's soft flesh, tearing her neck open. Her eyes shot toward Gardner.

Gardner stood, horrified, silent, as if the world had slowed to a crawl, while Donna's throat was torn open. Her eyes turned black. Blood gushed to the floor in a massive splash and soaked the wood planks. Her skin turned ashen. Gardner wanted to scream, but he could only stare. He watched Donna's eyes as her life left her.

Cherri screamed and ran to Donna. She tried to rip the snake from Donna's neck, but it recoiled. Cherri tried to cover Donna's wound. She pressed her hands against Donna's gash. The blood pumped between Cherri's fingers. She couldn't stop the bleeding. Donna was dead within seconds.

Gardner cried out.

He was angry with God.

3

Sammael's snakelike arm coiled around Donna's body. After it ripped her neck open, it tossed her down from the attic. It launched her into the hallway while Cherri attempted to help her.

Donna's lifeless body smacked the hallway floor. A heavy thud, her head slammed against the hallway wall. Her throat continued to bleed. Her eyes remained open. She stared, lifelessly, down the hall. The demon's satisfaction was accentuated. Its eyes gleamed white. He rejoiced with sinister pleasure.

He'd been allowed to kill her. He'd wanted this for years. His pleasure was heightened. He felt like a king. He was granted his kill. He hadn't been sure if the Unholy One was going to allow it. Earlier, he'd been denied. There were restrictions on what he could and could not do. It wasn't up to him.

Sometimes he was only able to encourage his victims. His encouragement would lead to self-destruction. He'd aided in many deaths and evil deeds. With a simple whisper, he would plant a seed. To a weak person—someone with lack of faith—a whisper would suffice.

In the end, the demon's whisper would destroy them, somehow. His whispers could show a man that his wife was cheating, when in fact she was not. The whisper encouraged the thought and the thought encouraged the action. Sammael was a master of deception.

He would watch his planted seeds bloom into despair. His victims would take their own lives or cause another person to kill for them. Sammael was good at his job. On many occasions, he'd been able to make men perform the atrocious. On many other occasions, he'd been able to let men destroy the lives of others, before taking their own life. Sammael enjoyed his dark works—*his whispers.*

Now, standing in the hallway, he relished at the sight of the dead woman, Donna, as she bled all over the floor. Sammael felt the lips of Garth's mouth stretch into a gleeful smile. He could feel Gardner's rage building. He was still in the attic. There was no way Gardner could resist vengeance.

Sammael placed Gardner in a weakened state. Gardner would self-destruct. And there was nothing that could make Sammael feel more content.

To Sammael, it would be ultimately satisfying to watch Gardner take his own life.

If Gardner died by his own hand, Sammael would dance over his corpse. He'd savor the body while it rotted.

Gardner's soul would burn.

4

Winny stood at the edge of the hatch in the attic, shocked. Donna's demise had taken him by surprise. He faced away, unable to look at what was happening to her. Agony stung. It felt like sharp needles dancing across the lining of his stomach. As best he could, he shook off the atrocity.

They needed their heads in the fight. Later, there would be time for grief and mourning. They didn't know if Gardner was out of commission. Plus, it was unimaginable to think about what was running through Gardner's mind.

Winny stepped away from the hatch. Sammael could easily grab him from where he stood and he didn't want to die, definitely not at the hands of Sammael. Also, he didn't want Gardner to slip into the hallway. It would be the end of him. This is what Gardner had told them about earlier, the demon had gotten to him.

It owned him.

Judging by the mad expression on Gardner's face, Winny knew what Gardner intended to do. Sure, he was going to fight. They wouldn't be able to stop him. His anger had gotten the best of him. But the fight would be useless. If he were to fight in the name of rage it would kill him. Gardner would defeat himself if he fought with no logic or reason.

Winny was easily able to understand that, in this moment, Gardner only knew vengeance. He would go into this fight with Sammael with or without the power of good. If he fought wild, he would be destroyed. Winny knew this in his heart.

"Father Gardner," Winny called out. "It wants you to go down there. Don't let it beat you. If you do this, you will fail the test."

Gardner turned to Winny with red fiery eyes. They looked demonic, like Sammael's.

"If you go down there, the demon will win, and you will…"

"It's already won," Gardner snapped back. His voice was low, monotone. The creases at the corners of his aging eyes folded deep. His tired, angry face suddenly sparked with determination. "And now, I need to do what is meant to be done—what is written."

Winny braced himself to hold Gardner back. He stepped in front of the hatch, looking back after each step. Sammael could easily make his way into the attic. Winny didn't like feeling this vulnerable.

Cherri stood in the corner, frozen with terror. She wiped her eyes. Winny wanted to comfort her. He knew she'd developed a connection with Donna. They cared for each other. She had died a horrible death. Winny stopped thinking about Donna. Right now, they needed to contain Gardner. Keep him sane until after they dealt with Sammael.

If Gardner went into the hallway, and let the demon destroy him, Winny and Cherri were destined to be destroyed as well. They didn't know how to fight such a powerful enemy. But the demon knew how to fight *them*. It had been destroying humans for centuries.

The reality of the situation took hold and Winny's blood turned icy. The sweat which ran down his forehead was cold, and his hands shook. If he were to speak, his voice would tremble. It would slur. And then, another terrible thing happened. Sammael began to cackle; mad like a loon. He stood, facing up, beneath the hatch. He called up to Gardner.

"Father Gardner? I know you can hear me. I think we have some business to attend to down here. Don't you think? I'll do awful things to her, Gardner. I'm not finished."

Gardner strutted forward. The wooden planks beneath his feet wobbled. Gardner put all his weight into each step. Winny stood in front of Gardner and grabbed his shoulder. Winny pushed forward. Gardner pushed back. Winny stumbled to the side and Gardner lunged with staggering tenacity. Winny was forced to let up. He couldn't stop him.

Cherri stepped forward and called out to Gardner. It was her last attempt. "If you leave us, we're done. That thing will kill us. We don't know how to fight it. We need you."

Gardner turned to Cherri. The madness in his eyes was present but diluted. He looked like he was going to scream. He settled. It was as if the gentle voice of a woman was enough. His eyes drooped and he stopped fighting.

"You will fight him. I've seen it in my vision." Gardner looked to Winny then Cherri. "…and you will walk out of this house, victorious. I can't say the same for myself. I don't know if I want to. My fate has been written. I accept my destiny. I'll do what I can, and I pray God will keep me."

"That doesn't have to be true. You can use your anger to fight. You can seek your vengeance. You can help us. We can all leave here together. We'll mourn Donna when we can," Cherri pleaded. Tears ran from her eyes, in quick currents.

Gardner pondered what she'd said. Cherri had gotten to him. It made sense. Winny loosened up for just a moment.

Cherri and Winny lowered their guard.

It was too late.

Gardner jumped down the hatch and into the hallway.

5

Gardner scurried down the hatch. Fury fused into every cell of his body. Rage possessed his thoughts and his soul. It drove him. For the first time in his life, he was angry with God; God who had tasked him with so much.

He spent so many years of his life serving him.

All he wanted was for his life to be simple and enjoyable. After fighting off so much evil, he felt entitled to it. It was his right. But now, his sweet Donna was taken from him. His reason for living was gone. All his focus funneled into fighting Sammael. He didn't care if he was to be killed. He needed to strike the demon. Afterward, if he were to be killed, at least the nightmare would be over.

This thought suddenly snapped his sanity back. The wellbeing of Winny, Garth, and Cherri weighed in on his mind, but he didn't know if it was enough to stop him.

Normally a logical man, even when it came to matters of the supernatural, Gardner controlled his anger. But now, his rage hit its boiling point. Gardner was going to explode. Even the power of prayer wouldn't stop him.

In the hallway, he gained his footing. Standing before him, the demon Sammael stood. His fists were clenched. Snakes slithered across and around him. They ran between his legs, around his neck, and waved up his chest. He was covered in the scaly creatures. They hissed and snapped at Gardner.

This was the demon. The demon he'd fought all those years ago…and had beaten all those years ago. Gardner's rage was going to destroy him. He didn't care. He lunged forward as the snakes sprang at him.

Sprinting down the hall, as though he'd be able to tackle Sammael to the ground, Gardner's logic sunk in. If he were to go through with this—let the anger and insanity of what had happened get the best of him—he would not only lose and be defeated, but he would fail the test. That's what this was—a test.

If he failed, his great works would be disregarded. He'd be sent to a place where Sammael would laugh and torment him, forever. But in this moment, he disregarded the idea. His humanity got the best of him.

He didn't care.

And as Gardner slammed his body into Sammael's torso and tackled him to the ground, his fury escalated, peaked, and then dissipated. The laughter on Sammael's face was overwhelming. The anger returned. It seemed like the child of his mind was turning the light switch of anger on and then off, over and over again. The switch released logic and anger, logic and anger. Sammael watched Gardner's emotions flash back and forth across his face.

Gardner saw how delighted the demon had become.

Gardner hoped for an answer, but there were no visions. There was only simple emotion and Gardner couldn't escape it. When he looked across the hallway and saw his wife's corpse lying in a pool of blood, his anger further reddened. It snatched the sanity from his weary mind. He screamed, "You vile piece of filth!"

In that moment, he didn't know if he was speaking to the demon or to his God.

6

Winny stood with Cherri in the attic. They were lost, excited, and didn't know what to do. Standing defensively, Cherri knew one of them or both of them would have to jump down and fight. Raising a finger, Winny snapped his attention toward Cherri.

"I think I can help him." Winny said.

Cherri watched Winny say this, but she didn't believe it. What she knew about Gardner was that he was a man who could fight and defeat something like a demon. Winny was a simple man. He couldn't defeat Sammael. Not even with an army of ten thousand. He just wasn't capable.

"When I was outside with Garth…well…not Garth, but that thing, I begged for it to let my brother go. For a moment, Garth came back. It worked."

"You don't know that it was Garth—not for sure. It was probably the demon playing his tricks on you, making you believe it was Garth when it wasn't. He was lowering your guard, trying to make you believe you could make a difference when you couldn't."

Cherri suddenly realized what she'd done. She'd stripped away Winny's hope. For a moment that was all he had. Without hope they might as well jump down into the hallway and give up. Let the demon destroy them. When Winny lowered his head to look at Cherri, her stomach felt like it was filled with ice. But Winny turned to her and said, "Maybe you've given up, but I haven't. You can either help me, or you can stay here and hope for the best. Either way, I'm going to try."

Before Cherri had a chance to retort, Winny jumped down the hatch, into the hallway.

Cherri's nerves shot into high gear. She didn't know what to do. She wanted to help Winny. Even if she failed, at least it would be a valiant effort, even if the outcome was death. *And maybe that would be fine.* If she fought, then maybe she would die quickly, with no pain.

Cherri stepped forward. She glanced downward. She heard the shouts and screams of Gardner and Winny. Above their cries, she heard the demon laughing.

For the first time, in a long time, she closed her eyes and prayed. She asked for guidance. She'd never gone to church a day in her life. She was vaguely aware of religion at all. She didn't know what she was doing when she bowed her head. She asked God to help her—*to help them.*

With shaky legs, Cherri stood and moved toward the hatch. Slowly, she stepped down into the madness that awaited her.

7

Sammael clamped his hand around Gardner's throat, tight. His elongated fingers dug into the skin on the back of his neck, palm smothering his Adam's apple. Gardner's feet dangled, scissor-kicking in the air. They danced, four inches off the floor. Winny dropped, slinked back, and curled in a ball behind them.

Cherri twisted in order to see Donna.

She was lying in a slippery pool of blood that formed above her head like a vile halo. Sadness consumed Cherri.

Quick as her sadness set, it was gone. It was replaced with fear. Sammael was watching Cherri and smiling. He'd taken the boyish face of Garth and turned it into a sinister grin, reflecting the death and destruction he sought. Cherri was sick of being tormented by this vile thing, tired of being bullied.

She was tired of feeling afraid. She was fed up with being exhausted. Most of all, she was sick of the unknown. Even more, she was sick of the demon, *her demon*. Sammael could see this. It was written upon her face. The demon received great pleasure in destroying Gardner, but still, he couldn't help but refocus his attention to Cherri, as though he couldn't turn away from the opportunity to destroy something new—fresh meat.

Gardner wasn't enough.

The demon savored the consumption of everything good. His appetite was insatiable. Cherri was mocking him; because her fear of him was diluted. The fear she should have felt was replaced with annoyance. Her limit had been reached.

Sammael's maniacal grin fell into an eager, fearfully intense stare. He tilted his head in Gardner's direction, eyes darting forward, intently. The demon was tormented. It couldn't choose—it's appetite for flesh was selfish. The demon wanted everything, to kill all.

He must be thinking: destroy what he had or go for the girl?

A scaly snake shot from Sammael's mouth, it coiled around Gardner's neck and, even though it was dark, Cherri could see Gardner gasping for air. His eyes ballooned and bulged. His skin flushed crimson and then purple.

The floorboards creaked. Dust jumped. Gardner hit the hallway floor like a sack of dirt. Sammael had squeezed the wind out from him, causing him to pass out—he'd choked consciousness from him.

Cherri didn't know what came next.

Sammael locked eyes with her. With each breath he took he seemed to enlarge. Looming larger again as he stepped toward her. Cherri didn't budge. She couldn't. The thought of death and dying swirled erratically through her spinning head.

Flashes of her childhood; all of the worst things she'd done in her life and all the good she'd done accumulated in her mind like cumulus clouds. It seemed, for the moment, that Sammael didn't matter. The only point that mattered was doing the right thing—now, when it counted.

It didn't matter if she died in the process, she would be redeemed. She didn't back down. She stood tall. Her stance was solid as the beast hovered near her. She smelled its foul breath. Its pungent odor was remnant of burned and rotting flesh.

"You can kill me, but you won't defeat me. So get on with it!"

The maniacal smile illuminated Sammael's face as though he'd never enjoyed a more extravagant invitation. His face was seized with sinister glee.

8

Sharp pins and needles struck every molecule of Winny's being as his consciousness returned. His legs, arms, body, and mind were famished and stung horribly. For a quick moment, he didn't know if he could rise. His body was giving up. Pain coursed his torso—every joint, muscle and bone ached.

The fight had taken its toll on him. He was beaten. He didn't know if he could handle any more strain. Shaking his head, facing forward, he looked to Cherri as she faced off with the demon, a stubbornly fierce aura radiated from her. It made the demon cringe.

The surge of energy that flowed through Winny when he realized Cherri wasn't scared inspired him to flex into a straight plank and then stand. He hobbled toward her.

Sammael didn't budge as Winny stumbled forward. A clicking sound tapped through the air. The *slithering thing* shot from Sammael's mouth. Its jaws snapped while it rounded the demon's lips and shot backward. The look upon Cherri's angered face seemed to be screaming: *grab that stupid thing and twist it till he chokes*!

As if synchronicity caught step with Winny's thoughts, he grabbed the slithery snake and held it tight in his grip. He pulled the fibered serpent taut and tried to rip it in two. Sammael stumbled backward. In the moment that it took for Sammael to spin around, Winny saw the fear of *falling* burn across Sammael's face. Mass confusion seized him as if he couldn't fathom being beaten by these *people*.

And then, Winny saw his brother return to his rightful body. Garth was back—in his own skin—where he belonged. It was miraculous. Winny had never felt a more vivacious sense of relief; never in his life.

Winny stretched the snake and yanked it hard. He was sure he'd ripped it from the demon's mouth. He hoped he wasn't hurting Garth in the process. It hadn't ripped free, but it wanted to. Grath was rejecting the snake, trying to spit it out, biting on it. Winny could feel the snake tearing when he shifted his hand and looped it. It was uprooting like a tree in a tornado.

"Let him go, you puke!" Winny screamed as the snake unhooked from Garth's mouth and shot forward, sliding through his hand and sending Winny to the floor. He let go of the snake.

Winny was utterly amazed by what had taken place. Determined, he quickly jumped to his feet. He'd hurt the demon. A surge of confidence ran through him. The beast that stood dominant throughout the night was being defeated. It was being reduced to a slim, muscle-like snake that slithered across the floor toward Gardner. It was pathetic looking.

Gardner stirred as the snake made its way toward him.

9

Garth was in a dark place. Screams rang out from every corner, but he couldn't see anyone or anything. The foul odor surrounding him kept him nauseated. The thin layer of skin shrink-wrapping him to the wall felt like acid on his flesh.

He was being held captive in a dark dungeon. Visibility was limited. His blood was oily and it burned. The skin restraints holding him to the wall felt loose and thin. The texture was deceiving; as hard as he'd been trying to tear through it, the elasticity was too strong. It only stretched when he attempted it.

He'd began to give up hope, fast. He didn't know how long he could stand being held here. But then, a *feeling* came to him, a welcomed sensation. It was as if someone had torn through his binds from the opposite side. *It was Winny.* He knew it. He could sense his brother.

Right then, Garth couldn't think of anyone he'd rather see than his brother. He wanted to see him badly. He began gritting his teeth as he did when excited. For another moment, it felt like the indestructible restraints binding him to this awful place had been disabled.

There were a few moments, earlier, when he'd gone from this dark place and wound up back in his own body. The last time he'd awoken, he'd been sitting on top of a garage staring down at Winny. It was like coming out of a blackout.

In that moment, he felt the same freedoms then he was feeling now. He wanted to break apart from this hellish prison. Suddenly, he felt his brother's anger. It sucked him back into the only world that made sense, the world of the living. Garth was punching through his restraints. He could see the layered skin of restraint splitting roughly as if being slashed with a saw. Wet, jagged pieces fell to the murky floor.

And then he was free, released from this place.

Sobering and quick, Garth stood. He didn't recognize where he was, but there was a familiarity about it. None of that mattered because Winny stood a few feet from him. He looked scared, relieved, and furious all at once. The redhaired girl was there, too. He didn't mind. It was even a relief to see her. His eyes focused on his brother. He fought to contain the smile. Reality struck. They were still in danger.

There was something very wrong happening.

Donna Gardner was lying on the wood floor. A pool of blood surrounded her. It soaked into her sun-bleached hair making it appear black. Father Gardner crawled in Donna's direction. His eyes were raw and fiery. His fury was unavoidable as he reached out to touch his wife.

Then, the slithering thing caught Garth's attention and he watched as it darted toward Gardner, wiggling fast in a smooth S-shape. Garth jumped forward, slamming his boot down hard on the snake. The snake screamed as Garth's boot crushed the middle of it. The head and tail leapt in both directions then settled. Lime green fluid ejected from its mouth, oozing yellow foam followed.

Leaning down, Garth tried to grab the slippery serpent, but it slipped through his fingers and slid across Gardner and underneath Donna.

10

Scratching, digging, and clawing at the floor, Gardner tried to grab the snake. It was threatening to touch Donna. Gardner wouldn't allow the vileness of Sammael to touch his sweet Donna, never. Sammael was able to kill her, but Gardner wouldn't allow the demon to possess her. Or desecrate her body in any way.

On the brink of madness, Gardner stood above Donna, his eyes frantically searching for the slithering demon. It was moving slow. It had a stammer to its wiggle—the result of Garth stomping on it.

Wait.

How and why had Garth done that?

Gardner's head spun toward Garth. Just seconds ago, Sammael had been wearing Garth's body as his black mask. Gardner half expected Garth's boot to slam down on his face as it had the snake. But then, he caught Garth's eyes and saw the life living within them. The demon had been expelled from Garth.

Gardner didn't think it could be done. He'd written Garth off for dead. Sammael was death to most of his hosts. For a moment, he forgot about Donna. He was ecstatic about this miracle, this strength. Winny was right when he said his brother wasn't doomed.

Most victims of unholy occupancy died during the period of possession. Gardner had talked with many surviving victims of possession and they'd all told a similar tale. That they'd awoken in a dark place. It was black and everything was foul. Gardner imagined the place as some kind of hellish lobby, where souls were imprisoned until the body died or was cleansed. It was a twisted sort of Limbo.

Logic crashed hard. Images of Donna drifted in. Gardner's last thoughts were of quitting. Donna was gone and he wanted to die. He wanted Sammael to take him. But now, even as sadness and madness melded together, the logic of what needed to happen started to set in. He needed to be strong for Garth, Winny, and Cherri. Not to mention Donna. She would be tormented by the thought of him giving in to the demon. He couldn't fathom disappointing her.

Together, Gardner, Winny, Garth and Cherri could win this battle. No matter how devastated Gardner was over what had happened to Donna, he needed to be strong for these kids. He'd held off from this fight for too long. He needed to step to the challenge presented before him.

He was being tested.

Prying his eyes away from his wife, he glanced to Garth and asked, "What's happened?"

Garth tilted his head, still looking for the *slime* trailing across the floor. "That thing…it came out of me and then it crawled over your way," he replied, still not looking at

Gardner. His eyes floated eagerly across the floor, looking for the snake. "Is that…snake…is that the demon?"

Then he saw Donna's chest rise and he knew, right away, it was the snake tearing Donna apart from the inside. It was feasting on her insides. It had gotten into her. That is what the demon did—devoured the flesh and destroyed life. Its nourishment was the taste of rotting flesh and tormented souls.

Gardner wanted to cry while he watched his wife's body being desecrated, vandalized. Cherri ran to Gardner and pulled on his hand. He resisted at first but soon allowed himself to go with her.

The three of them watched-on as the snake tore at Donna's insides.

The vision came to Gardner, bright and full of life.

11

Donna was present in Gardner's vision. She was well. She was radiant and more than beautiful. She was full of life and vibrant. She appeared young, no older than eighteen. She wore a white dress that waved in the light breeze. A haze of white light surrounded her flawless appearance. There was no smile on her intense expression.

Her youth was intimidating. She was the most beautiful creature that had ever passed Gardner's eyes.

In the vision, they were in some kind of paradise. The grass was long and silky. The water was blue. It looked turquoise. It was the clearest sky Gardner had ever seen. Massive white clouds floated by slowly.

Donna came to him and touched his face. Her fingers were warm. They felt soothing while they ran down his cheek. It felt like she was tracing his face with sunlight. Her smell was fresh as lilac as it swarmed him with ease.

Finally, she smiled at him and nodded. There were no words, only understanding. There didn't need to be any words. She was telling him to help the kids. To go back and display his goodness with the gift he'd been given from the highest power. And in that moment, he knew he would be with her again.

That was the message: Good men must strive for better. It was simple.

And when Gardner returned from his vision, he looked past the realm in which his hallway was made of a floor, two walls, and a ceiling. His sight brought on the true nature of their setting.

There was a parasite within the company of goodness. It needed to be cast away before *it* caused any more harm. Gardner looked to the vile thing as it lay on the floor devouring what was left of the human body belonging to Donna's beautiful soul. He reached down, grabbed the vile parasite, held it firmly in his hand and brought it to the backyard.

Gardner stood at the edge of the cornfield where the world of fire opened and the sky peeled back. He threw the demon like it was a bloodsucking slug, into the fire. It spun and convulsed as it was vacuumed into the incinerator.

While it fumbled and charred, Gardner felt the rage of defeat prying at the demon. Sammael had been defeated, yet again, by Gardner. And Gardner felt his wife's presence. She was his partner in life, and he would see her in the afterlife. He enjoyed her presence as the porthole between Hell and Earth closed.

There was only the corn again. The sky had begun to turn a magnificent orange. There were accents of purple in the clouds. It was a sight to savor.

Gardner walked back to the porch steps where he and Donna had spent many hours sitting. He wished he could feel her next to him. He couldn't, she was gone. There was emptiness. But what he could feel was the warmness of his new friends.

Garth, Winny, and Cherri approached carefully. Their footsteps were soft, almost silent. They looked to each other and then slowly to him.

"Is it over?" Cherri asked

12

"It's never over. The demon is gone, but not dead. Evil never dies, only suppressed. It's locked away for now and we can go on with our lives. We can leave these demons behind us and move on the best way that we know how. Our struggle is to be good. Being a good person is hard enough…for anyone."

The cool morning silence resonated. The birds began to chirp, and the first glimmers of sunlight danced across the cornfields. Standing side by side, they took in the first light of the new day. The moment didn't last. For now, they had many ordeals. A million details needed to be sorted out. The resting town would soon be plagued with the previous night's slaughter, the demonic crime.

Winny listened, closely, to what Gardner said, but he didn't know if the answer had been stated. It seemed odd that this nightmare had concluded. That in the end, all it took was goodwill and heart. The raging battle he thought would ensue wasn't as it played out in his mind. To Winny, it seemed as though, in the end, it would have taken a platoon of heavily armed Marines to destroy the evil that had torn into their lives on this hellish night in August.

"I see." Winny spoke up. "Those things. The Demons. They're gone for now. They sure took a lot from us. And we'll have to go through the rest of our lives tormented by what happened. But we'll manage. Life will go on," Winny continued saying while attempting to smile. He was trying to set everyone at ease, even if it was for only a moment.

Garth looked to his brother. He cupped his shoulder and said, "I thought I was in the worst kind of trouble. That place I was in, it was dark. I thought—I knew—that I would die there. But you never gave up hope. You saved me from my stubborn self, Winny. I don't know what comes next, but thanks." He looked to the liquor store down the hill. "We have a lot to answer for."

Gardner stood, staring at the liquor store along with the Gasper brothers.

"The answers will come. We'll let those who need deal with this, deal with this."

"I don't understand," Garth said.

"In the decades of dealing with this brand of…evil, I've found that a rational answer is always made available for those who need rationale."

"I think he's saying that everything is going to be fine," Winny chimed in.

Cherri dropped her small hand from Winny's grasp and brought it up to Gardner's face. Her fingers ran down his weathered cheeks. Her eyes were red with exhaustion. She managed a smile and said, "You'll see her again."

The corners of Gardner's eyes crinkled, and his eyelashes moistened. He nodded and said, "I need to be with my wife now." He walked across his lawn and entered his house through the back door.

Winny, Cherri, and Garth stood silent while the pink tone of the early morning sun rose in east. With the bright rays of the sun, they were famished. Not wanting to think about what would happen next, they couldn't help but think about the next few days, weeks, and possibly a lot longer. They would meet many trials.

Garth's lips stretched upward and his teeth jutted forward. A hearty chuckle fell from his lips. He turned to

Winny. "The last customer…The last customer is always the worst."

And despite all that had happened, Cherri, Garth, and Winny couldn't hold back their laughter.

Chapter 28

1

The laughing stopped. Garth's sentiment fell and he brought up the reality that they would need to explain what had happened at the liquor store, not to mention there were two dead bodies at Gardner's farmhouse. Garth had faith they would be able to answer the *questions* correctly.

The reality was that there were dead bodies, a liquor store had been destroyed and there was no logical explanation. Remembering what Gardner had told them about rational answers, they made their way down to the liquor store.

Chapter 29

1

A few hours had passed and the sun was bright in the morning sky. It was about to be another scorcher. It was Sunday. The first police car arrived while Winny and Cherri stood near the cash register debating whether or not they would talk of the robbery. The Gasper boys had decided they could leave Cherri out of it.

But Cherri felt that, given what had happened, she could no longer lie. *She didn't want to.* Winny couldn't bear the thought of what would happen to her if she were to leave him. Neither of them wanted her behind bars. Not even Garth.

And the thought of her going to jail for a long stretch was even worse. Besides, nothing had been stolen during the robbery. There was significant damage to the store, but they were willing to let that go. It wasn't Cherri's fault.

"We don't even know each other. What if we neglect to tell the police *exactly* what happened and then a few months from now you find that you don't want me around?" Cherri asked, her head low.

"We don't know our childhood history. We don't know each other's parents. We don't know a lot of things…but we made it through last night and I'd say that has to count for something. I trust you and you can trust me." He smiled. "Our souls are fond of each other. I want to be with you. I want to know you."

Cherri's raw face leaked tears and Winny knew she'd felt his sincerity. He couldn't explain it. *It was one of those things—indescribable.* He was destined to be with this girl and they both knew it.

2

Officer Rick Laymon was the first officer to respond to the liquor store. He walked through the parking lot, skeptical. His glasses kept slipping down the bridge of his nose. It annoyed him. Right now, it was even worse.

He had many things to deal with. At the start of his shift, he'd learned of what had happened in town. The townsfolk had found the dead police officers over an hour ago. There were detectives investigating an elderly couple who had been murdered and they'd found another woman dead in the back alley behind the ice cream shop on Main Street.

There was a mess to be cleaned up. There were many answers that needed to be found. The town wouldn't stand for this, not without answers. This was the worst crime wave to ever hit Dodge Junction. And Laymon wouldn't take it lightly. He would do whatever it took to do his job competently.

Walking through the parking lot, the glass crunched beneath his combat boots and his heart pounded beneath his ribs. His breath was quick. He was nervous. The violence that had gone nearly undetected throughout Dodge Junction was enough to have every law official in a state of paranoia.

Officer Laymon was no different.

When he entered the liquor store and heard Garth Gasper call out from the back office, "In here, officer!" he pulled his gun and held it shakily in front of his chest.

"Is everyone all right?" he asked, not knowing where he'd found the words.

"We're okay!" Winny called out from behind the register.

Laymon lowered his standard issue nine millimeter berretta. "Do we know what happened here?"

3

Surprisingly, Garth and Winny weren't as nervous as they'd assumed. The answers came easy. It seemed as if their mouths were moving, but the answers were coming from someplace else. Their faces held a blank pause when the officer entered the store.

Winny knew Garth would handle the immediate explanation. He was better at explaining most things. And Garth's face insinuated he would prefer to explain while he slightly frowned at Winny and nudged his head, motioning for them to go outside.

Cherri stood silent next to Winny. Her eyes were heavy. Bags had settled beneath them.

Winny looked to the officer and asked, "May we go outside and catch some air?"

Laymon nodded. Winny and Cherri stepped into the humid morning air.

Winny heard Garth speak with the officer. Garth was telling the truth yet leaving out the details which would not be understood by the officer.

Standing in the warm summer sun, Winny leaned down to Cherri and ran his fingers through her tangled red hair.

"I want you to stay."

"Are you sure? I mean, you won't get sick of me?"

Winny frowned. "I might get sick of you."

Cherri cringed.

Winny smiled. "But I want you to stay, anyway."

"I want to…stay."

Slowly coming together, Winny's eyes danced across Cherri's face, their lips met. And despite the adrenaline and the stress emanating from the hellish nightmare of the past night, they received heaven as they kissed for the first time. Her lips were paradise.

4

The farmhouse was a grim sight. The dead girl in the yard, baking in sun, added a macabre garnish to the property. Inside, upstairs, down the hallway, Gardner knelt beside his wife. The body lying on the floor hardly resembled his Donna. When he touched her, her skin was cold. Her face was turning purple, and her lips were blue. The blank stare in her dead eyes was hardening. They looked like small wax globes.

Gardner's grief hit heavier than he could have imagined. His heart ached. His stomach was hollow. He still wanted to die. Earlier, his vision of Donna had been pleasant. He attempted to hold onto that image, the one of her in his vision.

She'd been perfect; an angel. But now, the desecration of what had happened to her physical body was disturbing him. He began sobbing. If he was to die, then he would see her again, sooner. But there were things he needed to do before that could happen.

Gardner had kept his *gift* dormant for too long. He needed to work on becoming familiar with his blessing again.

He stood and strode down the stairs toward the living room. He pushed the large rectangular wooden door open. He squinted when the brightness of the fresh new day struck his gentle eyes. The red and blue lights flashing from the liquor store below danced in the bright morning sunshine.

Closing the door, Gardner walked toward the lights.

Epilogue

1

Gardner, Winny, Garth, and Cherri were able to answer the questions that had been asked by the local law enforcement. They'd left out the supernatural details, which hadn't been difficult. Gardner's group had been revealed as living victims.

Their explanations weren't received as mad, as they feared they would. And in the end, the murder, destruction, and blame fell upon Rod Barton and Patty King. It was unveiled that they were a team of serial killers who had left a trail of bodies and mayhem strewn across the entirety of the Northern Midwest, from Iowa to Wisconsin.

The statements made by Garth, Winny, Gardner, and Cherri were enough to bring logic to the night of disaster that had taken place in Dodge Junction, Wisconsin. The town would not recover for years to come. And stories, rumors, and nonsense took form as the horror story broke throughout the small town.

2

Winny and Cherri were married the following summer. Garth was the best man, and Father Gardner conducted the ceremony. It was a beautiful ceremony and a gorgeous day.

Garth finally found his calling as a writer. With his words, he was able to travel to the places he so desperately sought to visit. He even wrote a non-fiction book which ended up as a best-selling fiction novel based on his experiences of that hellish night in August.

The End

About the Author

Daniel P. Coughlin was born and raised in a small town in southern Wisconsin. At the age of 19 he joined the United States Marine Corps and served four and half years as a Machine Gunner in the infantry. After being Honorably discharged, Daniel attended and graduated from California State University at Long Beach. While studying screenwriting under the mentorship of acclaimed writer Brian Alan Lane, he also interned and served as a script analyst for his favorite director, Wes Craven. *Photo by Sipper Photography*

Daniel is the author of two commercially successful films *Lake Dead*, which was selected as one of After Dark Film's *8 Films to Die For*, and *Farmhouse*, Starring A-List film and television star Steven Weber (Wings, Desperation, Single White Female). He has sold numerous short stories to such publications as *Strange Tales of Horror, Macabre Cadaver Magazine*, and *Dark Gothic Resurrected Magazine*. Daniel was hailed by *Macabre Cadaver Magazine* as, "A promising New Voice in Old School Horror."

Other HellBound Books:

Satanic Panic

"A delicious homage to those 80's horror B-movies!'"

Satanic Panic, a mass hysteria created in the nineteen eighties, has returned to a small college town in the Midwest.

Ritualistic murders and the presence of the occult have bled below the surface of the town in the form of icy accidents and other coincidences.

And when three lifelong friends find themselves on the radar of a killer—and leader of a satanic cult—they must fight for what's good without being seduced by the evil that possesses their campus.

Ted's Score

"Shocking, psycho killer horror at its very best!!'"

When beautiful Jules Benton, a seventeen-year-old senior, goes missing after the spring formal dance in the small town of Watertown, Wisconsin, her father, Richard, becomes suspicious of Jules' boyfriend, David Miller, and his involvement with her disappearance.

When Richard confirms his suspicions, the brutality of his capability consumes him, and soon David will find out what that means...

Unbeknownst to David or Richard, a serial killer by the name of Ted Olson has more to do with Jules' disappearance than anyone might suspect.

As Jules' whereabouts unfold, the truth begins to bleed from a dark place, and the authorities begin to smell the criminal acts committed.

Murder and mayhem catch up with the slow pace of this ordinary Middle American town when evil, perversion, and death mislead these simple folks into a disastrous wave of crime that spirals out of control.

All the while, Ted collects his score..

NeverEnd

Inexplicably, huge locust swarms of Biblical proportions plague Austin, Texas: a sinister portent of terrifying things to come?

Dr. Jon Edom, hero surgeon, loving father, finds himself unwittingly drawn into the dark conspiracies surrounding the sinister Church of the Resurrected, which has uncomfortably close family ties to his wife, Rochelle. Rochelle Edom, daughter of the Church's founder, genius creator of the worldwide hit video game, NeverEnd, has left her coding days behind to focus on family life. She laments that the repetitive, highly-addictive game she designed shows an alarming increase in ill effects among its players: they emulate the characters' violent actions with increasingly brutal consequences – which her husband witnesses first hand.

When Rochelle unexpectedly goes missing, along with her and Jon's two young children, Jon all too quickly becomes a suspect once old infidelities are exposed.

As Jon fights to clear his name under seemingly impossible, tragic circumstances, aided by his close friend, Rabbi Max, he becomes inexorably embroiled in the evil undercurrent of the Church of the Resurrected's association with the enigmatic Coppersmith, who has a nefarious agenda all of his own…

Two Headed Alligator

Despite being conjoined twins with one heart between them, Deirdre and Desdemona Gardner lived perfectly ordinary lives until they turned fourteen, when strange clicking noises in the night and a string of missing girls turned their quiet existence into a waking nightmare.

In the wake of an unspeakable tragedy, the twins spent a summer away from home, visiting a small Louisiana town with a dark history of murder, unsolved disappearances, and lynching – all centered around two figures fascinating to Deirdre: Florence and Sage Labelle, conjoined twins, alligator farm heiresses, and suspected serial killers.

With the help of Florence's diary and a mysterious little girl whose uncannily adult mannerisms, antiquated vocabulary, and extensive knowledge of her town's history set Desdemona on edge, the Gardner twins set out to solve a decades-old murder mystery while struggling to cope with their own traumatic past.
Following a semi-successful separation surgery, the surviving twin, wishing to remain anonymous, invites you to read this, her life story.

splat·ter·punk
noun
informal
noun: splatterpunk

Definition: "A literary genre characterized by graphically described scenes of an extremely gory nature."

Welcome once again, fellow gore lovers, to HellBound Books' second foray into the deliciously bloody, innards-strewn world of splatterpunk!

Death, dismemberment, and destruction abound within these pages, as we bring to you nineteen perfectly ghoulish tales of terror that are definitely not to be read while eating!

Go on, we dare you!

You have short tales from: Shannon Blake Skelton, Juan Ozuna, Sarah Moon, Seaton Kay-Smith, S.C. Vincent, S. Michael Wilson, Carson Demmans, Diana Parrilla, Michael Errol Swaim, John Schlimm, P.J. Verfall, Karly Foland, W.L. Lewis, Caleb James K., Brian J. Smith, D.J. Tuskmor, Terry Grimwood, Dave Davis, and Paul Allih.

**A HellBound Books LLC
Publication**

www.hellboundbooks.com